COLD STAR

Dick Woodgate

First paperback edition June 2021

Cover design by Bob2412, coverbookdesigns.com
Formatting by Polgarus Studio

ISBN: 9798504262888 (paperback)

Independently published
www.dickwoodgate.com

The cold war just got hotter.

To Mum,

with all my love,

Richard.

X

Dedication

This book is dedicated to my Dad. I remember him reading Alistair MacLean novels when I was little and then, much later, telling me about his attempts at writing action-adventure stories himself when he was a boy. He laughed about it as he told me how he'd get his characters into such extreme situations that it was quite impossible for him to then write them out of them. I think he would have enjoyed this, my first novel.

Free Book Offer

Get your copy of *Treasure Hunter* FREE

Aboard a WW2 destroyer on Arctic patrol to hunt down a Nazi enigma coding machine.

For a limited period, you can download *Treasure Hunter* for free.

The story is exclusive to The Club (free to join) and features Dowling, the head of station in *Cold Star*, in an intriguing story set during his time as a young naval intelligence officer in WW2. Patrolling North Atlantic waters aboard the destroyer HMS Tartar, Dowling leads parties ashore to Arctic lands. Dowling is hunting down an elusive codex machine in a bid to unravel the secrets of the Nazi's enigma code.

Find out more at dickwoodgate.com

Prologue

Product

By mid-morning the snow had mostly been cleared from the Old Town Square. Having completed a circuit of the historic plaza, the agent passed by the clock tower again and walked south-west along Staroměstské nám. The snow shovels hadn't got this far and his brogues continued to battle the inches which had fallen on the city overnight. The empty streets of the old town led him in a winding path toward the river, which he crossed at Charles Bridge. It was almost into April but ice still clung to the banks of the Vltava. The air seemed colder here, and away from the protection of the buildings, the agent felt exposed.

His feet were numb but then the blood always ran cold in him. Long ago the reality of what he had to do for a living showed itself to him for what it was. But everyone adapted to their profession – settled into it eventually. He hadn't wished for it – the wave had come and he'd chosen to get on. It carried him along and he had to ride it out. Once it had run its course it would dump him in a place far from where he'd started, with no possibility of ever finding a way back.

An alley of baroque statues adorned the balustrade. With stone eyes, they watched him cross over to the Lesser Quarter –

the agent was sure they were the only ones to notice him. He doubled back across the bridge, returning to the east bank and continuing along the embankment, walking against the flow of the river towards the National Theatre. He carried on as far as Legion Bridge, turned onto Národní and climbed the steps of Café Slavia. The lobby was done out in green-veined white marble which reminded the agent of blue cheese.

The pillared interior was spacious and saturated with light. Intensified by the whiteness of the snow laying outside, sunlight came streaming in through a series of large plate glass windows. Positioned vertically on the pillars were tubular wall lamps with large-format, frameless mirrors below them, reflecting more light. The brilliant sunlight subsumed the opaque glow of chrome and frosted glass ceiling lights, geometrically grouped over the arrangement of café furniture – warm-coloured, wooden Thonet chairs with their distinctive latticework side panels, set around circular tables topped in the same marble used in the lobby and with thick chromed bands around their circumferences. The booths had dark wood banquettes upholstered in a deep green leather arranged around square tables of the same type as the others. Rich wood panelling on the walls radiated warmth. The style was unmistakably deco – simple, clean and elegant.

The large café was quiet and, at first sight, the agent couldn't imagine a less suitable location for the meeting. In such a visible space, concealment was impossible but, he reflected, sometimes the greatest cover of all could be achieved in the open – provided one was discreet. The agent was early but the soldier was already here, in one of the booths. He wasn't wearing his uniform but he sat so upright that he didn't need to – his posture said it all. The agent went over to the booth. Despite his body language, the man seemed quite at ease – which was good – and he watched the agent with calm eyes as he took his seat on the opposite banquette. Neither man spoke and there was no handshake. In the absence of any pleasantries, the agent called the waiter over instead. The smell of coffee had been powerful as soon as he'd walked in. He asked for his black and, taking a cue from the soldier's empty brandy glass, ordered him another and one for himself too – it was cold as hell outside and it struck the agent as an excellent idea. He left it for the soldier to begin.

'I have it,' he said, giving his jacket a firm pat.

'Good, so do I,' the agent replied.

'You want to look?'

'No. Just put it on the table. I'll do the same.'

The soldier placed a thin, brown envelope onto the creamy, white marble.

The agent contemplated the envelope for a moment. 'That doesn't look like much for the money.'

The soldier shrugged his shoulders. 'I can sell to Americans.'

The agent exhaled slowly. He produced a much thicker envelope and laid it on the table, alongside the other.

The soldier extended his index finger and lifted up the unglued manilla flap. His eyes shone for a moment, then he let the flap fall back again. 'Is all there?'

'It's all there.'

The soldier studied him. 'I will look.'

The agent watched in horror as the soldier went to open the envelope there at the table. The camouflage afforded by plain sight was often a missed opportunity but there was a limit and, behind the iron curtain, an envelope stuffed with American dollars was about it. Way too casual – it was obvious why this asset had been marked a risk. He caught the soldier's hand. 'Take it into a cubicle in the bathroom – you can count it in there.'

Looking peeved, the soldier casually stuck the envelope into his trousers and got up to go. Half of it was sticking out. The agent coughed and directed his eyes towards the man's waistband. Sloppy, really sloppy. The soldier harrumphed. Jamming the envelope a bit further down over his belly, he went off, the bulk of it lending him a peculiar gait. Arrogance and stupidity don't mix well. Put those two traits together and the result is destined to lead to misadventure. He didn't like the soldier's attitude – did this make it any easier?

The agent teased open the soldier's envelope and slid the header of one of the papers out. He noted the sheen of the cheap photostat paper and the blurred rendition of the state emblem of the Soviet Union – the hammer and sickle overlaying the globe, the rising sun below it and the red star of communism at its crest; the three celestial bodies cradled by ears of wheat, wrapped in ribbons. Though impossible to discern from the stamp, the agent knew the ribbons were inscribed in the various languages of the Union with the motto 'Proletarians of the world, unite!' He eased the paper back into the envelope and resealed it.

He looked around him while he waited for the drinks to come. A blood-red carpet ran centrally the length of the café like an artery. Over by the windows was a baby grand, for the moment silent. Framed photographic portraits, presumably depicting the café's illustrious past clientele, adorned the pillars. The agent examined the print closest to him. Taken in black and white it showed a man, perhaps ten years his senior, wearing a dark suit. Despite being well dressed, he was perched casually on an outdoor stone step, one hand cupping his cheek. He looked comfortable and relaxed. His eyes displayed warmth and his moustachioed mouth cast a confident smile towards the photographer. He seemed content. The agent had no idea who he was.

The drinks were taking a while to come but it was fine: he suspected the soldier would take his time counting the money – he might also want to use the facilities – and the agent was quick at this. Anyway, if it came to it, he'd go and fetch the bottle from behind the bar himself and curtly tell the barman that his friend wanted a drink *now* and not when it suited the waiter. In the end the drinks arrived in time and the agent felt in his pocket for the little bottle.

The soldier came out of the bathroom a minute or two later. Walking awkwardly back along the carpet, he returned to the booth and took his seat.

'Okay?' The agent asked.

'Okay.' The man noticed the drink which had appeared while he'd been gone and smiled back at the agent. 'Maybe I have more… tomorrow.'

The agent raised his eyebrows. 'That wasn't the arrangement.'

'Same price.'

The agent let it go. 'We'll see.'

'To our health!' The soldier proffered his glass.

The agent raised his briefly. But there would be no clashing of Czech glass – that would be too risky. The agent watched the soldier drain his, as was customary in his country, in a single swallow.

***

As the soldier left, the agent moved over toward the windows and perched on the empty piano stool. Through the window, he watched the soldier emerge from the foot of the steps onto Národní and walk over to the tram stop opposite the café. A few minutes later he boarded a tram going in the direction of the bridge. Tramway 22 would take him north first before changing direction and heading out toward the western perimeter of the city – good, he was going straight back to his hotel.

The agent ordered another coffee. He needed to wait a while and passed the time ruminating on his posting. He'd been in Prague for the worst half of the winter – the coldest he'd endured. He could trace the reason for his being here all the way back to '57 – to Sputnik. Following the success of the Russian 'moon', the immediate fear in the West had been that the Soviets might then set their sights on the real thing. And the worrying possibility of Russia militarising space had subsequently led to the missile gap becoming the overriding issue of Kennedy's campaign for office. With the threat of communism no longer seeming earthbound, the British government had become concerned too. In Prague it was possible for a British agent to operate behind the iron curtain but the meagre intelligence he'd managed to obtain since his arrival here couldn't have amounted to much more than titbits. Now he'd been told to close down permanently the channel of information from the only useful contact he'd made in three months.

**

He checked his watch. It was eleven. The soldier had been gone for about twenty minutes. He called for the bill, paid and left.

Out on Národní, he waited for the next number 22 tram. He jumped on and took a pew leaning against the rail at the back of the car – the tram wasn't crowded at this time of day and there were benches available but the agent preferred to stand. Though the soldier had never disclosed to the agent where he was staying, he'd easily worked it out from a small thing he'd said during their previous meeting. The agent had asked him if he would have time for any sightseeing while he was in Czechoslovakia. The soldier had shaken his head but said, 'I see castle from hotel – fifteen floor.' There was only one building in Prague with that many floors.

The agent prepared to get out as the tram approached the stop at Zelená. The shouting alerted him first. Heads turned along the benches as the tram drew up and came to a halt beside the stop. He knew at once it had gone wrong. Leaning, side-on against the window of a tobacconists for support and holding onto his chest with his free hand, the man was screaming blue murder to anyone who would stop and listen – most kept moving but a few concerned passers-by were gathered around him. The agent stepped off the tram and cautiously moved closer to the throng. He saw that the soldier had already emptied the contents of his stomach onto the snowy pavement. The warm vomit had formed a colourful pool of pink – to the spectators, the colour might have suggested a recent consumption of too much red wine perhaps but to the agent's more informed eye, the soldier was suffering the ill-effects of something far more serious than drink. Odourless, tasteless and within an hour or two, lifeless. But the complications which the poison was expected to bring on should have been crippling and followed by a swift death without fuss – certainly not preluded with the scene the soldier was making.

Within the tirade, the agent thought he recognised the Russian word *ubiytsa* (assassin) and an obscene coupling of the words *angliyskiy* (English) and *piz`da* (c***). The soldier quite literally spat these words from his mouth as if he were attempting to expel more of the poison which had nearly done for him. The bugger was making a scene in public, right out here on the street, with his mouth spilling the beans and his pants full of American dollars. Who knew what else he may have already given away? The agent couldn't afford the soldier the opportunity to blab any further – the VB would be along any minute to see what the fuss was about and that wouldn't do. The secret police would be called. An English assassin brought to light, loose behind the iron curtain, wouldn't look good to the politicians whom his chief had to report to back home. No, he couldn't have this. He must do something to stop it – and fast. But what?

The crowd parted as they heard the commanding voice shouting, 'Doktore, nech mě projít' (doctor, let me through). Then he told them – again in Czech – to get back, to make room. The agent had to be quick about this. He approached the soldier from behind so he wouldn't see his face. Adrenaline coursed through the agent's system causing his heart to beat faster – though not as fast as the soldier's, desperately fighting to rid his body of the poison. The agent took hold of him in the crook of one arm – holding him in a headlock and forcing his head backward – the other arm bringing the vial swiftly up to the man's mouth. The manoeuvre would have been far too quick for the ailing soldier to take in. Delivered in Russian, the agent issued an urgent command directly into the man's ear, 'Meditsina, pit' (medicine, drink). His Russian was extremely limited but just these two remembered words were sufficient – indeed, anymore and the soldier might have recognised his voice and gone haywire. Instead, he was compliant. There was no struggle, no need for further force – the soldier simply opened his mouth wide and allowed the agent to pour the lethal contents of the bottle right into it. He gulped it all down.

As quickly as he'd arrived, the agent forced his way back out through the small crowd, making sweeping gestures in an attempt to part the spectators once again. One of them stood in front of him, barring his way. He demanded to know what was happening. The agent had no time for discussion – he had to get away from here as fast as possible. He went to push past him but the man was big and he stood his ground, blocking his attempts to pass. The agent had no choice but to relent – in faltering Czech, he told him quickly that he was a European doctor on exchange from the West, working at the hospital. The patient needed urgent treatment. He would go to the kiosk and telephone the hospital to request an ambulance – and then he would come straight back.

The man wasn't satisfied. 'I'll come with you – to help with the call.'

'No, you stay here and look after him – I don't need help – try and get him to calm down – it won't help him, being so upset.'

The man seemed happier now he'd been appointed a role but still he wanted to know what the agent had given him.

'A vomiting suppressant. He's bringing up blood – and that's no good,' the agent said gravely. 'Look, there's really no time for this. He says he's been poisoned – he needs to be taken to the hospital.'

Finally, the man was satisfied and let the agent go.

Walking briskly along Jugoslávských partyzánů toward the hotel, the agent considered the situation. Certainly, his action should help speed things along – the remainder of the bottle must have contained at least another full dose, perhaps two. The soldier's rantings wouldn't last much longer. What was important ultimately was that it worked – though he had, of course, hoped for it to have taken effect in his room, with the soldier on his own. This scenario would have been more likely if, instead of at the Slavia, he'd agreed to meet the agent at the hotel.

The Hotel Čedok was located in the municipal quarter of Dejvice, in the north-west district of Prague 6. The agent had found out a few things about it: as well as being the city's tallest building, the hotel had nearly three hundred rooms, boasted two restaurants, a lobby bar, a rooftop lounge terrace (on the fifteenth floor – from where the soldier would have looked out across to the castle) and, unusually, an in-house laundry located in the basement. The agent gazed up at the towering edifice before him. The Čedok was a Stalinist behemoth. It seemed out of place amongst the comfortable homes of Prague's bucolic upper-class neighbourhood. From between its twin wings, the central tower rose sixteen stories and was adorned with a giant metal chalice. Atop this was a spire with a socialist star rendered in ruby-coloured glass at its pinnacle. The heavy stone façade of this socialist realist edifice looked to the agent more like an imposing government building than a hotel. A flight of steps led up to the grand entrance. Prominently positioned above the portico were three large stone-carved reliefs in the socialist realist style depicting the typical assemblage of workers, soldiers and mothers with babies in their arms. The agent passed underneath and went through the brass doors into the lobby.

The floor was a geometric design in black and white marble which extended to the formal pillars and the high, open space produced a hollow quality to the sound of the agent's footsteps. He quickly took in the layout of the lobby: the location of the staircases – carpeted in claret; the whereabouts of the lifts – their doors faced in gleaming gold plate; the situation of the lobby bar; the positions of the dark, marble-clad columns; the sightlines – particularly in relation to the desk. He noted the nature of the lighting produced by the vintage sconces – great glass goblets with brass rims and ornate fluted stems giving out a soft, yellow incandescence. And the furnishings: the comfortable looking armchairs upholstered in a rich, thick fabric – the design, a frightening botanical vision in swirling gold on a deep burgundy background; the dark oil canvasses – foreboding looking portraits of dead heroes in gilt-edged frames.

His observations were made in the few moments it took him to approach the outsized desk, rendered too in marble – just black this time and highly polished. Dropping onto it the loose change from his pocket attracted the attention of a bored-looking clerk. The coins clattered down on the obsidian-like stone. In the vacuum of the hotel lobby, the sound ricocheted like bullets. Sliding the scattered crowns across the cold marble towards the official gained his full attention – behind the iron curtain, it seemed everyone was an official. The agent enquired after the soldier – the particular acoustics of the lobby gave his voice a metallic edge. The windfall approaching, the clerk asked for the agent's name. The agent gave him the one he used on these occasions as the transfer of currency was completed. The clerk consulted the register, then the board of keys hanging on the wall behind the desk before telling him the comrade in question was out. His pockets now depleted of coin, the agent pulled out his wallet and withdrew a banknote. Folding it between his fingers, he proffered it to the clerk.

'Oh, and by the way, can you tell me the room number – in case I want to try telephoning later?'

The clerk didn't hesitate and received the note in a wholly practised manner. The agent reflected that, in the poor economies of the communist countries, bribes were as commonplace a necessity as, in combatting the damp British climate, umbrellas were to the English. He thanked the clerk and left the hotel.

Outside, he followed a signpost to the car park at the rear of the hotel and regained access to the building by a service door. When one of the hotel staff confronted him, he said he was looking for the laundry room to check on a suit of his that was being cleaned. He was told he should speak to one of the clerks on the reception desk and was directed down a corridor leading him through the labyrinthine heart of the building. Having followed the passageway back to the lobby, he strode briskly over to the rear stairwell and climbed the steps, neatly avoiding being seen by the clerk at the desk. On the first floor, the agent found his way along another corridor leading to the lifts. Inside the garish gold-lined interior of the elevator compartment, he pressed the button for the fourteenth floor and watched the floor numbers illuminate in turn on the panel as the lift ascended the tower. Army captains of the Socialist Republics wouldn't usually command a room with a view, least of all one in a hotel as sumptuous as this – it certainly couldn't be afforded on army pay alone.

Beyond the lower floors though, the opulence vanished as soon as the agent left the elevator. On the fourteenth floor, the golden outer doors of the lobby lifts were replaced by an institutional shade of dull green, framed by a utilitarian bare metal surround. The corridor had an insipid colour scheme, drained of hue as if in death. Padding along it, the agent stopped outside the soldier's room and put his ear to the door. All was quiet but caution had its place in the agent's oeuvre – you never could tell. The lock was easy. The cheap, East European mechanism took him less than half a minute to pick.

After the grandiosity of the building and the palatial lobby downstairs, the small rooms must have come as some disappointment to guests of the Čedok. A bland scheme of anaemic green, khaki and gloomy browns washed over the walls and furnishings. A meagre suite of drab wooden furniture appointed the room – each item clinging singularly to the wall like uncomfortable guests at a dismal party. The bed – not quite so narrow as the one at the agent's apartment in the centre of the city – was by Soviet standards, presumably intended to be a double. Even so, the faded pink bedspread barely covered it, throwing out its shiny pleated skirt not quite to the floor. Under the window was an uncomfortable-looking armchair and a small, round table with a full ashtray on it. The desk on the wall opposite the bed held a tray with two dirty-looking water glasses and a single, unused paper napkin. Next to the tray was a grubby telephone and a room service card. Finally, beside the door and of a similarly diminished scale to the bed, there was a wardrobe. This was all. It wouldn't take him long.

He started with the wardrobe – going through the soldier's clothes, hung on the pitiful rail and then checking the almost-empty suitcase which he found to contain only a small collection of dirty underclothes and socks. No one would be stupid enough to keep anything of interest anywhere obvious – but this was routine. The desk drawer was empty besides the room's thumbed copy of *Dialectical and Historical Materialism*. He moved on to look in all the usual hiding places. Nothing behind the picture of Stalin hanging above the bed, nothing in the bedding, pillows or under the mattress. He pulled the cushion off the chair and felt about in the upholstery – nothing there either. Returning his attention to the wardrobe, he eased one side of it away from the wall and slid it out so he could look behind – but taping something to the back would be too obvious. Netherthless, he did a similar job with the bed and the desk. With little furniture and no bathroom (he suspected that none of the Čedok's rooms would have an adjoining bathroom), the possibilities were running out. Methodically, he felt all along the bottom of the curtains – it would be an easy job to have stitched something in-between the material and the lining. Nothing. The room appeared to be clean. But the agent's suspicion that there would be something hidden here, prevailed. He prized off the electrical socket and the light switch. Not a thing behind either. There was nowhere left for him to look. Perhaps he was wrong?

The agent let himself out of the room. Dejected, he walked

back up the hallway. He'd walked right past them before he took in their significance – then he doubled back and went in. There were a pair of communal bathrooms next to the lifts and he found what he was looking for in the first one he checked. Standing on the lavatory, he reached up into the cistern and felt something bobbing about. He locked the door to the stall and fished out a package wrapped in plastic and thoroughly sealed with tape – it was about the same size and heft as one of Tolstoy's longer works.

He waited until he was back in his apartment to open it up. The tape had done its job and the contents were completely dry – three brown envelopes of the same type as the one he'd bought from the soldier earlier. The first was stuffed full with dollars – about twice the amount that he'd paid. There was no doubt in the agent's mind that the soldier had sold the same information to the Americans – only they would pay such a premium for this type of product. Inside the other two were identical sets of further material. The silly sod had planned on repeating the trick with the second instalments before returning to Moscow. With how things had gone, it was too messy for the agent to stay on any longer – he'd have to quit Prague early. Instead of passing the product on to the courier in the usual manner, he could at least take it home to London himself.

Part One
Casa

Chapter 1
The Club

Getting out of Prague in a hurry hadn't been easy and ten hours spent in futile attempt at sleep on the East German sleeper carriage to Hamburg had been hell. When he'd disembarked at Lowestoft, the agent had never felt so happy to be home. Following the drop at headquarters and the briefest of accounts to the Chief of Staff, he'd gone home. Refreshed from a decent night's sleep in his own bed, he was up bright and early strolling along Park Lane into Boodles. The chap at the desk took his name and showed him to the library.

The lieutenant-general was sitting at a table studying some papers – at the weekend he used the club's library as a second office. He looked up as the agent entered. 'Bring us some coffee, would you please James?' he said to the steward.

'Good morning sir,' the agent said as he took a seat opposite.

'Yes,' the lieutenant-general said, as if the agent had asked him a question. 'We found some interesting information in the product you turned up – very good stuff indeed. Some of it we knew already – the Soviet's plans to get a man into space, for instance. But beyond their immediate goals there's also some informed speculation about the future hopes of their cosmonaut programme and their overall designs on space.'

'Sounds fascinating sir.'

'Yes, I'm unable to share it with you in any detail but I can tell you it makes for compelling reading – even though a part of it sounds to me rather more like science fiction… Anyway, that's not what I want to discuss and your debrief will have to wait – I understand you had a little trouble?'

'Nothing serious, sir'.

The lieutenant-general made a brief, high-pitched noise that was somewhere between a snort and a strangled laugh.

The steward returned with the coffee tray and left, closing the door behind him.

The lieutenant-general poured a cup for himself then slid the tray over to the agent. 'There was something else in what you brought back – and rather than being ostensibly scientific, we think this document is unquestionably of a military nature. Take a look at this.'

The lieutenant-general passed a single page of translated material across the table to the agent. He read the heading and scanned the body of text. It was a consignment docket listing an equipment inventory. Despite being in translation, the agent struggled to understand what he was reading.

'You might need to fill me in, sir.'

'Yes…what's detailed there are ballistics parts – heavy weaponry broken down for transportation.'

'What sort of weapons, sir?'

'We're not entirely sure – they could be ground-to-air missile parts or perhaps components for something more powerful. And there's munitions of some sort too. Now, I know what you're thinking – what's unusual about it to cause us to take interest?'

The agent looked over the document. He read the transport details. The consignment was being transported by rail from *Plant 586 Glushko OKBM, Hartron OKB* to the *Port of Odessa.* 'What's this Plant 586, sir?'

'Actually, we've no clear idea what that plant manufactures, besides suspecting that it supplies the military. What's of more interest to us though is the destination. If something's being shipped out of Odessa, then it's most likely on its way out of the Soviet Union – our concern is where it's bound for. If the Russians are supplying arms – on a grander scale than a few cases of Kalashnikovs – to somewhere outside of their borders, then this presents us with a significant concern.

'We're already in the possession of other information which has given us cause to watch the ports recently – internationally, I mean. We'd not spotted anything untoward until last night, when something came through from Reuters which would have been difficult to miss even if we hadn't been looking. They reported a major incident at the Port of Casablanca yesterday. It would appear that there were a series of large explosions on the quayside leading to the sinking of a vessel – the casualties are already estimated to stand at over a hundred and the suggestion is that the damage may be colossal.'

The lieutenant-general paused to drink his coffee – he took it black with a thin strip of lemon peel to reduce the bitterness. 'The Moroccan authorities are playing the whole thing down, describing it as a minor industrial accident. Now this may well be just an unfortunate accident as we're being asked to believe – and have nothing whatsoever to do with what we're looking for

– but a common worry is that these sorts of things may be down to the other side. Should that prove to be the case, then it could be of serious concern as it might present a tangible threat to our national security. We have a station there of course but I'd prefer the matter to be dealt with by our office – long shot as it might be, it's the only event we've seen and, based on the date of our docket here, the timing looks to be about right.

'So, you'd like me to take a look, sir?'

'Precisely.'

For a moment the lieutenant-general looked as if he were considering how much more to say on the subject. Then he laid his hands flat on the polished table in front of him and spoke to the agent more frankly. 'But that's not quite the end of it. There's another angle. One from across the water.' The lieutenant-general paused to light a cigarette before going on to further sketch out the case. He would never offer one to the agent – the agent had no idea why.

'We have our eye on Morocco at the moment. You may be aware that they have a new king, Hassan II. His father, Muhammad, died a couple of months ago during a routine operation, which meant the throne was handed to his son, Hassan, in January. This new king's a progressive and it seems that he might be keener to work more closely with the West than his father was. Now, our friends across the pond are keen to cultivate a relationship with him because they feel he could be useful to them. For an Arab leader this Hassan fellow has an unusually moderate attitude towards the state of Israel and the Yanks think he could prove to be a valuable mediator in this regard. Kennedy will want to keep Morocco onside as well, if you see what I mean. But that's no good if the Soviets are already supplying the country with arms – if for a moment we allow ourselves to draw that conclusion. Equally, the Russians could just as well be backing anti-government groups within Morocco rather than Hassan's government.

'Delicate business forging political alliances. And these Arab countries – particularly those in Africa – are prone to more than their fair share of unrest – coups and the like. I'm sure you read about these sorts of things in your newspaper? The thing is, not everyone's happy when a new leader comes in – the opposition parties of course, but they've been pretty much gagged by Hassan already. But there are always enemies within and there's no exception here. This Hassan fellow appears to have been frustrated by his father's rule and there're whispers his death may've been suspicious. It looks like he has his fair share of enemies already – even within his own circle.'

'It sounds like a rather volatile situation, sir.'

'Quite so. And as far as the Americans are concerned... well, one needs to know that one's betrothed is on the right side and that all's well before walking down the aisle, so to speak. In plain terms, if Soviet arms *are* entering the country then it will make Kennedy think twice about allying with Hassan – whether he's aware of it or not. The last thing the Americans want is to get caught up in another country's internal troubles – they've enough of that going on in Indochina. And a bally mess that'll turn out to be too, mark my words... Anyway, you're probably wondering what all this political bunkum has to do with the assignment I'm handing you.'

'The thought might have crossed my mind, sir,' the agent had said respectfully. He knew better than to offer his chief a smart alec reply.

'Well, the answer to that is perhaps nothing. This thing may have little to do with Morocco at all – even if it *does* have everything to do with our mystery shipment. You see, the port of Casablanca is a gateway for a fair few other North African countries besides Morocco itself. But whichever way, North Africa's considered to be our patch in the worldwide scheme of things, which is why you're here listening to all this. I need you to go out there and investigate. It's not your typical assignment: find out what's happened – if it's the case that there *was* a munitions fire aboard then you'll need to discover who these arms were destined for and what they were planning to do with them – who their squabble's with. It might even have been a bomb – exploding unintentionally or otherwise. Report back to me – we can determine then whether it's likely or not of there being any remaining threat to the throne – or indeed, from it. Now, do you have any questions?'

'I do have a question, sir. If not the Moroccan government – or another even – do we have any idea what faction Russia might be intending to arm?'

'That's a reasonable question – but the answer is no. There are so many political groups operating in the region – many of whom will undoubtably have communist leanings –that it would be fairly futile to guess at which… Look, it could be nothing – a storm in a teacup – but I can't tell. You'll have to work that out for yourself. And if you turn up anything which looks sinister, then you're to close it down – immediately.' At this point the lieutenant-general had looked at him in a way his father might once have. 'And without any of the usual dramatics, you understand?'

The look of disapproval prompted an antagonised response from the agent. 'The usual dramatics being what exactly, sir?' He regretted his words at once.

'Good God man, do I have to spell it out?' the lieutenant-general leaned forward in his chair. 'I don't want more bloody fireworks blowing things to smithereens. And specifically, the diplomatic incident that would follow. The political situation there is delicate and I can't have the British government's relationship with Morocco damaged by letting an agent loose to cause mayhem in a foreign country. If you have good reason to, then simply put a stop to whatever it is without making a song and a dance about it. I don't want any fuss – and I don't want any repercussions.'

It was in these moments of bluster that his chief could so closely resemble the agent's memory of his father. The sudden squall passed quickly enough and, sitting back in his chair again and contemplating the portrait of Montgomery on the wall opposite, the field marshal seemed to relax him.

The interview was concluded by the brisk propelling of a slim manila folder across the table towards the agent. 'The reports, for what they're worth. You can read them on the aeroplane – there's a ticket in there for the morning flight from Heathrow, together with your other travel documents. And in case you wonder, we've put you up the front simply as a matter of expediency – it was the only ticket available. You'll also note that, on our behalf, the American Embassy have booked you into a fairly decent hotel – but I'll warn you, this isn't a jolly.'

Chapter 2
Comet

The hailstones crunched under the leather soles of his brogues as the agent walked across the runway apron towards the stairs beside the aeroplane – the freak April weather at Heathrow Airport had delayed boarding of the new transatlantic route for an hour. Inside the cabin he could hear the hail rattling against the fuselage, even over the noise of the idling twin Rolls-Royce Avon Turbojet engines buried in each wing. The agent took his seat at a table in the front cabin of the BOAC de Havilland Comet and soon the aeroplane taxied out onto the main runway.

The pitch of the Avons increased and the strengthened light-alloy fuselage of the Comet sped down the runway, leaving a spray of water behind it like the vapour trail of its namesake. The aeroplane lifted off and, gaining altitude quickly, circled over the river. The agent looked out at the capital flanking the Thames until the Comet hit cloud level and the wet city disappeared from his view – he felt relieved to be leaving the bad weather behind him.

The pilot settled the aircraft into a steady climb following the navigator's course southwest over Sussex and Hampshire, passing above Southampton where it continued across the Solent and out over the Channel. The Comet climbed towards its cruising altitude as it passed over Brittany and struck out over the Bay of Biscay. On the wing, water droplets froze with the sudden fall in temperature. Inside the cabin, cocktails were served. The agent swirled his tumbler and the ice within it cracked as it transformed, surrendering to the pale gold liquid enveloping it. Through the new-style oval window of the Comet 4, he watched tiny ice crystals forming on the outside of the glass, developing long, delicately branched filaments around the perimeter. The process held the agent's attention and helped to focus his thoughts.

What was this really about? His interview with the lieutenant-general had felt somewhat jumbled. Was the assignment concerned with tracing the mystery shipment or did it actually have nothing to do with that at all? Was his mission in fact purely politically motivated and instigated on behalf of the Americans? Whichever it was, he had an inkling there may be more to this than he'd been led to understand. He lifted the tumbler and sipped his whisky sour. It hit the spot. He lowered his glass, observing the ice being slowly drowned in the spirit.

The agent finished his drink and called the stewardess for another. He'd been told that he'd have to work this assignment out for himself and so the sooner he got started, the better. From his attaché case he brought out the thin paper file. He opened it and leafed through the various reports. He started with the despatch from Reuters which was fairly minimal in content and he quickly moved on to the police report. There were no numbers given for those who'd perished in the explosion – the report merely stated that there were *a small number of port workers being treated in hospital for burns injuries sustained in the accident.'* The report went on to say that, *'The incident occurred during the course of unloading a consignment of flammable material from a foreign cargo vessel. Part of the load was spilt and ignited, causing the combustion of the entire consignment and the subsequent loss of the vessel and also some localised damage to the pier.'*

It already sounded fishy. Paraffin or the like – a commonly used fuel in the Third World – wouldn't have just caught spontaneously and gone up like that. Petroleum was more likely to behave in this way, but the ship wasn't a tanker and so he doubted whether the quantities involved would've been enough to have sunk outright a freighter in harbour. Either Reuters had it wrong or, as his chief had already suggested, the police were deliberately masking the true nature of the incident. The agent was already fairly certain of the cause being something other than that which had been officially reported but if so, then why exactly was it being covered up? After the police report, he read his own department's report and an attachment from the diplomatic office which together covered ground his chief already had during his briefing. He concluded with the submission from the head of station in Casablanca. Though factual, again, this added little useful information. It was, however, plentiful in speculative analysis of the economic implications of the incident.

'The Port de Casablanca is the largest artificial harbour on the African continent, a busy terminus annually handling a tremendous amount of cargo. The incident occurred on the Jette Transversale (the largest of three principal piers at over two and a half thousand feet in length). The whole of the pier remains shut off to all commercial trade whilst an investigation is being carried out by the

local police. The pier is expected to remain closed for the rest of the month at the very least. This will prove costly for the port authorities to mop up, not to mention the loss of trade to the city. The knock-on effects will also be noticed well beyond Casablanca's urban perimeter and in fact, throughout the country–'

It sounded more like a pessimistic report to the city's stakeholders than a document authored by a member of the Secret Service. These poor sods posted on long commissions out in the colonial backwaters were somewhat prone to losing their way. This one sounded like he should be working for the mayor's office. The agent skimmed through the report which, moving on from the prospect of harder times ahead, went on fairly pointlessly to state, *'It has not yet been possible to identify the ship in question nor to verify the presence or nature of any cargo aboard it, in transit nor on the pier.'* Giving up, the agent slipped the report back into the folder with the others, groaning at the thought of shortly having to deal with the stuffed shirt who'd written it.

He ate a decent luncheon. From the list, he ordered a half bottle of a simple red from the Languedoc to match the roasted quail and he had a glass of Sauternes from Château La Tour Blanche to accompany his tarte au citron – he thought the Sauternes a good wine to be stocked aboard an aircraft. The agent detested the snobbery surrounding wine. Certainly, he didn't find the complexities of viticulture impenetrable but he chose not to over-familiarise himself with the world of wine. This stance didn't prevent him from enjoying a crisp glass of sauvignon blanc or a robust red – he particularly enjoyed Primitivo, a heavyweight from the Apulia region in the south of Italy. And though he happened to know, he couldn't really have cared that this particular variety of Italian grape actually originated across the Adriatic, in Croatia. He appreciated the wine but didn't feel compelled to understand anymore about the cultivation of the grape used to produce it. Indeed, the agent's idea of hell would be to endure a wine tasting. The same could be said about his attitude towards good food. Though he liked the sophisticated French cuisine popular in some London restaurants, he hated all the chatter about it. To the agent's mind, food and drink should be a visceral experience, not an intellectual one – he'd no sooner want to talk about it than he would about sex.

The aeroplane had already reached its cruising altitude of forty-two thousand feet. At this height, the temperature outside was minus fifty-eight degrees. The stewardess served coffee and Madeira. Shortly afterwards the plane began its descent as it passed over the Strait of Gibraltar and continued south over the tip of the North African continent. As it lost altitude it became warmer outside. It continued its descent and at around seven and a half thousand feet, the temperature had reached thirty-two degrees and the ice on the wings began to melt. It flew down the Atlantic coastline and then came in low over the ocean to land and refuel at Casablanca.

As the aircraft approached the airfield, the agent looked out of his starboard window onto the endless blue-grey of the Atlantic. He would of course miss the tea and scones which would be served once the aeroplane regained cruising altitude – and later the canapés and champagne as it approached New York. Whilst he might enjoy that another time, for now he'd settle for fragrant scents and exotic spices. After much of the winter spent in Prague, the pleasant climate of a North African spring would come as a relief. There would be warmth and vivid colour by day, and by night – out in the Berber villages of the interior – smoke from the fires and the sound of the bendir drum being played. Across the Strait of Gibraltar, Europe was left behind and the north-western tip of Africa was a taste of things to come from this vast continent.

His mind wandered. It was here, where the Mediterranean was squeezed to its narrowest point between the northern peninsular of Tangiers and the southern tip of Spain, that there existed a crossing point between the two continents which had allowed the division between them to blur slightly. And it was from this point he reflected that the Moors had set out to invade Iberia and where they left behind – at the Alhambra and beyond – distinctive Islamic ceramics and Moorish architecture. European design has since felt the legacy of Moorish style which has had a heavy influence too on Western architecture. More recently the French established their protectorate over much of the country, which in turn infused its commercial capital with a cosmopolitan, modern-European style. Where Europe meets Africa, the agent would shortly be arriving in Morocco.

Chapter 3

La Jetée

When the Comet touched down it was over eighty degrees on the runway at Casablanca's Anfa airfield and the ice was long gone from its wings – the brittle heat of the coastal scrubland destroying any trace of water the plane had brought down with it from the heavens. The searing heat was momentarily shattered by the release of cool, conditioned air which scythed into it when the cabin door was opened. The agent was the only passenger to disembark and he emerged from the aircraft, for an instant still coolly enveloped in its micro-climate, then made his own final descent down the steps to the scorched concrete pad.

The agent could pick out a member of the service with little trouble and, in the arrivals lounge, he walked straight up to the man in the cream-coloured, colonial-style linen suit and introduced himself.

'Ah, yes. Pleased to meet you,' the man said. 'Clyde Dowling at your service. I'm the head of station here. Thought I should come along myself to meet you.'

The head of station asked after the agent's flight and, as they walked out to the car park, outlined the arrangements he'd made on his behalf.

'I cleared it with the head of the Sûreté for us to pay a visit to the port this afternoon in case you wanted to get straight down to it,' Dowling said. 'I wasn't able to get over there any sooner myself what with all the business of writing up my report and getting your car arranged and so on.'

'That's thoughtful of you Dowling – yes, I'd like very much to do that.'

Amongst all the tired-looking French imports and the odd new Moroccan-built Renault (the Casablanca plant had been open for a couple of years now) the car was a jewel in a sea of mediocrity.

'The car comes courtesy of the American Embassy – by way of the Italian Consulate,' Dowling said. 'Seems a better bet than one of the old Simcas from our car pool, what? Though I couldn't say how happy the Italian consul general is about the arrangement – it's his own car, you see. Oh, and if you didn't already know, it's also the Americans who're responsible for putting you up in the best hotel in town – they obviously have high hopes for you bringing home the bacon.'

The agent walked around the car. Long low and elegant – were it human, it would possess exquisite bone structure. With the prominent front and rear wings hinting at the car's muscularity, it projected a feeling of quiet strength. He recognised it instantly as having been bodied by Alfredo Vignale. The agent knew his cars well enough and he didn't need to see the trident badge on the front grill to know the maker.

'Maserati GT Spyder,' Dowling declared. 'It's a bit of a special apparently,'

Bologna manufacturer, Maserati produced some of the finest

coupés and sports cars in Italy and would never put its badge on anything remotely run of the mill. In midnight blue with a white removable hardtop and polished chrome spoked wheels, the car was a rare beauty.

'It's a Vignale,' the agent qualified. 'Built on a hundred-inch wheelbase – slightly shorter than the production coupé.'

Dowling looked upstaged.

The agent lifted the bonnet to examine the engine compartment and noted the six cylinders and the triple Weber carburettors. 'I hope the roads are up to it,' he said, slamming the bonnet shut.

'I thought you'd like it,' Dowling said as he tossed the keys over to him, 'but do look after it will you dear chap? It's me who'll get it in the neck if you prang it.'

The agent wasted no time in deciding about Dowling. The car though, would do. While Dowling clambered into the passenger seat, the agent put his bag in the boot and, jumping in behind the wheel, turned the ignition. The twin tail pipes tore and spat as he revved the engine then settled down to produce the rumbling purr which came from the three-and-a-half-litre, double overhead cam, inline six-cylinder engine – the signature note of a V6. He understood the relationship between Italians and their cars and there was only one thing the agent could think of that would have persuaded the Italian consul general to let this machine out of his sight.

'I don't need to ask how our American friends got the CG to agree to it,' the agent said, 'but she must have been quite a girl.'

'I'm sure I don't know what you mean, dear boy,' Dowling said to him, looking blank.

But to the agent it was clear that political strings had been pulled and lengths gone to over this assignment. He should take it seriously.

Possibly in an attempt to move things onto a more stable footing, Dowling opened the glovebox and pulled out a small packet which he handed to the agent. 'We've had these made up for you,' he said.

The agent took the packet from him and opened it. Inside was a small stack of professionally produced business cards.

'We've another few hundred or so back at the station if you find yourself running low. Even so, the printers still complained at it being far too short a run.'

'Who thought up the name?' the agent asked, not worrying to conceal his irritation.

'Why, don't you like it?' Dowling asked defensively. 'Coldblow is a place I used to know, when I was young. I had to come up with something quick if we were to get them printed in time and it seemed as good a name as any. It's in Kent as a matter of fact–'

'And Jenson?'

'Like the carmaker. Thought it might be an appropriate sort of name – kind of racy. Isn't their coupé named the Interceptor?'

'It was, but there's a new one now – the 541 – the bodywork's made from fibreglass to keep the weight down... But anyway, that's Jensen spelt with an e.'

'Oh dear, I'm afraid that motorcars aren't my strong point, but it seems you know your stuff – spot of luck, eh?'

The agent, rolling his eyes, tossed the cards back to Dowling and engaged first gear. He steered the car out of the car park and into surrounding Anfa, where he picked up the road heading into town towards the medina. Filling his lungs with the cool ocean breeze that rushed at him through his open window, he drove the car at a good pace along the wide boulevards of the new city centre. The striking modernity of the buildings paraded past his window – the agent thought it expressed hope in the future. The late afternoon light of northern Africa intensified the colours and the grey skies of home were quickly forgotten. Driving the car, with the city rushing past him, he felt completely uplifted.

Dowling was now busy providing him with an (unsolicited) potted social history of Casablanca to which the agent was only half listening. '…And for those who come here, the city has always provided a version of the American dream. Countless Muslims and Jews have migrated from the arid interior to work in the factories, leaving the droughts behind–'

The agent interrupted the lecture to move the conversation onto matters of more immediate concern, asking Dowling to fill him in on any other salient details about the incident.

'Well, I was in the embassy of course, so I didn't see anything but I could certainly hear well enough. They were extremely loud detonations – the pier must have gone up like a damn rocket.'

'How many blasts were there?'

'I couldn't say precisely, but there must have been at least half a dozen. It sounded like a bloody war.'

'I've read the police report – and your own – on the way out here. What have the authorities here got to say about it – what's the official line?'

'There isn't one. The minister for the interior – who would usually be responsible for issuing statements on things like this –

has gone missing. I already thought to make enquiries myself, you see,' he said, shooting the agent a look. 'At first his office told me that he wasn't available for comment, then they said he was out of the country and, at lunchtime, they finally admitted to having no idea of his whereabouts – all rather mysterious, wouldn't you say?'

'Perhaps,' the agent said dismissively. He'd already decided to play things cool with Dowling. He swung the car around to the left and drove into the port entrance. The gates were down and security had obviously been beefed-up at the sentry post. He stopped the car and waited for one of the guards to come over. The agent left it to Dowling to show their papers and to mention the name of the regional captain of the Sûreté Nationale. The guard retreated to the sentry hut to make the necessary checks and a telephone call later the gates were lifted and they were inside the port compound.

A pall of grey smoke hung over what remained of la Jetée Transversale like a great length of dirty lace. Below it was a twisted mess of steel and still-smoking timbers – all that was left of the wharf buildings which were either gone or may as well have been. It looked like the scene of an apocalypse. At the landward end of the quay, a mobile crane was being brought into position, blocking the way. Stopping the car, the pair got out. Ahead they saw the blackened body of an unlucky docker being brought out of the wreckage of the wharf. It was not a sight for the fainthearted. There were a great number of people working on the search and rescue operation, all too busy to notice the agent and Dowling as they picked their way through the carnage and onto the pier.

The grotesque form of what had been one of the great cranes loomed above them. The steel latticework had sagged and been partially melted by the intense heat from the blast, causing molten metal to ooze down toward the quayside. In the process of cooling, it had now fused to form an extraordinary new structure, looking like a monumental dripping sculpture by Salvador Dali. The fireball must have been horrendous to have caused damage on this scale.

Dowling appeared horror struck and gaped at the scene in disbelief. 'The whole thing has gone up,' he said.

The fires were all out but sea water was still being pumped from the harbour on the smouldering remains of the wharf – a full twenty-four hours after the incident. The agent quickly realised there was something missing and his eyes darted up and down the quayside. At first it appeared that perhaps by some miracle the blasts had occurred whilst there were very few ships berthed at the pier. A medium-sized freighter was half-sunk near the landward end – presumably the one which had been reported lost – and he could see another, afloat still, towards the far end but there was nothing between them but the ruined quay itself. Dowling had told him that the port was one of the busiest in North Africa – this pier was over two and a half thousand feet long yet it had only two ships on it. Curious. The agent steered Dowling along the quay.

There had been no miracle, far from it. Beyond the first ruined ship, the agent cast his eyes over the upturned, fire-blackened hull which protruded from the water below – the capsized ship looked to be a good hundred feet long. But beyond this, the agent now saw the partly submerged wreck of another, bigger vessel. The men exchanged bewildered glances. Approaching the wreck, it became clear that this ship must have been close to the epicentre of the blasts. What they saw would have been difficult for the agent to easily describe. At this point, the harbourside wall had been completely blown away as if detonated by a charge. What remained of the ship was on its side in the harbour but at the waterline a part of it had become embedded in the side of the pier itself.

The source of the devastation became a little clearer as they came up alongside the wreck. What was visible of the hull revealed it to be mostly gone, blown out from within the hold – but what the hell was it that had gone up? Surely this had to have been a bomb rather than any kind of accident.

The Royal Gendarmerie were in attendance in addition to the Sûreté, which had a cordon in place around the shattered section of what remained of the seaward-side of the pier. The regional captain of the Sûreté was a personal friend of Dowling and it was he who had been at the other end of the telephone at the gate. Dowling pointed him out. He was standing behind the cordon, about forty feet away engaged in discussion with two others. A big man, he filled the dark-blue uniform – with the shoulder epaulettes and the trouser piping – of the state police. Of the two police forces operating throughout Morocco, the Sûreté played second fiddle to the more politically-directed Royal Gendarmerie. Attached to the military, the Gendarmerie took their orders directly from their Supreme Commander, the King himself.

The agent looked over at the remains of a wharf building – the jumble of bent and tangled, blackened steels resembled a giant raven's nest. From the other side of the cordon, a raised voice was quickly followed by the sharp exit of the Sûreté captain from the huddle. Cursing vividly in French, he stormed over to the edge of the cordon where the agent stood with Dowling.

'A fool and a crook,' the captain shouted, still visibly angry, 'and neither understands police work.'

'Whatever is it?' Dowling asked him.

The man took a deep breath and seemed to let it go. 'Just police business… and politics. It's nothing for you to be concerned about. Please forgive me, my friend, it's been a hard day – and a long night.'

The agent introduced himself. 'A terrible business,' he said.

The captain agreed and spoke about the difficulties they were having – the mobile crane which had finally arrived would make the work easier, he said. The captain talked about the victims of the fire. His eyes looked hollow and haunted – he'd evidently seen things that he wished he hadn't.

The agent asked if the police had established the cause of the explosions. The captain, clearly voicing the official line, said that the incident was thought to have been caused by a paraffin spillage catching alight aboard a ship which in turn led to the ignition of gasoline in the fuelling tanks staged along the pier. Privately discounting the explanation given to him as being naïve, the agent disagreed, saying that if either fuel were present, neither paraffin nor gasoline would be capable of causing damage on this scale – nor even propane for that matter – and besides, he reminded the captain that marine engines run not on gasoline but on diesel oil which is far less flammable and not explosive. The captain looked a little pained and shot a questioning glance at Dowling who in turn gave a small nod.

The captain ushered them away from the cordon to where there was less activity. Keeping his voice low, he said, 'The Sûreté's only providing policing support – the Gendarmerie is leading the operation. The investigation's being run by the Special Administrative Police – the Explosives Unit. So far as I can tell, they've actually no idea what caused this and nothing's been found yet to point to anything specific… but it certainly has the characteristics of a bomb. That's as much as I know – they don't share any more information with the Sûreté than they have to. I don't need to tell you that this information is confidential and highly sensitive… I could lose my job–'

'But of course,' Dowling reassured him.

The agent looked over towards the broken ship. The parts of it which were not wedded to the concrete of the pier or hidden below the waterline were too blackened to see any markings or means of identification.

'Do they have divers examining the wreck?' the agent asked.

'No but I think they'll send a team down in the morning once the search and rescue operation is over.'

'You mean, in case there's another bomb down there?'

'It's too dangerous at present, until they're certain what they're dealing with.' The captain paused and nervously glanced back at the group still gathered behind the cordon. 'But also, the Special Unit will want to ensure the proper security for their procedures.'

'Meaning it'll be a closed investigation?'

The captain gave a tight-lipped smile.

The Gendarmerie wanted the Sûreté out of the way. The agent wouldn't receive any further information on it through this channel. He took a closer look at the pair the captain had left so dramatically. One – dressed in a cheap dark suit – looked like he might be an official of some sort. He was clearly North African, most likely Moroccan. In early middle age, he could be a civil servant or perhaps even a politician. Watching him, the agent ruled out the latter. The fellow lacked that certain swagger which comes only with office – or money. The other man also had the dark skin of a local but he wore a better suit and held himself with ease. A third man had joined them. This one with a receding hairline giving way to the pallid complexion of a more northerly climate. There was something about him – though he too wore a suit, it was tailored in a particular way that led the agent to believe the man wearing it had a military background. It looked too buttoned-up and the man wore it stiffly, like a uniform. Unlike the others, he seemed to have noticed the attention of the agent and there was perhaps something sinister showing in the eyes which had settled upon the agent's own.

'Who's the fool and who the crook, Captain?' The agent asked.

The captain gave a short laugh. 'To the left, that's the attaché to the minister for the interior,' he said, indicating the one in the cheap suit. 'The head of the Special Unit is to the right. The foreigner between them, I don't know. I'll leave you to draw your own conclusions as to which category each of them belongs.'

Appearing jittery at the thought of further bombs, Dowling was clearly not keen to remain at the scene any longer than necessary. He began concluding the interview fairly briskly, telling the captain he quite understood the need for him to get back to work. He thanked his friend for his help and said, 'I'll look forward to seeing you along with the other chaps on Friday – if all this has blown over by then that is, and you're able to make it this week? Otherwise, we'll keep your seat warm and see you Friday week.'

The agent thanked the captain too for his time and that was that. Dowling, who seemed hugely relieved to be leaving behind him the threat of being blown up, hastily led the way back along the pier to the car.

'What on God's Earth was aboard that ship?' Dowling asked, having put some distance between himself and the peril. 'Makes the mind boggle to think what might have caused that sort of carnage. I've never seen anything like it, not even during my time with the Royal Navy in the war…'

But the agent wasn't listening to him. He cast his eye back down the length of the pier as, mentally, he compiled a list of what he would need.

Chapter 4

Star

The cold North Atlantic water was black – there was no moon and the stars were the only thing to distinguish the sea from the sky. The horizon was out there somewhere and beyond that the ocean stretched for another three and a half thousand miles before finally making landfall on the eastern seaboard of the United States. The agent bobbed about in the water while he got his bearings. In the absence of moonlight even the multitude of lights from the shore weren't sufficient to fix his position. Looking up at the constellations, he found Ursa Major then Cassiopeia and traced a line between them to locate Polaris, the north star. He needed to swim due south a little further before he would come to the breakwater. Pushing the salty rubber mouthpiece of the aqualung back into his mouth, he sank silently below the surface once again.

The thing loomed up ahead of him in the light from his diving torch – a towering wall rising from the seabed, made from enormous quarried boulders dumped into the ocean to form the foundation for the largest manmade breakwater on the continent. The agent followed it seaward. As the water deepened, so the breakwater grew until it reached colossal proportions. He swam along the steeply pitched slope of rough boulders which descended to the sea bed, now deep below. And then, finally the wall came to an end, sloping off into the depths – he'd reached the mouth. He must be careful here at the entrance to the harbour. Though the Jetée Transversalle was closed, the rest of the port was still operating and he was now swimming in a busy shipping lane shared by large ocean-going vessels, one of which he could now hear wasn't far away. The dull drumming of the pistons provided backing percussion for the shrill emitted from twin screws. He swam quickly, hugging the inner edge of the breakwater, his torch searching for a safe haven. The beam illuminated a large crevice between two rocks – it looked to be just large enough. Like a small fish burying itself to hide from a larger predator between the corals on a reef, the agent squeezed himself into the crevice, wedging the cumbersome tank on his back between the rocks.

The noise was thunderous as the ship passed by almost above him. He braced his body against the rock and waited for the wash. It came, at first driving him deeper into the crevice – the tank scraping against the rough stone – and then it pulled at him, sucking his body back out of the hiding place again, the current determined to fill the void of sea suddenly displaced by the passing vessel and to drag his body along with it towards the slicing propellers. He held on. The current eased. He checked for any obvious damage to his aqualung – there was no sign of a leak and the pressure looked good. Carefully, he extracted himself from his hideaway and swam on towards the Jetée.

The agent reached the pier and swam alongside it until the wreck of the big ship came into view. He surfaced cautiously to check on the activity above. Lighting set up on masts floodlit the scene for the recovery operation still continuing above him in what had been the main wharf shed but there was no sign of any divers on the pier. With stealth, he descended again. The sight he'd seen from above the water earlier in the day was only one half of the story – the mangled ship had been split into two along most of its length. Much of the hull now lay on the harbour floor, with the remainder of the ship – opened up like a pea pod – lying on its side, half buried in the tremendous crater which had been blasted out of the quayside both above and below the water line. The agent had dived on a good few wrecks in his time but he had never seen anything like it. He swam underneath the upper part of the ship, its lower decks laid out above him in near perfect cross-section. It was extraordinary. Locating the deckhouse, he swam up and found the ladder to the upper decks. The body of a sailor blocked the way. Blood streamed from the dead sailor's ears as he propelled the corpse away through the water – the sonic blast of the explosions must have ruptured the sailor's eardrums. Passing through the upper decks and on up to the bridge, he saw the surface appear above him and checked his depth gauge. This couldn't really be the surface – he was still too deep to have reached that – it was an air pocket. He rose, his head breaking through the water. Pulling out his mouthpiece, cautiously he took a short breath. The air, of course, smelt of combusted material. The pocket would have been created soon after the blast – the fireball it made would have sucked oxygen from the air, leaving it stale and acrid. It wouldn't do to breathe it in for too long. He pulled the mouthpiece of the aqualung back on and looked around him. The air pocket extended to the doorway into

46

the passageway beyond. The agent swam over to it.

The deck was only listing at about thirty degrees and here the water was shallow enough for him to stand. He saw that the pocket continued on beyond the passageway but the doorway was partially blocked by a jam of buckled steelwork. He began trying to heave it away but out of the water the oxygen tank strapped to his back was a dead weight and using the mouthpiece to breathe through whilst he exerted himself only added to the difficulty of the task. Frustrated with the situation, he pulled the mouthpiece away, removed his mask and unstrapped the tank from his back. His flippers would be too cumbersome to walk in and so he pulled these off too and set all the gear down by the doorway. The air smelt vaguely gassy and whatever this was could either be poisonous or volatile, or both – he had better make this reconnoitre a short one. Without the aqualung, it was much easier for him to finish pulling enough of the steel away from the doorway and soon he'd cleared enough for him to squeeze past and into the passageway beyond.

The first door opened into the captain's quarters. There were two portholes both doing the job of holding back the pressure of water outside but looking as though they might give way at any time. The seals had gone and water was spraying into the cabin. The captain of this ill-fated ship was slumped against the bulkhead below the portholes, the seawater spray gently dousing over him. He had a large gash on his head and before the wound had clotted, the blood had turned his white shirt a dirty red. The agent went over and took a closer look at the dead sailor. A fat man, he certainly wasn't African – nor did he look to be European for that matter. The seawater sprayed the agent's face, stinging his eyes. The precariousness of the situation struck him – he had better be quick. He went through the captain's pockets. Just some foreign coins and a pack of foul-looking cigarettes. The water was knee deep here and was covered by a flotsam of soaked charts and other nautical items. There was a table in the corner, set for an unfinished meal. He went over and inspected it – you can tell a lot about a man by what he eats. In this case it was soup. Morsels of bread floated in the water under the table. On it, the bowl had been upturned and the contents were all over a sodden chart.

What chart had the captain been studying while he ate? The soup was blood red and had turned much of the chart the same colour. It had been largely ruined but the agent could see that it wasn't a maritime chart but a topographical land survey map. What was curious about it was that there appeared to be little of particular interest shown on it to warrant the thing – it was mostly desert plain, devoid even of contour variation. Upon closer inspection, the agent saw that towards one side of the map, contour lines were closely packed indicating a sudden and steep rise to higher ground. Bisecting this was a steeply sided valley with a thin blue line (presumably representing a stream) running along the valley floor. Another line, hand drawn in pen, traced the path of the stream to what appeared to be the head of the valley almost at the very edge of the map. To one side of where the penned line finished, the agent noticed a small symbol, carefully inked onto the map – a square with lines projecting inward from each corner to a much smaller square at the centre. A symbol, but for what?

The agent saw some printed information in the bottom

corner of the map but there was no legend here for him to refer to. It showed only a reference number and various other, now undecipherable, details below it. The lettering had bled and was lost under the swathe of soup stain and seawater. He bent down to see what he could make out of it. An inked stamp showing a name and company details was still just visible below.

'Zarauz Architectes, Casablanca, Morocco.'

If this was an architect's drawing, it was one without any building in evidence. Curious. What about the symbol though? What if it weren't a symbol at all? The agent visualised the elevated form of what was shown here in plan-view. A pyramid? With a flattened top?

There were no points of reference shown beside a small settlement which he noted towards the opposite corner. The agent stood up and moved over to it. He stooped down again to read the name. He felt sick at once. It was the air – it was polluted. He looked again at the map but was losing his ability to focus – he was becoming oxygen starved. He needed to get out of here.

The ship suddenly lurched, then a low rumble preceded the explosion which brought a column of seawater spewing into the cabin through one of the now ruptured portholes. It threw him over, cracking his head onto the bulkhead on his way down, almost knocking him out cold. As he went underwater, he saw above him the flash of white and yellow light. He stayed under the water and held his breath until the fireball had gone out above. The sudden dunking had saved him from instant immolation.

Dazed, he pulled his head up from under the water and

attempted to get to his feet. At the same moment, the other porthole went too and the torrent of water which engulfed him knocked him back down again. The water level rose rapidly and while the agent fought against the tide of it, the cabin quickly filled up. Gasping for air, he got himself upright again – the water was now up to his chest. What about the map? He thrashed about in an attempt to recover it but it was futile – it was already soaked and would probably have been torn apart by the sudden rush of water anyway. Time to leave. He waded out of the cabin and stumbled back along the passageway to the bridge where he'd left his scuba gear. The water was shallow here still and he squeezed passed the blockage in the doorway and onto the bridge deck. An awful groaning came from the wrecked ship as the agent reached for the aqualung. And then he was violently thrown across the bridge, his body smashing against the far bulkhead.

The displacement of the air pocket had unbalanced the buoyancy of the wreck, causing it to list suddenly by around forty-five degrees. There was a roar from the passageway as a huge wall of water thundered down it and slammed into the remaining mangled steel sections at the entrance to the bridge. The force of the water took the steels with it and hurled them towards the agent. The jagged metal smashed onto him, ripping through his wetsuit and cutting into his flesh. A flood of seawater followed, the tremendous weight falling onto him knocked every last breath from his lungs. The steel sections had him pinned against the bulkhead. The increasing volume of water inside the bridge added further ballast to the wreck and it screeched and whined as it tore away from the concrete of the ruined quay, gravity winning the fight to drag it further down. The shipwreck sank into the darkness of deeper water. The agent, already suffering the effects of oxygen starvation, had lost his aqualung and now found himself dazed, winded and trapped underwater in the pitch dark aboard a sinking wreck. Suddenly the assignment was not going so well.

The wrecked upper deck section slid further down into the deep water below the broken quayside and, as it plunged to the harbour floor, the wail of shearing steel was replaced with a grinding metallic shriek as the deck reunited itself with its sunken hull. The collision was as if in slow motion, the upper section of the ship colliding side on with the hull then rolling back over and settling on the harbour floor in a new position. Inside the bridge, the heavy steel sections – which would have been his coffin – shifted. Fighting against the involuntarily reflex to breathe, the agent – with the weight on him now eased – was able to push some more of the steels clear and begin to force himself free. The exertion caused him involuntarily to fill his lungs with sea water and though he forced it out again immediately, his chest felt as if it were on fire. He was drowning. With the other flotsam, his life drifted cruelly past him through the water.

He felt for his torch, found it and put it on. Wildly casting the beam about, he saw it by chance – the aqualung wasn't far from him – only twenty feet or so along the bulkhead. With one last, desperate push he freed himself from the remaining steel and swam to it. Making a lunge for the tank, he pulled the mouthpiece of the aqualung to his face, opened up the valve on the tank and took a deep breath. Oxygen poured into his lungs, mixing with the residual seawater. He coughed the water up as best he could and took a series of short steady breaths. He was going to be okay. Once he had regulated his breathing, he pulled the tank onto his back and strapped it on.

Now that the shipwreck had changed position, the way he had come onto the upper decks was barred – it seemed that after everything he might be trapped on the bridge deck. Was it going to add up to a bad day after all? No, he saw there was an exit via one of the bulkheads through a new hole created by the latest explosion. Swimming through it, he cleared the wreck and was into open water. It had been a close call – he wouldn't want another like that on this mission. He headed back towards the breakwater, swimming broadside to the wrecked vessel. As he passed the stern, he shone his torch towards it and peered through the gloom. With the position shifted, the name of the vessel embossed upon the stern was now visible.

'Star of Odessa.'

The dirty coins in the captain's pocket – how had he failed to recognise them at first sight? And of course, the soup. It had been borscht – a classic Ukrainian dish. So then, this *was* a Soviet affair. The agent didn't need London to trace the vessel – he knew he'd found his mystery shipment – but whatever it was which had been shipped out here from the Crimea was now lost along with the ship and the many lives.

Chapter 5

Orca

The agent had slept deeply and woken just before midday feeling well and refreshed – assignments often required him to adopt a semi-nocturnal regime and he was used to it. He'd showered and then, with a luxuriously soft white cotton towel wrapped around his waist, went to the bathroom mirror to comb his hair. Dark and long, with a tendency to curl when left to its own devices, he rubbed on a dab of hair cream before reconstructing the side parting and finishing off by running the comb down his sideburns. His skin had a certain natural roughness which lent a ruggedness to his face, added to by the fact that he hadn't shaved since the day before. The build-up of heavy, dark stubble would be attended to next. The mirror man looked back at him with minimal interest.

After shaving, the agent put on a fresh shirt and a pair of lightweight trousers, stepped into a pair of German black leather sandals and went down to the hotel restaurant. He'd already had coffee brought up to his room and now he moved straight onto luncheon. It wasn't bad – opting to go with the local cuisine, he ordered a lamb couscous – finishing with an espresso and a cigarette. He gazed out through the large picture window of the restaurant to the casino – a separate building set in the gardens of the hotel, it was a striking piece of architecture and, while he drank the coffee and smoked his cigarette, he studied the unusual form it took. The building seemed to command his interest – this time not only for the usual reasons. He left the dining room around half-past-one and went back up to the fourth floor where he'd been given a large suite overlooking the pool.

Ordering a drink from room service, he took it out onto his balcony where, beyond the pool and the cultivated palms of the hotel grounds, he had a reasonable view of the Port de Casablanca below and the old quarter of the medina beyond. The agent surveyed what he could see of the Jetée while he took a sip of mint julep – the aromatic fresh local mint combined with the bourbon perfectly. He began running through what he knew so far about the case but his thoughts were interrupted by squeals of girlish laughter from the pool below – and then the telephone rang in his room. It was Dowling with some information for him. The agent arranged to meet him in the hotel bar at five o'clock – which allowed him a few hours to himself.

***

The fronds of the date palms fluttered in a light breeze which cooled the warmth of the spring sunshine and made for an agreeable temperature. At this time of year in England the mercury struggled to reach fifty under the inevitable low grey cloud which the agent found particularly oppressive. And after the winter he'd endured in Prague, it was joyful. He took off his Aviators and worked some coconut-scented sun oil onto his face, chest and shoulders, enjoying the way it made his skin glisten in the sunshine. The agent felt good again. Lying on the lounger he relaxed, savouring the pleasure of being in a warm climate.

Where it had been chopped up by the bathers, the water in the pool was dazzling as it caught the sunlight. The agent put his sunglasses back on to follow the progress of one of the swimmers in particular. After the previous night's antics, he wasn't in a hurry for another bath himself yet but he was more than happy to watch the lithe figure who, in her black and white all-in-one swimsuit, reminded the agent of an orca. In place of a tail, her long legs powered length after length of the pool, her long black hair streaking out behind over her shining wet back like the trailing tentacles of a jellyfish. The agent beckoned the waiter.

'I'd like a half bottle of Veuve Clicquot if you have it.' Which champagne to order and to be seen ordering was fast becoming a thing of fashion and whilst the producers of some of the more expensive champagnes were much in favour, the agent chose to eschew these for a wine which he chose not on name but on merit.

The girl was getting out of the pool. He watched the water running off her, describing the contours of her body in little streams and rivulets of silver. Her body had the well-toned physique of an athlete – all that swimming. Her calves were well defined and muscular though not in an unattractive way. The backs of her thighs shone in the sun like polished amber and her behind, black and taught in the swimsuit, was a picture. Her decorously long legs were further exaggerated by the high cut of the bathing suit – the one-piece affair had a plunging neckline edged with gold, framing the glistening cleavage of her breasts.

'Make it a full bottle and bring two glasses – saucers not flutes.'

While he waited for the champagne, he watched her wrap herself in a towel and dry her hair – she was superb and he at once felt hungry for her. She was busy pulling at the cellophane wrapper of a packet of cigarettes as he approached. He brought the Ronson out from the pocket of his shorts.

'Permettez-moi?'

Reclining now on her lounger, she looked up at him. He was from the tall, dark and handsome mould – a well-proportioned face with a strong, square jaw. The agent had no facial scars, no identifying features – he could be anyone. He had kept his shirt off and beyond the superficial grazes of the night before, she would see a toned and powerfully muscular physique. Though he looked fit, the agent knew he drank too often and smoked too many cigarettes – but at thirty he had youth playing for him still and his body would, for now at least, tolerate the abuse.

Presumably liking what she saw, she shot him a smile. 'Merci, vous êtes tres gentil,' she said, accepting the offer and opening the packet of Sobranie with long dextrous fingers, extracted two Black Russians. 'Vous en voulez?' she asked, holding up the cigarettes, the gold filter tips emblazoned with the Russian imperial eagle.

The agent didn't care at all for Russian-blended tobacco and actually thought it quite absurd that Sobranie had sometimes been compared to Dunhill. He wouldn't normally smoke these unless there was nothing else and his first instinct – as it always was in similar situations – would have been to reach for his own. But he was unable to resist the intimacy suggested by the way in which she'd offered him the gaudy-looking thing and he found himself saying, 'Oui, merci.'

He lit the cigarettes and bent down to give the girl hers.

Lifting her head, her eyes met his. Blue shot through with hazel and set slightly wide in the face giving her a touch of the feline, they were quite remarkable. Her skin was clear but tanned, setting off those beautiful eyes which remained locked on his. They watched each other smoke. The Sobranie was dreadful but he resisted the urge to put it out and light one of his own.

'Your French is excellent but you're not a native are you – where are you from?' he asked, trying English on her now.

'I am Russian, like my cigarettes.'

But she didn't fit the picture of a typical comrade of the Soviet Union. The characteristic pale Russian complexion had been lost to an established suntan – suggesting she'd been living abroad for some time. The agent was surprised at himself for not seeing beyond the colour of her skin immediately but now, of course, he recognised the Russian in her. Her face came from the classic Russian stable – even if her voice didn't seem to.

'And you are English,' she declared – with no trace of any accent but the perfect elocution of a good Swiss finishing school. From her voice alone, you wouldn't take her to be anything other than a well brought-up English rose. She was certainly well educated and, for a Russian, an unusually international type.

'I admit that I am.' Flirting with her, he added, 'I hope you're not disappointed?'

'I won't be if the champagne is for me,' she said, shooting a look at the bottle the agent was holding.

This girl didn't seem to recognise the fact there was supposed to be a cold war on and, for a moment at least, the agent allowed himself to forget about it too.

'I suppose I could spare a glass for you,' he said teasingly. He had the stems of the saucers tucked between the fingers of the same hand and he kept them there while he peeled the foil away from the muselet. 'I find champagne most reviving after a good swim.'

He had time now to appreciate her more fully. If she had the body of an athlete, then she had the face of a model to go with it – she was stunningly beautiful. In her late twenties, she had that particular bone structure of a Russian woman of good lineage: strongly defined cheekbones and an angular jaw line. She had a petite, elegantly pointed nose and a small mouth with perfectly formed pale pink lips, now pursed around the cigarette.

'Are you holidaying in Morocco?' she asked.

'Actually, I'm here on business,' he said, as he pulled the cork and filled a saucer for her. 'What about you?'

'I work here,' she said, taking the glass from him. 'I just come here to use the pool in my lunch hour… but there's been a stink on this week so I can't linger – one drink and I must get back.'

'Oh dear, what's up?'

She said nothing but gave him a look which said it was none of his business, that she was still making her mind up about this man. She sipped her champagne with that delicious little mouth.

He tried a different tack. There couldn't be that many Russians living here – she may possibly know something of interest. The agent took a punt. 'I only arrived here yesterday but I've heard all about that big fire down at the port – there was a Russian ship lost, wasn't there? I hope that no-one you know was hurt.'

'Well… no, fortunately not,' she said, somewhat taken aback, 'but I didn't know it had been made public yet.'

'One of my people here mentioned it.'

'Oh, I see... only we were told that, for the moment, we shouldn't talk about it.'

'Who told you that?'

'The Consulate.'

He calculated the girl for a moment. 'You work there?'

Saying nothing, she gave away everything.

'I would imagine it's all fairly hush-hush in your game.'

'Well, if that's so, then it hasn't worked,' she conceded. The girl's eyes narrowed for a moment. 'And what is it that you do?'

Remembering he'd put some of the cards Dowling had given him into his shorts pocket earlier, he pulled one out and handed it to her.

She took the card and read it back to him.

'Mr Jenson Coldblow
Director
Coldblow Ltd.
Fine Italian Sports Automobiles.
Park Lane, Mayfair,
London W1.'

Her eyes darted up to his. 'Italian sports cars, how exciting,' she said, dropping the card into her bag (as she did so, the agent noticed her glance at her wristwatch). 'But now you have made me late, Mr Coldblow,' she chastised him, 'and I must rush.'

'Maybe I'll see you here again tomorrow,' he said.

'I'm afraid not, I'm busy tomorrow.'

'That's a shame, you'll miss your swim,' he said, thinking how much he'd miss it too.

'Well… actually no,' she said, almost blushing.

'Why so?' he asked, probing.

'It's just work – well, sort of anyway. My job comes with certain… privileges.'

'Sounds intriguing – anything interesting?'

'Yes, quite interesting as a matter of fact,' she said, smiled and drained the remainder of her glass. 'But I'm not going to tell you. I think perhaps you have asked me enough questions already.' She gathered her things together and stood up to leave.

'But you haven't told me your name,' the agent protested. 'I couldn't possibly let you go before you do.'

The girl held his gaze, her face quizzical as she seemed to be deciding how to field this, the agent's parting shot. 'It's Valentina,' she answered finally. 'Valentina Primakova.'

'Valentina, what a lovely name. Perhaps I might run into you again another time – I'd love to take you to dinner before I have to return to London.'

'Perhaps,' she said with a smile. 'You know where to find me. Goodbye Mr Coldblow.'

***

Dowling arrived looking like the cat who'd caught the canary – he couldn't wait even for his drink to arrive before showing off his catch.

'I've run the checks you asked me to do on these architects of yours and – well, they threw up a bit of a surprise – a coincidence really. Now, their main office is in Spain but it appears another office was set up in Casablanca a few years ago, after the firm won a big contract here…' Dowling paused (likely for impact – he appeared to be enjoying his moment), 'and it certainly was a big contract,' he concluded, theatrically casting his gaze out through the picture window, taking in the gentle sweeping curve of the hotel's frontage.

The agent caught his drift. 'This place?' he said, raising an eyebrow.

'The fellow in charge runs a successful outfit – his firm not only designed the hotel but the casino as well.' Dowling waited in vain for the agent to react.

'Anything more?' he asked dismissively, hoping there would be.

'Yes, I've a bit more for you. Your man is highly regarded in his own country as well as being highly respected abroad. Belongs to a school of architecture known as the *International Style*, whatever that might be, but he's certainly worked all over: South America, Portugal, France, Italy, Lebanon, Algeria – but the hotel and casino represent his first major North African contract. I've scribbled the address of the office down here for you.' Dowling passed the agent a carefully folded sheet of plain paper (all foreign stations – and not least the agent's own department – never used printed stationary unless it were fake).

'Good work, Dowling,' the agent said taking the note, though he only half meant it. 'What about a pyramid?'

'You say you think this thing could be out in the desert?' Dowling asked, the gleam in his eye betraying what was coming.

'Yes,' the agent replied, levelly.

'Well, there aren't any pyramids that I know of between here and Giza, old boy.'

Once he had recovered himself from a fit of guffawing at his own questionable humour, Dowling admitted that actually he hadn't turned anything up on it. 'Nothing about any pyramid I'm afraid, dear chap – the planning department has no record of anything like that and in fact there are no pending applications at all lodged with them from their office. As far as they're concerned, the practice has been dormant since the hotel complex was completed at the beginning of last year.'

The agent took a mouthful of bourbon and pondered the information Dowling had brought him. Unusual to go to the trouble of opening a second office purely for a single job, albeit such a large commercial one as a hotel. But more than that, it was curious to keep it open when there was no more work forthcoming. 'Can you think of anything else which might help here?' he asked.

'Such as? Give me a clue old boy.'

'That's precisely what I want, Dowling – a clue. I don't know what I'm looking for. Maybe there's been something else going on here which you're aware of but that you don't connect with this business. Anything out of the ordinary – something happening in the desert regions possibly.'

After a good two minutes spent staring into his glass (while racking his brain, the agent hoped) Dowling piped up again. 'Here, now I think about it, we did have a queer report about a thing we never quite got to the bottom of. I think it was last year as I remember it but this wasn't in the desert itself, mind. Some fuss about a stream running dry up in the mountains – now… what was it exactly?' The head of station appeared to search for this half-forgotten piece of intelligence.

'Damn, I can't recall the details of it now but we'll have the file on it somewhere – if it's of any interest to you. I don't see how it could possibly relate to this pyramid of yours though.' He drained his glass and beckoned the bar steward. 'Another for the road?' he asked, turning his head to the agent.

'No, thank you.' It wasn't any wonder the man's memory had gone – he'd most likely pickled it. 'Dig that file out for me would you Dowling? It'll probably be of no use as you say, but you never know.'

'Shall do, my dear chap. Now, you've yet to tell me how you got on last night with your... (the bar steward was now in attendance) little excursion.' Dowling looked at the steward and jabbed his index finger into his glass by way of ordering a refill.

'It went alright,' the agent said, flatly.

Dowling waited for his glass to be refilled and, once the steward had retreated, said, 'Nonetheless, I wish you'd asked for some backup. I'm sure my duty officer would have been able to get his hands on another frogman's suit and what-have-you... if you'd wanted some company.'

'Thank you, Dowling but I really only needed the one suit.'

'But it must have been just hellish for you down there all on your tod.'

'I'm quite used to that sort of thing – that's how I work,' the agent said, nipping the topic in the bud. It was time to leave.

Chapter 6
Le Petit Poucet

Wonderful as it was, the car was a mistake – the Maserati was far too conspicuous for covert work, and most especially in a third-world country. The architects' offices were not located in the modern part of the city as the agent would have expected. Instead, the address Dowling had given him was in the old quarter, on the edge of the medina. The sun had set about an hour before and the narrow street, densely populated with ancient buildings crowding out the remaining early evening light, provided pockets of deeper shadow which played to his advantage – as did the dark blue paint job on the coachwork of the Maserati which, from a surveillance point of view, was the car's only saving grace. He'd parked a little way along the street from the offices, where a gloomy pool of shadow had been created under the overhanging upper floor of a building.

From the undeniable comfort of the leather driver's seat, the agent had been observing the office frontage and pondering what he'd found on the Star of Odessa for about a half-an-hour. What the devil was a survey map, from the offices of renowned international architects, doing in the procession of a Russian merchant navy captain? And why on earth would the man have been studying the damned thing while he ate his last supper? For the moment, the agent was puzzled. But it wouldn't do for him to go marching into the architects' offices suggesting that the explosions, which had certainly emanated aboard the Star, might in fact have been intended for this pyramid or whatever it was of theirs – he could leave all that to the Sûreté Nationale if it came to it. And anyway, he doubted the secondary blast he'd been caught up in aboard the ship last night had been caused by the detonation of another bomb. The agent had smelt the gaseous residue left from the original blasts – it had been trapped inside the air pocket on the bridge deck, remaining unignited until what was left of the ship had moved again. He reasoned that what he'd smelt and what had ignited must have been a volatile and highly explosive gas of some sort – which led the agent to believe that there were perhaps no bombs at all in the first place. If not explosives then what had been responsible for causing such damage?

Suddenly the front door swung open and the figure of a man appeared, crossed the street and began walking in the agent's direction. The agent carefully took him in as he went past, noting what he could of him in those moments in the half-light. He adjusted the rear-view mirror to watch as he continued along the street, the image of the figure getting steadily smaller. Before it shrank away completely, the agent was out of the car and walking briskly after him. Ahead, the man stopped for a moment and the agent instinctively went for cover in a doorway. He gave it only a second before he tentatively put an eye out, but showing too much caution can lose you your prey. The man was gone.

The agent carried on to where the figure had been. The man

hadn't disappeared – there was bar. He must have ducked into it through the open doorway. Realising this, the agent doubled back and, walking past the car, carried on to the front door of the architects' offices. He buzzed the intercom. A girl's voice answered. The agent asked if he could possibly have a word with the senior architect.

'I'm sorry but you've just missed him,' she said. 'He's left the office for the day, I'm afraid. Would you like to come in and leave a card?'

The girl's voice was inviting and in any other circumstances it would have been nice to have put a face to it, but he had other things to take care of this evening. 'Thank you but no,' he said. 'I'll call another time.'

***

An international crowd, one of those places where expats go to drink in a way that they wouldn't dare to – nor even want to – back home. Being on foreign soil somehow granted them permission to indulge in gross quantities of spirits. What might have been a quick pre-supper G&T at the clubhouse in Surrey, mutated here into a seemingly endless cocktail hour of pure abandon which might easily last all night. At le Petit Poucet the drinks were expertly mixed by a pair of skilled marseillais barmen and flawlessly dispensed to Casablanca's hedonistic clientele by the well-presented local waiters rushing about in their smart black coats. Dinner in the adjoining restaurant was tagged on at some point – almost as an afterthought.

The evening already had the signs of being a night to remember – the jazz trio were playing up to the Friday night party mood (though it was only Tuesday) and although it was still but dusk outside, there were already a couple of early starters making the most of the little dance floor between the tables. The volume of chatter from the growing crowd steadily increased as the musicians played on and the drinks kept coming. The bar was pure Thirties Deco blended with Moorish style. Beautiful Islamic patterns of green and black ceramic floor tiles worked with the bold curves of a swooping red lacquered bar inset with Bakelite panels. Exquisite chromed European table lamps sat on ornate handmade metal tables – no doubt produced in the local bazaar – the smooth brass-covered tops softly reflecting the lights on their polished surfaces, creating a rich, warm glow.

The maître d' quickly saw the agent to a table in the corner.

'Champagne,' the agent said to the waiter. 'Veuve Clicquot.' The occasion might not have been quite up to the one which had gone before it at the pool but still the setting appeared to demand it. The agent scanned the room. He hadn't much to go on – it had been the briefest of encounters. He might have recognised his gait but here in the bar that was of no use. He was tall though – a good six feet – with a dark complexion and very dark, possibly black hair. He'd been wearing a double-breasted coat in a dark colour – brown perhaps. And he'd worn a tiepin. The agent had noticed it flash for a moment amid the gloom as it caught a light from somewhere. That was all he had seen.

It was busy in the bar – there were easily forty, maybe even fifty in already. The waiter returned with the champagne and while he fussed with the cork the agent methodically dismissed them one by one – too fat, too short, the wrong hair, tall but with no hair etc. He wasn't in a hurry – the bottle was open now, resting in a silver bucket beside the table, and his saucer had been filled. The agent lifted it and took a good-sized mouthful. Not all the men wore their coats but for those who did, the garments too came under the agent's quiet scrutiny – boldly checked, only single-breasted. He reduced it down to two possible candidates. Both men met the physical characteristics of the figure he'd watched pass by him earlier and both wore double-breasted coats – one charcoal black, the other a dark grey pinstripe. The charcoal black was engaged in conversation with another man at a table a little way across from him. The pinstripe occupied a high stool at the bar and was alone. The agent watched these two men a little longer. Both wore equally sober looking ties – and both ties were worn with a pin.

At this distance, the table in question wasn't close enough for the agent to be able to hear any of the conversation emanating from it above the general hubbub of the bar – but his eyesight was sharp enough to be able to make out the design of the tiepin worn by the man in the charcoal coat. At first, he thought it to be an aeroplane before realising that, oddly, it was in fact a miniature brass rendition a cruise missile – a surface to surface job. Discreetly, the agent studied it a moment longer. It was a Martin Matador MGM-1. The distinctive US air force decal was emblazoned on the fuselage below and slightly forward of the tail fin. The Matador was similar in concept to the German V-1 but with the ability for in-flight course corrections made through a radio command. It was certainly an unusual pin for a fellow to be wearing sitting in a North African bar. No reason for this to discount him from being his man – nor to suspect him either. What of the other fellow at the bar in the pinstripe? If it was him, then would he not be more likely to drop into the bar near his office before heading home? Perhaps. Instinct would have to come into play at this stage. If he were wrong then, provided he established this quickly, he would still have time to try the other fellow.

The agent got up and walked purposefully over towards the man at the table with the Matador pin – and then he walked straight past him. As he'd approached, he was able to overhear some of the conversation – the man with the pin had suddenly cranked up the volume seemingly to combat the noise of the bar. Perhaps the pin wasn't too unusual a thing to be seen… on a Yank. The man's nationality was instantly given away by his loud, Southern drawl. This wasn't his Spaniard. It had to be the other man. Practicality was on his side here – the agent could more easily approach a man who was alone. He continued on across the room and went over to the bar to buy cigarettes. After discounting all of the French brands on offer he was left only with Lucky Strike (which he hated) or Camel – and the local affairs which were undoubtedly much worse than either. When the barman came over to him, he opted for the Camel.

Casually, the agent asked for a light from the gentleman in the pinstripe seated at the bar. He had one of those strong Latin faces which convey great confidence. The Roman nose could have belonged to Michelangelo's David. The hair though was nothing like – thinning, oiled and neatly combed back. Not a trace of grey in it yet though – it was black as space. The agent had the measure of him immediately. As his cigarette was lit for him, he casually took a moment to look at the man's pin. It was a bold, golden 'V' overlaid by a gold-rimmed, black-enamelled badge containing the profile of a white stallion, air-born and at full stretch. Where he couldn't simply walk into the man's office and strike up a conversation about God-knows-what, the etiquette of a drinking establishment allowed for such familiar behaviour and so it seemed perfectly natural for the agent to talk to him – particularly here at the bar. 'Going by that clip, I would say the Z 102 out there has to be yours.'

The badge was the emblem of the Spanish auto manufacturer, Pegaso and the horse was Pegasus – minus the wings (the agent recalled that Mobil Oil had beaten the company to registering the flying horse as its trademark). Owned by a parent company, Enasa, who traditionally built all manner of commercial vehicles including coaches and trucks, Pegaso was a division of the company set up to produce high-performance sports cars. However, the factory near Barcelona only succeeded in producing a single model, the Z 102, of which very few were actually manufactured during the past decade's seven-year period of production. It was a rare car to see anywhere, even more so here. But on his way back up to le Petit Poucet, he had been surprised to see a particularly rare version of the model, parked on a driveway near the architects' offices. If he were looking for a Spaniard, then surely the driver of this enthusiasts car had to be his man.

It was clear to the agent that, like himself, the man wearing this pin knew a thing or two about cars. After initial small talk, the agent thought to drop casually in a comment about the Maserati he had with him here. The man's interest was immediately piqued and he asked what he was doing with it in Casablanca. The agent, privately pleased that the car might now be of some use in his assignment, presented him with the cover story. In under a minute, he had secured the man's full attention and they were now deep in a discussion concerning the finer details of a shared passion. After another minute or two, the man paused to offer the agent a drink. Now he knew he had him.

'Actually, my friend had to leave unexpectedly,' the agent said, 'and now I've a full bottle of Veuve Clicquot to get through alone, which I couldn't possibly do. Would you care to continue our talk at my table? I would hate to see good champagne go to waste.' Before the man had a moment to answer, the agent called to the barman. 'Have a fresh coupe taken to my table, if you please,' he said, and then returned his attention to his newly acquired companion. 'My name's Jenson,' he said, happy to stick with Dowling's alias for the time being at least and fishing out a card from his pocket, 'Jenson Coldblow.' Time now to check if he'd picked up the right fellow. 'Now do tell me, what is it that *you* do?'

***

After the champagne, the cool night air on the agent's face had a sobering effect. He would need to be sober if he were to catch up with the Pegaso, which was being expertly negotiated through the narrow section of the Boulevard Mohammed V and away from le Petit Poucet. The braking lights flashed only briefly as the car slowed for the intersection at the Poste Maroc and then shot through a break in the traffic – the architect then accelerating hard as the boulevard widened to become two lanes.

The agent, meanwhile, was blocked by the station wagon he had narrowly avoided and which was now inching its way out of his path. He hammered on the horn – there was a distinct possibility of this becoming a one-horse race. Finally, the bloody car pulled clear and the agent jammed the Maserati into first gear, gave it full throttle and dumped the clutch. The Pirellis screamed as they fought for grip and then finding it, shot the car forward once more. The Pegaso was still in view – just – he could see it careering on through the next intersection. The traffic was heavier here and, as the agent approached the junction, he saw the Pegaso having to weave its way slowly through. On an impulse, he pulled the wheel sharply and the Maserati slewed to one side, the back end hanging out as the agent threw the car into a left turn onto the Boulevard Hassan Seghir. He thought he could find a better route, away from the centre and out towards the docks where the roads would be less congested.

As he'd hoped, the boulevard took him in the right direction for the port and from the terminus he got onto one of the wide avenues which ran alongside the Port de Casablanca. It was, no doubt, a less direct route than the one the Pegaso had taken but it would be quicker – and it needed to be, for although the Maserati was quick, the Pegaso was the faster car. To the Maserati's more than respectable two hundred and twenty horsepower, the supercharged V8 of this Spanish high-performance machine produced a dazzling three hundred and sixty. The agent had turned on to the Avenue des Far and was soon on the long and straight Avenue Pasteur – now he could properly open the car up. The V6 snarled like a big cat as the power from those two hundred and twenty draught horses below the bonnet threw the Maserati forward, pushing his body back into the luxurious tan leather upholstery.

The race had been his idea – a gentleman's wager of one thousand francs to the winner provided the opportunity to get the Spaniard fired up. At the end of the straight, the agent approached the turning to Aïn Harrouda. The Pegaso would surely have had to come along the Boulevard Emile Zola, which must join this road. And there it was – he watched as it flashed past him. The lightweight alloy coachwork of the Pegaso was designed and built by Touring in Milan and the car's high-winged profile with the side vents and sloping rear roofline was not dissimilar to Aston Martin's DB4. The chromed spoke racing wheels completed the picture. The agent went into the turning at speed, dropping his own car into third gear but with his other foot stamped firmly on the accelerator pedal, keeping the power at full revs. The roads around the port were fairly clear of traffic at this time of night and once he was onto the boulevard he was able to work his way back up through the gearbox and into fifth.

Attempting a road race in an African metropolis was a perilous undertaking. Like many large African cities, Casablanca was schizophrenic – the modern city fought with the traditional way of life here. The boulevard had been built by the French and was a wide, two-lane affair. Unlike Paris however, motor cars had to share the roadways here with tractors and carts pulled by animals piled up with produce and other goods. The pedestrians didn't confine themselves to the imposed colonial pavements either, ambling along on the highway also. Despite the difference in horsepower, both cars could achieve a similar top speed on the track of around a hundred and forty miles per hour. Heading away from the centre of Casablanca along the boulevard, the agent dared to get the Maserati up to seventy. Weaving a path for it around the livestock, the V6 growled as he shot past the donkey carts and brought the car up into the wake of the Pegaso. Then his ears were treated to the deep, throaty roar produced from the Spanish beast's all-alloy, four-cam longitudinal V8 running at full tilt.

The architect could not have failed to spot the Maserati on him in his rear-view mirror. The agent closed on his rear, forcing the race leader into braking late for the next bend. The two cars entered it at close quarters but the Pegaso couldn't carry its speed through the corner and with the car beginning to drift, the architect was forced into taking a wide line. The agent seized the opportunity, pulling out from behind the slewing Pegaso, he threw the Maserati toward the apex. He may have just clipped the rear of the Spaniard's car as he had pulled out to undertake it, confirming an appointment for it with the curb – the car obliged, mounting the pavement. The architect, braking hard, narrowly avoided hitting a barrow piled with cages of live poultry. Sailing past, the agent watched the Pegaso fishtail as its driver fought to bring the car under control. It was a convincing manoeuvre but had the agent merely forced an error or was this plain ungentlemanly racing? Whichever it was, it made no odds on this occasion because it just wouldn't do for him to allow the architect to win the race. His competitor wasn't a child after all and the agent didn't need to suck up to him in order to gain his confidence. He needed to impress him by winning – by whatever means necessary. This would buy him time with the man afterwards. Time for the architect to warm to the agent, to come to like him, to get drunk with him and finally, to trust him enough to tell him everything he wanted to know.

The approach road to the Casino Park Hotel foretold the architecture. The roadway rose gently up on a series of piers and then turned, describing a tight circle while gradually sloping back down under itself in an elegant loop to arrive at the hotel lobby. The Maserati flew onto the elevated section and the agent wheeled it expertly round the circular roadway as if the car were locked in orbit. The architect had proven his mettle, keeping control of the Pegaso during its brief excursion away from the tarmacadam and had quickly recovered his race – now he trailed behind the Maserati by only a few feet. With a cacophony of noise, the two cars arrived side by side at the agreed finishing post outside the hotel lobby almost as one – but the agent had won the bet.

Chapter 7
The International Style

The road was now above, cleverly providing an awning for the hotel lobby. The main building drew an arc across the plot, the curved section of a circumference belonging to a larger imagined circle. At the centre of this unseen circle was a smaller, round building which was the casino. It was cradled by the arc of the hotel, with the looped roadway connecting the two like a tether. And the man who would have first sketched out this relationship on a page in his drafting pad was united again with his creation. Despite his loss, he looked across at the agent and smiled broadly at him – likely though, it wasn't the architecture making him feel quite so buoyant. The stench of burnt rubber hitting the agent's nostrils was inhaled by the architect with real Latin gusto.

'I thought I had you there, until the corner,' he shouted over the noise of the idling motors.

'And for a moment so did I. You drove superbly and the Pegaso really is one of a kind.'

'It is our secret weapon,' the Spaniard exclaimed, almost breathless from the exhilaration of the race – and he slapped the polished hardwood wheel as if were a girl's behind. The men cut their engines and got out of their cars. The architect came over to the agent and they shook hands but then, keeping a firm hold on the agent's hand and narrowing his eyes, he said, 'I think perhaps that there was a little contact back there – no?'

A wry smile crept onto the agent's lips. 'I wouldn't like to say.'

'No, I'm sure you wouldn't. However, my congratulations to you – I will settle with you inside,' he said unfazed, indicating the casino across the lawns.

On the face of it, the architect appeared to be in good spirits but the agent sensed this man had troubles which, as the evening progressed, he intended to unearth. The agent was playing the long game and, for the moment, was in no hurry to crack him and besides, it gave him the chance for some fun along the way. What was it his chief had told him? That this wasn't to be a jolly? Well, he would see about that.

They left the cars with the parking valet and together walked along a path through well-maintained gardens to the casino building at the centre. The casino itself was a hyperboloid structure supported by numerous, curved external buttress piers. These piers were narrow and at a distance appeared almost two dimensional. Like ribs, they expressed a containing force on the captive, tapered structure at the centre. They also gave the casino the appearance of something else: a motor surrounded by cooling fins or perhaps some machine part or a small manufactured item, blown up to a ridiculous scale. Inside, the ground floor was dramatically lit by rings of red neon lights recessed into wide channels in the ceiling and the whole circular space was filled with the colour and noise of the gaming machines and the cosmopolitan clientele playing them. The agent and the architect walked through this gay scene and ascended a gently sloping ramp which looped around the curve of the outer wall.

The architecture was magnificent and the agent felt it appropriate to ask the architect what his approach had been to the particular design. He explained that, as with all his work, he wanted to explore the formal possibilities of the particular material in question solely for its aesthetic impact – in this case, reinforced concrete. The concrete construction which formed the core of the building had deliberately been left exposed. The unashamed rawness of the rough finish expressed an artistic confidence in the lean, simple forms of the building. But the agent also noticed the restrained use of some superb detail. Part of one wall had been tiled using a combination of snow white and rich blue rhomboid-shaped ceramics arranged to form a bold geometric pattern. The design clearly drew upon Islamic style but was filtered through the European minimalist sensibilities of the new decade, to produce a fresh and stylish mural.

The serious gambling was conducted on the top floor where the tables were set up for baccarat, black jack, poker and roulette. The two men had bypassed the bar and the restaurant on the first floor and gone straight up. The architect steered the agent towards an already busy roulette table, where he pulled out his money clip, peeled off several notes which he handed to the croupier and indicated to him that he would like a thousand-franc chips apiece for himself and his companion. The agent smiled his acceptance of payment of the wager in this way – it was a commitment to spending the evening at the tables with him.

With roulette, the agent always liked to bet on the street at the start of any night in a casino. He enjoyed gambling a moderate-sized stake at higher odds, and eleven to one suited him to begin the evening with. As he would do for the next half dozen spins of the wheel, he placed a hundred-franc chip halfway over the line forming the end of the row of three numbers which formed the street ending in twenty-one. The architect bet on red. The croupier gripped the spoke and spun the wheel. Then, with a flick of the wrist, he set the little ivory ball into an opposing orbit about the more slowly rotating central column of the wheel. At first, the centrifugal force held the ball inside the outer rim of the wheel as it raced around it, but then inertia took hold of it and the ball began to lose its momentum. Gravity pulled the tiny sphere towards the centre where it collided with the pins to be shot off on a series of ricochets – it was at the mercy now of the slowing revolutions of the wheel. The crazed, haphazard course finished with the ball landing neatly within one of the divisions – a red division. It was number twenty-one. Both men had won on the first spin.

At the end of the first half dozen spins, the architect's luck hadn't held – just like in the cold war between East and West, red was losing to the opposition. The street however, had continued to pay dividends for the agent, with twenty black coming up for him on the fourth spin. His chips had multiplied rapidly and his capital now stood at three thousand francs.

'Lady luck is with you tonight,' the architect commented.

'I believe that you make your own luck,' the agent said dryly.

The main casino bar was located on the floor below but up here on the top floor there was also a smaller bar, just off the main gaming area. Standing at it was an attractive-looking European girl – most probably French – who'd caught the agent's attention earlier. Now he noticed that her eyes were on him and he got up from the well-padded stool.

'Excuse me a moment, won't you?' he said to the architect and walked over to her, discreetly engaging the girl in a brief conversation before returning to the roulette table where the architect had remained, his eyes clearly fixed on the girl as he'd observed this exchange.

'Come on,' the agent said, pushing all his chips onto the table and telling the croupier that they wished to cash out, 'let's go over to the bar – there's someone I'd like you to meet.'

'I'm not sure if–'

'Oh, but I insist – I told her who I was with and the girl's all aquiver to meet the casino's creator.'

The croupier exchanged both the men's roulette chips for normal casino chips – the agent stuffing his own into his coat pockets as he left the table with the Spaniard in tow. What was it that excited women so much about watching men gamble? The agent mused as they walked across a gaudy salmon-pink carpet towards the bar. The girl was a Parisian and it transpired that, as luck would have it, she had a friend with her. The agent chatted up the pair of them and ordered a bottle of champagne – and with the benefit of further lubrication, the architect then conducted a fair job himself with the girlfriend. When the girls went off to powder their noses, the agent turned the conversation to architecture again, asking his companion to expand upon the central theme within his architecture.

'I want my buildings to embody a simplification of architectural forms,' he said, answering with great enthusiasm. 'I wish to discard anything extraneous, leaving behind a pure expression of structure. My architecture attempts to prioritise aesthetic qualities over pragmatic concerns. When form creates beauty, beauty itself is its justification.'

The man felt an obvious passion for his art which the agent hoped would keep him talking. He asked him what he was currently working on, 'Another hotel perhaps?'

'I have been involved with the construction of another project which has in fact just been completed here in Morocco,' he said rather coolly. 'Not an hotel. In a way, not really a building at all,' he added with intrigue.

Presented with a perfectly good opportunity to fish, the agent did so – and the architect took the bait readily, going on to outline what sounded like rather a radical structure which he had built somewhere out in the desert. Though he clearly enjoyed talking about his work, he was however vague about the details of the project and his description of it was somewhat abstract.

'Artists talk about sculpture as being either subtractive or constructive. Subtractive sculpture is a term used to describe the shaping of a sculptural form from a solid mass by a process of considered removal of material to produce the finished artwork. Constructive sculpture, on the other hand, involves the manipulation and assemblage of one or more raw materials to construct the work. If architecture were viewed in this way, then it would, of course, be considered to be constructive – how could it be otherwise?'

'I've no idea. You had better tell me.'

'But what if these notions were turned on their head? What then would the architecture look like?'

The architect was steadily becoming drunk and the agent was

quite happy listening to him as he meandered his way towards telling him what he wanted to know about this building that wasn't really a building at all. To the agent, it was starting to look highly likely that he was talking about the thing he'd seen depicted on the survey map aboard the Star of Odessa. He let him go on for a while, before choosing his moment.

'It all sounds terribly interesting but I can't quite picture how the thing must look. I would love to see it, perhaps you'd show it me – is it far?'

The architect seemed to sober up at this and now he looked pensive. He apologised and explained that while he would be more than happy to do so, his client was a very private individual and that unfortunately this would not be possible.

The agent was coming to understand this man and he knew not to push it any further. He needed another way in. He lit a cigarette – his own brand, the nearly full packet of Camel having been discarded already in the footwell of the Maserati – and looked out onto the gaming room. The casino was beginning to fill up now and the tables were getting busier. He might like to play some black jack when the girls returned, the agent thought distractedly, before he returned his concentration to the matter in hand. He realised that he needed to come at this from the side.

'You know,' he started, 'It's interesting talking to you about your work but I must confess that I do, at least in part, have an ulterior motive.'

This only seemed to make matters worse – the architect looked visibly concerned now. He'd better get on with it and quickly, before he lost him altogether.

'You see, I've been thinking for some time now how I'd like

to expand my business back in London – I've already a large showroom in Mayfair. Now, the business has done me very well indeed, especially of late, and just before I came away on this trip I was offered the opportunity to buy up a vacant plot of land in another part of the city – in Chelsea. I've been mulling over the idea since I've been here. You see, if the estate agents are to be believed, the area's set to be the next big thing. They say that all the fashionable artists are already moving in and that trendy boutiques are starting to appear along the Kings Road – of course, this sort of thing attracts young affluent types, not without a discerning eye, who might be interested in purchasing an Alfa Romeo or perhaps even a Ferrari.'

The architect now seemed to come back from wherever his paranoia had momentarily taken him. The agent's mind raced as he thought about quite how he should put it. He was, after all, making this up on the hoof.

'This plot I'm talking about was a former bomb site – there's still quite a few of them left in this part of the city that haven't yet been redeveloped. Now, having had the good fortune, quite by chance, to have run into you and to have enjoyed the pleasure of your company for last couple of hours, I'm thinking to go ahead with it. You see, I should want to build something very special there. Not just some run-of-the-mill, utilitarian affair – a great empty garage to park the cars in – but something unique and exciting, modern and stylish. Rather like the very latest models I sell… and expensive too. And so, I was thinking, if I were to invest a great deal of money on a new building such as this – and for it to represent my company properly – then I'd only want to employ the very best firm of architects to design it for me. Having seen what you've done here and having listened to you talk about it all so eloquently, it has left me in no doubt at all that you would be the man for the job.'

The architect had, much to agent's relief, relaxed again.

'That is most flattering,' he said and asked him about the requirements for the new showroom.

The agent kept his reply short. He was on more solid ground talking about cars than about buildings – especially ones for businesses which didn't exist.

The architect listened to the agent's rather truncated brief and looked thoughtful. 'I have worked in many places around the world but I have never been offered a commission of any significance in London and certainly not one which would so well combine my second love – of sports cars…'

Now the agent felt he had him hooked – he'd better get to the nub it. 'Of course, while I think that what you've achieved here is wonderful, they say success can only truly be judged by one's last work.' His story was as big a carrot as he could muster and he'd said as much as he could. Now the agent just let the idea hang in the air. He took a small mouthful of champagne and casually lit another cigarette. He looked round the room again and then back at the architect who was fiddling with his remaining five hundred franc casino chip, turning it over slowly between his fingers. He appeared to be lost in thought. The agent smoked his cigarette and waited for him to come back to him – hoping that he would before the girls did. Whatever it was that women found to do in the Ladies' room which took them so long, for once the agent felt grateful of it.

Finally, the Spaniard spoke. 'I have the models at my office,' he said, looking up but still fingering the chip. 'If you are interested, I could perhaps show them to you tomorrow.'

The agent knew that the architect's offer had come well lubricated and would not survive until the morning – this had to happen now or it wouldn't happen at all. 'I'm so intrigued,' he said. 'This project of yours really has sparked my interest – let's go now, we can take the girls with us.'

'No, that would not be a good idea.'

'Okay, then just the two of us. We can leave the girls here to spend my winnings on the slot machines downstairs – there's more than enough to keep them occupied for an hour or so until we return.'

'I don't know, tomorrow would be–'

But the agent was already fishing chips from his pocket. 'Come on, let's go,' he said, cutting him off once again. Laying out his handkerchief, he placed a neat pile of chips on it, leaving out a single one hundred franc chip 'I'm sure the girls won't mind waiting for us,' he said and with a mischievous look, he threw his room key in on top of the chips and tied the handkerchief up into a parcel.

He called over the bar steward. 'Please convey our apologies to the ladies, would you? Tell them we'll be back soon and make sure they get this,' he said, indicating the bindle he'd just made and handing the barman the lone chip with a couple of bills to pay for the drinks. The architect looked on, dazed – the agent had already made the decision for him.

'We'll take the Maserati,' he said and then, playing his best card last, dropped the car keys onto the bar in front of the bemused architect. 'If you are to design a new showroom for me, then it should only be right that you're given the opportunity to experience the models I'll be displaying there at first-hand. Anyway,' he added – quite untruthfully – you've had far less to drink than I have and so it should be you who drives.' The art of seduction, cultivated through years of practise, was one in which the agent was masterful.

'You can test my little Italian out for yourself,' he said as the architect, finally submitting to the agent's charm and persuasion, obediently rose from his bar stool.

Chapter 8

La Pirámide

The large topographic model provided the context for another, altogether different structure to the casino building and the agent knew for certain the moment he saw it that this was what he'd seen represented in plan-view on the map he'd found aboard the Star. A large section of mountain had been rendered in modelling cement. From it rose the precise form of a shallow Perspex pyramid – only the pyramid was upended, its top buried into the cement. It was now past midnight and the agent looked at the architect who stood – on a tasteful pallet of threads spun by hand to produce the carpet on his office floor – gently swaying in an alcoholic breeze.

The agent pondered the upturned pyramid and felt drawn to the use of this powerful shape. In a sense the chosen form was classic – like the dark grey double-breasted coat the Spaniard wore – but it was also striking and completely at odds with the natural form of the hilltop. The result was a strangely beautiful piece of architecture. The architect said that he had been careful in his choice of this particular form for the building and he reminded the agent of the celestial connections that the pyramids of Central America, Egypt and Cambodia all shared. They spoke for a little while about this and the mystery surrounding the engineering prowess of the Maya and the ancient Egyptians. Then the agent asked him what his client had thought about the association of the architect's design with the pyramids of these great civilisations.

'It had greatly appealed' he said, the booze wiping away any trace of modesty. 'I remember he said too that the inversion of the pyramid made it look as though it was not of the Earth at all, rather more like something from space had landed on the mountain. He liked this notion very much – that it appeared to have fallen from the sky and, in the process, had upset the natural order of things. He said that the premise fitted precisely with his vision…'

He trailed off here and the agent watched the architect carefully. For the first time, the trouble which he'd suspected lay buried in the man showed on his face.

'And what exactly is his vision?' the agent asked.

The architect gave him a heavy look. 'Do you know, I am not sure about that,' he said. 'It might be something wonderful…or it could be diabolical.'

The melodrama piqued the agent's interest. 'Whatever do you mean?'

'It is a scientific installation, that is all,' the architect said dismissively and, recovering himself, went on. 'But come, let me show you something else. With the pyramid, I have quite literally turned constructive architecture on its head, but this is only the tip of the iceberg.'

The architect led him over to another table where a smaller secondary model was set up. 'I give you, *subtractive architecture*,' the Spaniard proclaimed, somewhat drunkenly.

This model detailed extensive subterranean accommodation and service spaces carved out of the mountain, below the pyramid. The model accurately illustrated these areas in cross section.

'My God,' exclaimed the agent. 'It's an underground lair.'

At this, the agent sensed the architect stiffen by a degree and he quickly asked a question to relax him again.

'What are these large vertical chambers?' he asked, pointing at a pair of vertical void sections.

'Ah yes, they are ventilation shafts for the underground areas,' the architect replied, brightening once more and clearly excited about showing the agent this extraordinary model.

'But they must be enormous – this model is to scale, isn't it?'

'Yes, they are much larger than required but they utilise two existing shafts, naturally present in the rock – the geology is quite unusual you see. I have connected them to the subterranean sections of the installation to provide ventilation to those areas. The client was particular that he wanted them to be incorporated exactly in this way.'

'Yes, I see, making good use of what's there already, I suppose.'

It was obvious that the installation would have cost the architect's client a small fortune to construct. From what he could see here alone, the agent was none the wiser as to what particular branch of science it might be used to serve. Thrilling architecture demands an equally thrilling purpose and it was the specific nature of that purpose which was of concern to the agent. He asked him what the brief had been.

'My client is a man who enjoys privacy, Mr Coldblow. He

wanted me to design an installation where he could carry out his scientific work and not be bothered by the outside world – a retreat, if you like.'

'I see, well an underground labyrinth hidden somewhere in the world's largest sub-tropical desert would certainly fit the bill. But what about the pyramid – I take it that the actual thing is made of glass? This element surely though doesn't fit at all with the brief you've just described to me – in fact it might serve rather the opposite function wouldn't you say?'

'The walls are indeed made entirely of glass and so, yes, I would have to agree with you. In fact, you are quite correct, the pyramid has not only been conceived using constructive – as opposed to subtractive – architecture, but it also serves a different purpose to that of the subterranean chambers.'

'What's the pyramid for then?'

'It is a look-out of sorts…' he said, trailing again.

The agent recognised an opportunity to push the conversation along from architectural terminology to the specifics of location. 'I imagine the view would be impressive,' he said, then added casually, 'Where did you say it was?'

The agent at once sensed the architect feeling probed by the question and he appeared in a moment to almost sober up before delivering his long-winded answer.

'I really don't know you at all, Mr Coldblow – but I like you and for some reason I feel that I can trust you. That is why I have allowed you to see these models and have discussed a private project with you – this is my work after all and so I think that it is up to me. I can see that you are understandably curious and so I would like to be able to tell you more but, as I have already said, my client is a private person and, unfortunately, I am unable to elaborate any further without breaching client trust. I am not at liberty to reveal the location without putting myself in... well, to be frank with you, a perilous position. The whereabouts of the pyramid is a secret which my client would like very much to remain as such.'

Despite the architect's grandiose speech, the agent continued working to glean a little more about his client but, from then on, he seemed to slide away into a funk, retreating into himself in that particular way which can be brought on in some men by drink. He had become maudlin now and this was no good at all. The agent had manipulated the architect into showing him the models through a combination of flattery, good impression and subtle coercion. It had got him this far but the technique had now run its course and he required a new method. He needed to find out who the architect's client was and if he wouldn't talk freely any more, he needed to switch tack and apply pressure to extract the information.

The Berretta was nestled in the shoulder holster where it had been all evening. Casually, he felt inside his coat for the butt of the gun but in that moment, the architect stirred from his reverie and suddenly piped up.

'A nightcap,' he said determinedly, then sprang up too quickly from his chair and stood there wobbling for a moment before stumbling off into an adjoining room in search of a bottle. The agent let him go. He'd have a final drink with the man and see where that went.

The bottle was clearly taking some time to locate. In his absence, the agent contemplated the models again. He went over to the table with the smaller one and took a good look at it. He had an idea. Carefully, he lifted it up from the table and turned it over in his hands, revealing a wooden base on which was a medium-sized label with the architect's details printed at the top of it. Underneath this, it read:

```
Modelo numero: 1902/b
Fecha: 17 de Diciembre, 1958
Proyecto: la Pirámide
Cliente: Sr. de Sauveterre
```

With the elusive bottle in hand and now beaming drunkenly as a result of the find, the architect returned to the room. He saw the agent had the upturned model in his hands. The label was clearly visible. He stopped dead and his face fell.

'I am curious,' the agent said to him. 'Who is Senor de Sauveterre?'

The architect's face turned pale but, to the agent's relief, he didn't drop the bottle – it looked to be a good single malt. The man opened his mouth as if to speak but, instead of words, what he ejected was a great billowing wave of vomit. The architect crumpled, his demeanour stripped now of any remnant of style and sophistication, he fell into his chair with his head in his hands. He made no effort to clean himself up at all, the vomit soaking into the lapels of his coat reeked of bile and would have made a lesser man than the agent retch himself. It did, however, quite turn the agent off the thought of having a whisky.

'I should never have told you anything about this,' the architect said, slowly shaking his head in his hands. 'What was I thinking, allowing you here, showing you…?'

The agent kept his silence, simply watching the architect as he unravelled before him. The man had tears in his eyes now as he looked up at the agent. Then it had all simply poured out of him, like the contents of his stomach had a few moments before. He told him that de Sauveterre was a Frenchman, an industrialist and a scientist of some sort but that he really didn't know very much about him beyond that. The pyramid had been built out in the Sahara, on top of a ridge on the edge of the desert plain. He understood that it had been built as a centre for science – though which particular branch of science and what exactly the nature of the work intended to be carried out there was, had never been made clear to him. He said that what he had been told was always vague, ambiguous. He was aware only that both the pyramid and the underground areas were required to accommodate some extremely large, presumably scientific, instruments.

The agent reminded him of his earlier comments and asked him what his instinct had been about what de Sauveterre planned to do in the building. His face darkened. He told him that the more he had worked on the project, the more he had suspected that the nature of the science might not be wholesome and that, by the end of the commission, he wondered if in fact it might be something sinister – perhaps even evil. He couldn't say why exactly, he had just felt this was so.

The agent asked him what the Soviets involvement was in it all. The architect was stunned.

'How could you know that?'

The agent gave the man a look of utter seriousness and spoke to him harshly. 'It doesn't matter. But you had better tell me.'

'I don't know what would happen to me if they found out that I–'

'I do,' the agent cut him off. Firmly, he said, 'And I'll do it right now if you won't tell me what I want to know.'

The architect looked down at his lap where the mess had pooled on his trousers. The agent recognised the shape of fear in the man. He had allowed the agent to learn something private, something secret – something dangerous. But it was too late now. He resigned himself to the agent.

'I know they're involved, that's all. But I don't understand how. I felt threatened by them…'

'By who? Give me their names.'

'It was run through the Soviet Consulate. I…I don't know any of their names – it was all kept under wraps.'

'I'm sorry but that's not good enough.'

'I think he's an air force colonel – the one who's in charge of their end of it. I've never been told his name but I can tell you that he's not a pleasant man.'

'And who else there – at the Consulate?'

'There were a couple of other Russian military types who I met with de Sauveterre out there – at the pyramid, but we were always talking through their interpreter. It wasn't very personal.'

'Okay, and who else is in on it?'

'I think there are some fairly high-ranking local officials who know about it – in Hassan's cabinet even. It's not good – the whole business disturbs me. I think perhaps that my involvement in it has left me in a seriously uncomfortable position with the government here.'

'Poor you. Where is it – the pyramid?'

'I've told you all I know already…' he started but then, shocked, he trailed off. Disbelief was written across the architect's face as he watched the agent slide his hand into his coat and coolly withdraw the Beretta.

The agent held the gun quite casually. He said, 'You strike me as a man who cares very much about his work. As the architect of this building – or whatever it is that you wish to call it – I do not believe that during the course of its construction you would not have needed to make at least one visit to it. Where is it?'

'I don't know. That is the truth. Yes, of course I was required to make several visits to the site but I was taken there on every occasion at night and in a Land Rover with blacked out windows. It was around a three-hour drive from Casablanca – I timed it once. It had all seemed very "cloak and dagger" to me but I had accepted de Sauveterre's terms, respected his desire for privacy and I suppose I had secretly rather enjoyed the sense of mystery surrounding the whole thing.'

The agent doubted he would be enjoying his current predicament much. De Sauveterre – or was it the Russians? – certainly had the man spooked enough for him to keep quiet even at the risk of having his blood spilt over his rug.

'I really don't know the exact location but I suppose it must be somewhere in the High Atlas Mountains, possibly out towards the border with Algeria. You must believe me, please–'

'Are you left or right footed?' the agent asked him suddenly.

'What?' The architect was thrown by the question. 'Left, as a matter of fact, but why do you–'

'You told me earlier that you liked me. Well, I like you too and so I wish to show you some leniency,' the agent said, and he shot the architect in his right foot.

A quarter of the bones in the human body are in the feet and there are twenty-six of them in each. The effect of a gunshot wound to the foot is not life threatening but it is extremely painful. A bullet will shatter most of these small and delicate skeletal components and usually result in a permanent disability. The agent sipped his whisky and watched the architect, now lame and writhing in agony on the beautiful geometric design of the Berber carpet.

'Now, if you would rather not spend the rest of your life in a wheelchair, you had better tell me the truth before I put a bullet into your left foot as well.' But he doubted he'd need to go that far. A shot in the foot was excruciating and one foot had always produced a result – except in the very toughest of cases. He repeated the question, 'Where is the pyramid?'

Desperately the architect tried to recall details of the journeys to the site, but there aren't many landmarks in the desert at night and in the end the crying became too much for the agent to bear. After receiving a gunshot to the foot, he had known most men, including some of his opposite numbers, to tell him everything – even what they really preferred in the bedroom. He was convinced now that the man didn't know any more than he'd already told him and there would have been no advantage to gain by the agent carrying out his threat. The night been productive enough and amongst the information he had extracted, the agent now had a name and at least a vague notion of the location and some idea of the function of the pyramid.

Also, along with some (probably corrupt) government officials here, he now knew for certain that the Soviets were in on it. He had something to go on which would do for now. He told the architect to be quiet, that he'd heard enough. He was satisfied.

The man stopped talking at once. Despite the anaesthetic effects of any remaining alcohol in his system, he would be in great pain. He lay still now, softly whimpering.

'Who are you, really?' the architect asked him in a whisper.

'There are no names in my business.'

Though in shock, the architect appeared haunted by the further worry of retribution. He spoke again.

'What if they find out what I've told you?'

'We had better make sure they don't,' the agent replied, raising the gun again – this time pointing it at the man's chest. Was this merely a threat or was he actually taking aim? It wasn't easy to kill somebody whom you've just spent time getting to know.

Chapter 9

Kingfisher

The coffee in Morocco is superb. Freshly roasted Arabica beans from the Côte d'Ivoire are prepared in the Turkish manner to produce a dark, strong cup. It had taken a few of them though to shift the agent's thick head. He had left his room quietly that morning, leaving the girls to sleep. They were both petite with young, lithe bodies and had that very French way about their sexuality which he found particularly alluring – at least he had done after all the drink he'd consumed last night. The sex had been the usual story though. Automatic, mechanical – a means to an end, and once it had ended he didn't want either of them there. He didn't know them and he didn't want to. Take away the desire and you're left with nothing, unless there is love – and that's another story.

In the end, of course, neither of the girls were needed but, when the agent had had his quiet word with Lilly at the bar, the deal he'd made with her was for two. And so, he'd decided that he may as well make the most of it and get his monies worth. He'd recognised the pair as working girls from the off – all those women in casino bars wearing cocktail dresses weren't there waiting for their husbands. Casinos the world over quite happily allowed these girls to pick up business inside their establishments, or at least they tolerated it and turned a blind eye – the bars would be empty otherwise. He had left the fold of notes for them on the nightstand, wondering what he should put it down as on his expenses sheet.

He had put the call into London requesting information on this de Sauveterre character from the station inside the British Consulate. He wouldn't hear back for at least another 24 hours – the department responsible for tracing that sort of information wasn't ever quick off the mark and the staff didn't work shifts. Rather, it was strictly office hours only and so there was little hope of him getting a reply the same day – certainly not, given that he happened to know that they regularly sloped off for the day not very much later than tea time. In the meantime, he intended following up on another lead while he waited for the reply.

The agent finished his fourth coffee, put down his copy of *Le Monde* and lit another cigarette. The French paper was full of the news of Gagarin's orbit around the Earth – the manned space flight meant the Soviets had taken yet another step further ahead of America in the space race. They certainly had made great gains over the past few years. First the Sputnik satellite, then the dog, Laika and now this. On the other side of the coin, it was Russia who were trailing behind its rivals in the arms build-up. And by some margin as, contrary to Kennedy now claiming there to be a missile gap in order to justify America's arms spending, the agent knew full well that the Stars and Stripes were in fact well ahead on this front. While the Soviet missiles had been proven to work well in delivering payloads into space orbit, their design wasn't so well suited to carrying intercontinental ballistic missiles.

Gagarin's flight had been announced to the world's press by TASS, the Russian news agency. The Soviet authorities had described the flight as a complete success going exactly to plan – from the launch to the precision landing of the capsule at the predetermined landing site. But the agent knew a thing or two about the Soviets and about how the authorities there managed their own press. Only good news was ever reported in Soviet Russia – news that helped underline the supposedly inevitable march of the Union towards utopia. But it went further than that. The Soviet authorities were also masters of obfuscation and so bad news could quite easily be manipulated into good. In a land where things were often called precisely the opposite of what they really were, in reality the flight could as well have been lost forever in space or even have ended in a ball of flame on the launch pad before ever leaving the ground. The agent knew full well that in Russia words and appearances were meant to be deceiving. And so, for the moment at least, he took the details of what he'd read in the report with a large pinch of salt.

The waiter came over to where he was sitting at one of the tables set up on the wide pavement outside the cafe on Rue Soumania and asked if monsieur would care to inspect the menu de jour. The agent looked at his watch. It was a minute before noon. He'd been here for too long. He ought to leave or he'd begin to look suspicious. Anyway, he'd finished reading the newspaper and nothing interesting was happening at the building on the other side of the road from where he was sitting. Amid a row of colonial edifices, now looking distinctly worn around the edges by the North African climate, the building in question bore all the fading decorative flourishes of the French Colonial style. Maybe he'd missed her already. He asked for the bill. The waiter came back with it in a saucer which he put down on the table. The agent fished out a few francs from his pocket and dropped them onto it, then he folded away his paper and, gathering his things, was about to get up and leave.

At precisely midday the main door of the Russian Consulate in Casablanca, which occupied the building opposite, was swung open by a doorman and Valentina Primakova stepped out onto the pavement. She pulled out a pair of sunglasses from her handbag, put them on and headed west along the wide pavement of the Rue Soumania. She had on a tight-fitting dark skirt which finished at the knee. Below the hemline, her fine legs were bare. She walked briskly along in matching low-heeled shoes, her breasts shivering beneath her cream silk blouse.

He watched as she walked towards a lovely little turquoise Alpine Berlinetta A110 that he'd already noticed parked a short distance away, then got to his feet and moved quickly to the Maserati which he'd parked directly outside the cafe – on the opposite side of the road to the Berlinetta. He got in and started the engine. As he had walked to the car, he'd seen her fish in her handbag and pull out her keys. Now the little sports car was already pulling out into the steady stream of midday traffic. Wasting no time, he pulled out into the opposite lane and executed a U-turn which brought him neatly around facing the same direction as the Berlinetta.

The traffic in the centre of Casablanca seemed particularly bad for the time of day and he crawled along the congested French boulevards, maintaining a safe distance. An intersection came into view – there were a couple of Sûreté Nationale motorcycles stationed there, stopping the traffic, apparently at random, to inspect drivers' papers. So, this was why they had been moving so slowly. It would cause him trouble if he were to be delayed here by an inspection. Ahead he saw the little Berlinetta just breeze through the checkpoint and accelerate off like a rocket along the now clear road ahead. The agent knew that the Maserati was just *too* flashy – and nor did he have the smiling eyes of Miss Primakova. He wouldn't get through so easily. In readiness for being stopped, he pulled out his passport and driving licence (both in the name of Benson – his usual alias) but realised he had no idea where the papers were for the car. Hoping Dowling might have left them in the glovebox, he reached over. Damn him – nothing in there but a bottle of Acqua di Genova. He looked up. Ahead he could only just make out the little turquoise shape of the Berlinetta now. Looking dead ahead of him, he inched the car towards the police checkpoint. One of the gendarmes waved him over to stop. He mustn't lose the girl.

The fact that, unusually for a Russian, she spoke both very good French and perfect English hadn't escaped the agent. Surely it had to be more than a coincidence. How many Russians working at the Consulate were as proficient in languages as this girl? The architect had mentioned an interpreter and the agent had a hunch that interpreter's name was Valentina Primakova. And if she *had* been in those meetings at the pyramid then it was just possible that she might lead him to someone involved. Looking back to when he had met her, she'd certainly been cagey with him about what she had planned for today.

He couldn't risk being held up at the checkpoint. He gambled. Quickly he opened his notebook and extracted two five hundred franc notes. He placed them inside his passport and returned his notebook to his pocket. He wound the window down. The gendarme looked in at the luxurious pod which cosseted the agent: fine Italian leather upholstery, woollen carpeting and the polished wood dashboard and trim. The policeman held his hand out for the documents. He was going to need to trust to luck here – he handed him the passport and driving licence. The gendarme took them from him and, as he opened the passport, the agent apologised for not carrying the car's documentation with him. He said he hoped that it wouldn't be a problem.

The officer handed him back the driving licence and then the passport – now minus the cash. 'Pas de problème, monsieur,' he said blandly and waved him on. The agent slung the documents onto the passenger seat and pulled away sharply. Quickly, he got the Maserati into third but there was more traffic ahead. He'd need to do some fairly smart driving now if he were to catch up with the girl. He kept the window wound down to let the rushing wind cool him as he pulled out and overtook a lorry. He'd left the wide French boulevards of the city centre behind him now and was travelling southeast along the main road out of the city, through the scrappy edge of town. Casablanca disappeared behind him as he gunned the Maserati along at fifty miles per hour and then up into fourth gear, weaving himself a path through the traffic. He was beginning to enjoy this assignment.

Up ahead there was another intersection where the road branched off for the coast route south to El Jadida. Where was the Berlinetta? Valentina had told him she was going to get her swim today – did she mean to go to the beach then? She'd mentioned 'privileges' to him too – could this mean the use of a beach house perhaps? In his induction, Dowling had talked at some length about there being some quite expensive homes to be found down on the coast towards the region's second city. In fact, he seemed to the agent such an authority on the subject that if it suited him, he could leave the service and quite easily set himself up as a property agent – if his civic leanings failed him first, that was.

He decided she must be heading for the coast, but just as he approached the junction and was about to take the turning, he caught sight of the car again. It was racing off down the other fork onto the southern highway which ran through the dry scrubland interior plain towards Marrakesh. He'd very nearly lost her, but he had her again now. The three and a half litres of power under the bonnet of the Maserati had no difficulty in catching up with the Berlinetta, after which he sat the car a comfortable two hundred yards or so behind, making sure there were always several vehicles between himself and the girl. She was charging the little French sports along the highway at over sixty and slaloming between the potholes. Either she was late for her appointment or she simply liked driving fast – the agent wouldn't entertain the idea that she'd spotted him. The girl, on the other hand, had certainly caught his attention.

After half an hour, the car pulled off the highway and he watched it throw up a great cloud of dust as the girl made a sharp left turn. Dust hung in the air as, slowing, he approached and pulled in just before the turn. Signposted to Tagadert, the road was an unmade, gravel track which wound its way up a gentle series of hills. The whereabouts of the Berlinetta was given away by the rising column of dust – it described the progress of the car in a thick, ochre stain on an otherwise clear sky. He turned in and drove on along the track, following her trail on the map she drew for him above.

Set brightly upon the furthest hill was the village of Tagadert. There were only about twenty or so houses – simple dwellings for the peasant farmers and herdsmen who made their existence here. There were a couple of tractors and trailers beside the road in the centre of the village but there were no other cars besides a battered old Mercedes taxi which had pulled up outside the village store – a folded down wooden flap on the side of one of the shacks which served as a counter for the meagre looking supplies contained within. As he drove past, he could see unmarked sacks of dried goods and large dirty white plastic tubs of heaven knows what. He passed a man dressed in tattered old clothes riding a donkey and leading another behind it, packed to the gunwales with sacks of half dried up, dirty yellow corns. What was a smartly dressed, sophisticated young Russian woman doing in this place?

The trail she'd left him stopped on the other side of the village. The agent pulled the Maserati over and, from his carryall, pulled out the small sniper scope which he quickly buried in a trouser pocket before getting out of the car. Ahead of him the track narrowed and dropped away down the side of the hill, revealing the mountains in the distance. A high drystone wall ran alongside the track for some way, smothered in the rich fuchsia and purple blooms of bougainvillea. He walked down the track looking to see where the girl had left the Alpine – he didn't have to look very far. After a short way, the wall turned sharply by ninety degrees and described a large rectangular double carport.

He could hear the Berlinetta before he saw it – the hot metal of the exhaust system plinking as it had begun to cool and contract. He walked cautiously towards the carport. The rear end of an Alpine Renault A110 Berlinetta is every bit as good looking as any Italian's rear. The vents with their scoops sculptured into the rear wings, directing the air to the rear mounted engine and gearbox, gives the body an impression of animal physicality.

The roof of the carport was constructed simply from wooden rods spanning the width of the space and supporting a weave of dried grasses. There was a Land Rover parked in the other space. But the rustic appearance of the setup was subverted by more than just the cars: mounted above a fairly innocuous-looking door set within the wall, was a closed-circuit television camera. The girl was gone, though a trace of her lingered in the dry, sterile air. The spiced pear, jasmine, rose and honeyed broom that was Arpège – an expensive scent for a Russian girl to be wearing, even for one working overseas in the diplomatic service. He filled his lungs with the unmistakable French perfume made by Lanvin and ducked down behind the Alpine on the opposite side to the security camera. Stealthily, he moved along to the driver's door and lifted his head just enough to see in through the side window. He saw nothing in here that he wouldn't have expected: a few items of make-up and a packet of cigarettes on the dashboard, a magazine stowed in the side pocket of the passenger door.

The agent ducked again and, crouching behind the car, made his way back out of the carport. Giving the camera a wide berth, he walked on. The wall was about fifteen feet high and, as he walked, another wall came into view, rising up behind the outer one – a second structure built of concrete and dressed in baked ochre-coloured mud. There were no windows but it was clearly the exterior wall of a building. He walked on past it and along the track which continued to dip down into a small valley. There were no houses now – the village stopped here and the land around opened up to his right and ahead to give a good view of the mountains beyond.

Here, the wall was lower and it allowed a glimpse of a garden which lay within. Eventually, the track rose up again on the other side of the valley and the agent was able to stop and look back across it, over the wall at the garden and finally see the villa built on the opposite hill. The sight was surreal: a well-manicured carpet of lush, bright green lawn extended away from him and up to the house. The grass was being watered by a series of lawn sprinklers. Greys and browns coloured the arid landscape either side of the perimeter walls – the contrast with the garden was startling.

The villa itself was of Modernist design and comprised a large cuboid structure arranged over three floors. With the entire front wall of the building glazed, the aspect would take in a superb view of the mountains with the lawns in the foreground. On a raised terrace in front of the house he thought he could make out a figure, reclining by the unmistakable azure shimmer of the oasis that was a swimming pool – well, well.

The villa had been cleverly positioned on the plot to make the best use of the terrain. The absence of any windows on the street side of the property and the employment of the high perimeter wall made for complete privacy. In fact, to get any view of the house at all, one would have to get so far away that the occupant's privacy remained fairly intact – that is unless one happened to have a telescopic sniper sight upon their person. The agent pulled the thing out of his pocket and brought it carefully up to his eye, mindful of its lens catching the sun and giving him away.

Wasps and hornets danced about just above the surface of the water, looking for a suitable place to drink without drowning. The agent let the focus out and settled it on the previously blurred figure behind them, lying beside the pool. Dressed in colourful Hawaiian beach shorts with an open white silk robe over the top, he was slightly overweight with very light grey – almost white – hair which was worn long for a man. His body had the deep golden sunburn of the very rich. The agent put him at being around fifty. Through the powerful lens of the sniper sight, he could see in the crags and lines that the face had been given character by long exposure to a hot climate. Between the glossy black orbs of his sunglasses, emerged a strong nose and below it a wide mouth which opened to reveal the results of expensive private dentistry – white teeth flashed as he spoke.

The agent panned the scope over the man's shoulder and saw the girl appear from the house. Now there was more of her to see. He reminded himself that he'd followed her here on a hunch and that, therefore, this was supposed to be work – pleasant work mind – but work all the same. From behind him, the girl approached the man on the sun longer and spoke. She was facing the agent dead on. Carefully, he studied the shape and movement of her lips. She was speaking French – but what was she saying? She bent down to him for a brief kiss, then she moved forwards to the edge of the pool and stood – for only a moment – at the water's edge. The gold trim of her swimsuit sparkled in the sun as she dived, like a kingfisher, swiftly and cleanly into the water.

He remained at the end of the garden observing the villa – or rather the girl – for a while, training the sight on her as she emerged from the pool and savouring again the image of her wet swimsuit clinging to her trim body. He spent an enjoyable fifteen minutes voyeuristically watching her sunning herself on the terrace before she went inside with the man. She appeared again briefly in one of the vast picture windows of an upstairs room before the agent pocketed the sight and walked back up the track towards the house. But as he approached the carport he heard the engine of the little Berlinetta start up and he immediately dived into the bougainvillea, flattening himself against the wall. He could hear the sound of the car reversing out from the carport and once he'd heard it diminishing as it went off up the track, he stuck his head out from beneath the flowers to look. The girl was now in the passenger seat. The long white locks of her boyfriend in the driver's seat were briefly visible as they caught in the breeze before the car disappeared from view.

His time spent skulking in the shrubbery like a peeping Tom had not been wasted – now he had a chance to get in and have a good look around. The agent knew he couldn't approach the villa from the end of the garden where the wall was lower and so easier for him to get over. Though he'd watched the house for a while and had only seen the two of them, he couldn't be sure that there was no one else here. The villa belonged to a wealthy man and was sizeable enough to warrant a semi-permanent staff. With all those picture windows, if anyone were at home, they wouldn't miss him approaching the house that way – the great swathe of pampered lawn would offer him absolutely no cover. No, if he wanted to get in then he'd have to either tackle the perimeter wall where it ran nearer to the house or find another way altogether to gain access. He didn't want to risk being spotted scaling the wall where it rose up higher and was in plain view of the villa. There was only one other option. He walked back up to where he'd left the car, opened the boot and pulled back the cover on the tools compartment. He extracted the wheel brace, slid it inside his coat and closed the boot again. It was fairly short but the L-shaped brace with its pry bar should provide enough leverage.

The door gave fairly easily and with the painful sound of splintering wood, the brace persuaded it to part from the doorframe without much fuss – so much for the security. The path leading to the house was made from paddle stones which ran through a pleasant section of garden planted with lush, tropical flora. Once he reached the house, he looked for any evidence of a burglar alarm but couldn't see anything. Forcing the door again, he went inside, thoroughly scouting the ground floor before going upstairs. Here, there was a vast master bedroom which occupied much of the front aspect with an adjoining room built to one side. At the back of the house were three large guest bedrooms all with en suite bathrooms. There was also a second staircase leading to the top floor. The agent climbed the staircase up to it.

This level provided a smaller penthouse floor and a flat-roof terrace. It was open plan and taken up entirely by a study. The views from here were spectacular. In the foreground beyond the unnatural green square of garden were miles of dry desert scrubland – gently undulating hills of parched earth. Featureless apart from the occasional run of dry-stone wall in various states of decay and the scrubby broken lines of spiky plants intended to demarcate the land, barely getting off the ground without the water necessary to sustain any serious growth. In the middle distance a shepherd guided his goat herd – from this distance they appeared as small white dots swirling about like snowflakes. But the scene was dominated by the horizon and the mountain range of the High Atlas which filled the skyline. The snow-topped peaks were clearly visible rising through a thin band of cloud and though magnificent, they seemed a perverse sight in the desert.

In the centre of the room was a monstrous computing machine buzzing away, with another large metal cabinet to one side of it steadily spewing out a ream of printed paper. Next to this and connected to the machines by a number of wires, was a sort of electric typewriter which had been set up on a polished metal framed desk – one of the modern chromed steel affairs with a thick glass top. The agent held a dim view of these sort of machines: surely, they could never be relied upon to do the job any better than a decent secretary – and they were a damned sight less attractive than some of the girls working in the typing pool at headquarters back in London.

A bookcase lined the rear wall and the agent went over to look at that instead. The shelves were filled exclusively with reference volumes, largely scientific and seemingly covering all disciplines of the subject. Scanning some of the titles, he tried to pinpoint the major interest of the library's owner but there didn't appear to be one – the man was a polymath. And there were numerous periodicals too – everything from Time magazine to publications on the most specialised areas of science. There were reams of scientific reports and a whole shelf dedicated to plain-bound reports carefully organised and indexed. The agent pulled a couple out at random. They were geological surveys. One for an area of the Kalahari Desert, the other covered a section of the Western Sahara. He pulled a few more out. They were concerned with mineral analysis data and soil samples pertaining to a region in the Eastern Sahara. On the shelf above were a number of geological maps. He took one down, again at random: Sahara Occidental. Another: Great Sand Sea. Yet another: Grand Erg Occidental. They all appeared to be concerned with desert land – had he found a common theme? He walked the length of the bookcase – how could a man possibly read everything here? Molecular biology, plate tectonics, astrophysics, agriculture…the breadth of knowledge was staggering.

Reluctantly, the agent returned his attention to the metal cabinet which he could ignore no longer. Whatever was being printed out by the thing was strewn all over the floor. The agent picked up one of the fan-fold piles. The green bar paper was filled with figures. At first glance, their meaning was not clear but studying them, the agent realised that the numbers were a series of co-ordinates. The print-outs appeared to be recording a movement. But movement of what exactly? There were a couple of notebooks on the desk next to the typewriter machine. Opening them he leafed through. Full of figures too, these were handwritten calculations and recorded in the most compact of hands. The scientific shorthand was indecipherable to the agent

– it would even give Bletchley Park a run for its money – he was mystified. Beside these machines, were a couple of serious-looking telescopes set up by the window with various bits and pieces of scientific-looking equipment, the purpose of which the agent had no clue. He decided to have another look downstairs.

On the landing a framed poster for a science fiction film caught the agent's eye. A man's face starred out solemnly from inside the helmet of his red spacesuit. Over his shoulder in the background, planets and other celestial bodies were artfully depicted. Towards the bottom of the poster, the spaceman's suit had been cleverly merged by the artist with a scene showing a city on fire and, in the centre foreground, people running for cover from an explosion. It was a powerful composition. Dramatically overlaid obliquely across the artwork, in modern lettering, was the film's title – spelt out in capital letters: *'LA MORTE VIENE DALLO SPAZIO'* (*Death Comes from Space*).

In the lounge on the ground floor, he went over to the small semi-circular bar built to face the pool and sun terrace. He looked out through the giant picture windows to the garden where miniature rainbows were being created by the sprinklers. On the bar was a plate with some left-over blinis and a single, empty shot glass next to it. The agent picked up the glass and held it to his nose. Russian vodka – grain, if he wasn't mistaken. He spotted a small refrigerator behind the bar in which he found a bottle of good vodka and a jar of Black Sea Beluga caviar. Pouring himself a generous shot, he opened the caviar and dug into it with a finger – the vodka simply demanded it.

The Russian newspaper caught his eye on top of the refrigerator – absently he picked it up and opened it. A double page spread featured an illustration of Gagarin wearing a space helmet with the stars behind him. In the foreground, the Boctok rocket which had carried him into space, streaked forward emitting a blaze of fire from the engines installed behind the tail fins. It was clear to the agent that the representation of both the rocket and Gagarin's space suit were heavily stylised and he was struck by the similarity between the portrayal here – supposedly of actual aeronautical hardware – and the fictional image created for the film poster which he'd seen upstairs on the landing. The choice to print an artist's impression rather than a photograph would be more than simply censorship of the press. In Soviet Russia, it went deeper than that. The information would have been supplied by the authorities and would not have contained any details beyond those required for the propaganda. The newspaper editors would have had no clue as to what the rocket nor the cosmonaut's apparel actually looked like and their artists would have had to rely solely upon their imaginations. No wonder then that the result ended up looking so much like a film poster for a piece of space fiction.

Putting the newspaper down, he spotted a telegram lying on top of the refrigerator, previously hidden from view by the paper. It had been sent from Moscow and was addressed to the Soviet Consulate in Casablanca. The agent's knowledge of Russian was thin but the message was short and he understood all he needed to.

    SPECIAL CONSIGNMENT. THURSDAY.
    ADVISE DS.

'DS…' Whatever had been shipped out of Odessa hadn't been destined for some rebel faction. The Russians weren't arming a group – they were supplying an individual. The agent popped a blini in his mouth and poured himself another shot of vodka.

Chapter 10
Dowling

Leaving the villa, the agent walked back up the track to the store he'd seen on his way through the village. He bought a packet of local cigarettes which he had no intention of ever smoking, and attempted conversation with the man behind the counter. 'Who lives in the big villa?'

'The Frenchman,' was the unwilling reply.

The agent raised his eyebrows, a gesture indicating that he was looking for more than this, but the shopkeeper simply shrugged his shoulders and shuffled off into the back of the store where he was immediately lost behind the piled-up crates and sacks. His response had been adequate enough though – the agent had little doubt who this 'Frenchman' was. It was time for him to report his discoveries to his chief.

Back inside the British Consulate, he wrote his report privately in the station's signal room and sent it to London himself before going to find Dowling, who was in his office. The room had the unpleasant, sour smell of a men's changing room. The windows were shut and the fan in the corner succeeded only in distributing the acrid aroma produced by the man with the sweaty underarms sitting behind the desk. It was only teatime and yet Dowling was already well into the whisky.

'I've been trying to reach you at your hotel all afternoon – where have you been?' Dowling asked him as he entered.

'Actually, I decided to go in for a spot of bird watching.'

Dowling looked at him quizzically through the soft focus of eyes which had seen too much drink.

'I found a rather good spot for it as a matter of fact, about twenty miles out of town on the Marrakesh road. There's a village, if you can call it that, up on one of the hilltops. It's called Tagadert – ever heard of the place? There's a large modern villa there. Splendid views – enough to make you weep.'

'Yes, I know Tagadert and I know the villa you're talking about – it went up only about a year or so ago. There was a hoo-ha over the thing at the time. Seems the owner intended to draw water from the village well to irrigate some tomfool garden he had planned.'

'Any idea who owns it?' the agent said, taking the seat across the desk from Dowling and pulling it over near the window.

'French money – some sort of business consortium if I remember correctly. I don't have a name for you though I'm afraid. What's your line on it exactly?'

'Just fishing really.'

'Ornithology and ichthyology too?' Dowling retorted.

The agent conceded a smile to the head of station. 'Mind if get a bit of fresh air in here?' he asked, easing the window open. The stored up heat of the day fell heavily into the room like a drunkard falling off a chair. 'What was it you were wanting to get hold of me for so urgently?'

'Well, while you've been off gallivanting around the place

stalking the local wildlife, there's been a development or two here which should interest you,' Dowling said, visibly savouring the titbit of intelligence that had come his way. Announcing, as if he were on the stage in an amateur dramatics production, he said, 'The Interior Minister has made an appearance, finally.'

'That's hardly a newsworthy piece of information, is it?' He looked across at Dowling sitting there impassively, his head gently bobbing in time with his own pulse, waiting for the agent to bite. 'Well, what did he have to say for himself?' he asked him irritably.

'Not very much as a matter of fact,' Dowling managed to say quite casually – and then concluded with a flourish. 'His body was pulled out of the harbour at lunchtime.'

Why Dowling had to make it sound so much like a paperback thriller was beyond him.

'Must have been caught up in the blasts,' Dowling added. 'But one might wonder what business a government minister had to be down there on the pier watching a Soviet freighter being unloaded.'

The agent already regretted having shared the information on the ship so readily with Dowling. 'Best not to jump to conclusions,' he said. 'The explosions might also have provided someone with a convenient cover for foul play. Any reason why anyone might have wanted to be rid of the Minister?'

'Any number probably, although you could say that about the entire Cabinet. There's another thing too. You remember my pal, the police captain from the Sûreté?'

'Yes of course, what about him?'

'Well, it's looking as though he's not going to be with them for much longer. Seems the blame for the explosion has been laid with him personally – for not ensuring proper safety measures were observed at the port, would you believe? He says the Interior Ministry has made a scapegoat of him. That's what all that nonsense was about yesterday.'

'Really?' the agent said, interested though unsurprised – he hadn't forgotten the rumpus the captain had been having on the pier with the 'fool and the crook'.

'He's convinced of it. It'll not be about the loss of life though – a bunch of dockers getting fried won't upset the King. No, it'll be the material loss that bothers him much more and someone has to take the rap for it.' Dowling had launched into full flow. 'The Jetee is an important trading post, you see, for–'

'Yes, I read you're report on all that,' the agent quickly interjected. He certainly didn't want to hear it again.

'Yes, quite,' Dowling said but went on unperturbed, finally getting to the point. 'Well, it's not just the loss of the port infrastructure. You see, whatever the cargo was that went up aboard the ship, it appears to have been of some national importance. Anyway, it looks as though they're ready to give my pal the old heave-ho over it. Damn shame, he's a good man to lose – and, from our point of view, a valuable source of intelligence to boot. I'll have to start the whole bloody process all over again with the new man.'

Wistfulness blended with annoyance on Dowling's face almost as well as the scotch in his glass. He took another draft and picked up a file sitting on his desk.

'My DO managed to locate this for you,' he said. 'It's the file on that business I was telling you about. Having looked at it, I realise that it's not really your line at all – but here it is anyway,' he said, dropping it on the desk in front of the agent. 'I'll leave you to make up your own mind.' He picked up the bottle and held it out to the agent. 'There's a tumbler in that filing cabinet behind you if you'd care to join me, old boy.'

The agent shook his head. 'Why don't you just fill me in on the salient points?' He certainly didn't have the time nor the inclination to wade through another of Dowling's epics – with or without the anaesthetic properties of the proffered bottle.

'Oh, okay – right you are then. I did give it a quick look through earlier to familiarise myself with it again,' he said and promptly deposited a large volume of whisky in his mouth which he swirled about in an unsavoury manner, before swallowing. He began his account: 'Bit of background on it for you first (the agent winced). As you would expect, there's not a great deal of rainfall in Morocco. We get a bit falling on the coastal regions but it's virtually non-existent in the desert of course. There's snowfall mind – in the mountains of the High Atlas range in the centre of the country. The surrounding foothills and scrubland are arid regions though, with the mountains fairly much abutting the desert to the south. Now, the villages in these areas rely heavily on the meltwaters to provide them with water in the form of streams carrying the run-off down to the foothills – and these streams run at their strongest in the spring.' Dowling paused to refresh himself once more.

The agent wondered where on earth this lecture in geography might possibly be going. He considered helping himself to the bottle – if Dowling carried on like this for very much longer then he'd surely need to – but then he thought better of it. He didn't want to encourage the man any further.

Dowling churned his mouthful once again as if the whisky were mouthwash before gulping it down and resuming his monologue. 'Well, it seems that, despite there being a particularly heavy snowfall on the summits the previous winter – fifty-nine that is – the spring thaw which followed brought significantly less water down from the mountains than in past years – only a trickle. But the funny thing was that this change was only seen on the southern slopes, specifically those near the Erg Chebbi – they're the first dunes of the Sahara proper – close to the border with Algeria. The conclusion was that either there had been some sort of unknown geological movement resulting in the water being subsumed underground, or that it had somehow been directed elsewhere.'

'Do you mean naturally redirected or by means of an intervention?'

'Well, I seem to think there was a rumour at the time… but it's all in the file if you'd care to read it for yourself, old boy?'

'You're doing an excellent job – what was the rumour?'

'Ah, well I can't recall the detail of it you see,' he said, thinning his mouth into a minor grimace while giving the bottle a look, 'but I do remember there being some mystery as to where exactly all the damn water had gone. Of course, it would have been of the utmost importance to the poor sods affected – the peasants up in those villages in the foothills. They must have been up in arms over it all. Having their principal water supply cut off like that. They'll have relied on it you see for growing their…vegetables and whatnot…'

In the apparent absence of any clearer idea as to the lifestyle and particular farming practices of the inhabitants of the region in question, Dowling trailed off, eyeing up the bottle again before rounding off his summary. 'As I've said, I doubt it's at all up your street. I just remembered that there was this local furore over it all last year. I'm afraid that nothing much of note happens out in this country's hinterland, so this business rather made the front page as it were.'

The agent gazed lazily about Dowling's office, taking in the framed photograph of an old wartime destroyer hanging lopsidedly on the wall above the head of station's head. *HMS Tartar*, the caption below it read. The agent sensed Dowling notice him looking – he certainly didn't want to be regaled with his war stories and he quickly focussed his attention away from it and back to the man sitting below.

'Thank you, Dowling. That was most illuminating – but you can keep hold of the file,' he said and abruptly changed the subject 'What do you know about flights into Casablanca?'

It took Dowling a moment to switch gear before he answered. 'There's a fair bit of commercial traffic coming in: Paris, Marseilles – and there's the Atlantic stopover from London you came in on of course. A couple of national routes between here and Rabat and Tangier – though most of that's airfreight, perishables and the like. Then there's the military. There's no dedicated airfield here for military flights, so they have to use Anfa for that too – military manoeuvres tend to happen at night, presumably so there's less interference with the commercial flights which operate during the day. Anything in particular you have your eye on?'

'I'm not sure. It could be commercial or otherwise. Are you able to find out what arrivals are due for the rest of today and over the next few days?'

'I can lay my hands on the information concerning the commercial flights fairly easily but not quickly enough for it to be of any immediate use,' Dowling glanced at his wristwatch. 'It would all be over for today by the time you got down there. And as for the military, not at least through any official channels – they don't share that sort of information.'

'Whatever you can find out.'

Dowling took the opportunity to administer himself another large tot from the fast-evaporating bottle – he was steadily heading towards drunkenness.

It was time to get out of here. 'Thanks for finding that file,' the agent said, giving the thing a tap as he stood to go.

'You're sure you don't fancy a quick snifter for the road?' Dowling called after him – but he was already halfway through the door.

Chapter 11

Riad

There was a message for the agent when he returned to his hotel. The note couldn't have been any more concise – it read

'Riad Mogador. Dinner, 8 o' clock. VP.'

Having consulted the concierge as to the whereabouts of said riad, the agent went up to his room to shower and change. The image of Valentina Primakova's lithe swim-suited body was still fresh in his memory. Now he was going to have the pleasure of seeing her again today. Shame there wouldn't be a pool.

***

The agent walked past it twice before he found it. It was as if the entrance were consciously hidden. A nondescript street deep in the medina, little more than an alley, rubbish piled high against the opposite wall. In the fading light, the frontage was far from salubrious, amounting merely to an aged wooden door, set into the wall and a completely missable plate with the name of the riad written in a tiny script. He knocked on the door. After waiting for nearly a minute, he was about to knock again when, with a screech, the decrepit door was swung open. A dark-skinned man looked out from behind it and flashed the agent a warm smile. 'Mrehba' he said, and then, in faltering English, 'Come in, come in.'

The agent stepped over the threshold and followed the man down a long, curving flight of steps which led immediately from the doorway. The enclosed stairwell was softly lit by lamps set among ornamental ferns, planted in a series of little recesses in the descending wall. Everything here was whitewashed, clean and well-tended – the antithesis of the street outside.

At the bottom the stairwell opened onto a large atrium. Leading off from all sides of the central space were inviting rooms, furnished with comfortable-looking divans, spread with richly coloured fabrics. The walls of the atrium rose high above, open to the deepening blue sky. The floor was tiled in large, worn, antique floor tiles of a typically Moorish design in cream and black. In the centre of the space was a small, square, tiled pool (the agent had been wrong). The still, turquoise water reflected the shimmering flames of a multitude of candles illuminating the interior of the riad. The serenity of this space was quite sublime.

A few metal-worked chairs were set around small tables by the pool. She sat, with her back to him at the only one occupied. On it stood a silver teapot on a silver tray and he watched as she lifted her glass and delicately sipped the pale-green mint tea. Her long, dark hair fell over the back of the chair, its gentle curls lost in the whorl of wrought iron. If she were aware of his presence, knew that he would be watching her, she chose for some reason to pretend otherwise. She set her glass back on the tray carefully as he approached and circled the table.

She was dressed for dinner in a black, one shoulder evening

dress. The tailored silk was taut around the bodice, flattering her slender figure and a fold-over collar fell over her bust in four loose pleats. On her shoulder, gathered silk formed a black rose and a black moonstone set in an oval scalloped nest hung on a short chain around her neck. A single natural pearl hung from each ear on platinum pendants with rose-cut stones – diamonds. The agent was only marginally disappointed not to be seeing her again in her swimsuit.

'Hello Valentina,' he said.

Her beautiful face looked up – magnificent blue eyes, like the pool, shining deep and warm in the candlelight. 'Hello Jenson,' she said. 'How nice of you to come.'

***

They dined on the rooftop. Here the heat of the city was gently ushered away by a cooling breeze which made the parasols stir and flap. The sun was down and the lights of the old town sparkled against a backdrop of deepest orange. They began with a classic Casablanca-style dish – couscous bidaoui. As ever, the agent was reticent to discuss his personal life in anything more than broad strokes and it had seemed that so was she. Childhood, though, can often seem so far removed from one's adult life that it's almost as though it might belong to another person. Disconnected then, as it was from the complexities of life here and now, the subject of their respective upbringings proved to be safer ground for both, and the agent was surprised to hear himself speaking to this girl freely and candidly about his time as a boy.

With the girl whom he'd spied upon that afternoon now sitting across the table, he told her about the loss of his mother and about the years he'd spent living with his aunt and uncle when afterward his father had been unable to cope. It had been in that village in Hampshire, he said, where he'd developed a love of the outdoors. He told her about the time his uncle bought him a tent for his birthday – an extravagance he could probably ill-afford but a gift which certainly helped the agent as a young boy to cement his relationship with the landscape. He recalled the trips he'd made in the surrounding countryside, sleeping out in the tent alone, a full day's walk from home and not yet ten years old.

'Thinking about it now,' he said, 'it's odd that I hadn't any concern for danger – real or imagined. The woods were deep and full of noise at night, which might well have frightened other boys, yet I don't remember ever feeling scarred. I was happy being alone in a field surrounded by woodland, miles from the nearest village, with only my fire and my mess kit and a tin of corned beef.'

She smiled warmly at him, allowing herself to enter his world and be transported back to his dream of a pastoral idyll. 'And what did you think about all by yourself in that field?'

He was halfway there now. 'Besides the things which all boys of nine think about? (she smiled again, waiting for him to tell her). 'About how one day I would just keep on walking – not have to go back home. That was one thing.'

She narrowed her eyes. 'You were unhappy there?'

He pushed his plate away, finished now with the couscous. 'They were not my parents,' he said, matter-of-factly, 'but I was loved by both of them and given a good home. I don't think it was that.'

'Then what?'

He fiddled with his cigarette case. 'I suppose it was a yearning for adventure – for the possibilities of an ever-changing horizon.'

'You were bored?'

'No, not bored. I just sought more.'

'I see,' she said thoughtfully, spooning more couscous onto her plate. 'And now you travel a lot with your business, selling motorcars?'

'Exactly.' He voiced it a little sharply – brought up too quickly from his recollections of what seemed now to be an almost imagined world and jolted back into one which truly was.

'And so, you're happy.'

She hadn't framed it as a question, more a statement, but he answered it anyway. 'I suppose I must be.'

He sat back and lit a cigarette. The sky had darkened and the first stars were out. 'I used to lie in the long grass next to my tent and look up at the stars, marvelling at the immensity of the universe. I'd wait half the night to catch a glimpse of a shooting star.'

The girl's eyes widened. She leant her head back and looked up. 'I've always been fascinated by the cosmos,' she said. 'When I was young I had a telescope and I spent every night I could looking at the stars (perhaps to her it felt as though they'd found a common ground). When we were able to, my family used to leave Moscow at the weekend and go up to the dacha. It was wonderful there. The skies are so clear once you get away from the pollution and the lights of the city. Here it's even better, if you go out to the desert or up into the mountains. There's virtually no light pollution in these places and so you can clearly make out the full sweep of the Milky Way – it's quite magical. I used to look at the planets a lot through my little telescope. It's the most incredible thing to look up at another world with your own eyes.'

The agent wanted to ask what her lover – if that's who de Sauveterre was – was looking at through the telescopes at his villa. Instead, he said, 'It sounds wonderful.'

'With that small telescope trained on Mars, I could just make out the north polar ice cap as a tiny, blurred patch of white…'

'But surely a telescope must've been a difficult item for your parents to come by,' he said, casting a line into the river of her history. It broke the surface, stirring her from her reverie.

'My father was able to get it for me – through the Party,' she told him, matter-of-factly.

The girl obviously came from a well-connected family and her father must have held a fairly high position within party ranks to have procured such an expensive gift for his daughter. 'What does your father do?' he asked.

'He works for the Party.'

'And what is it that he does for the Party?'

'He works very hard so he can buy nice things for his family,' she said, tightening up.

The main course arrived in a traditional tagine – chicken cooked with preserved lemons and green olives. The agent served the girl first. Salty, sharp and zesty, it was delicious – with saffron adding fragrance.

Switching tack a little, he asked her about the family dacha.

'Oh, it wasn't ours – it belonged to the Party. When I was a child, my father enjoyed certain privileges within the Party – one of which was that we sometimes had use of the dacha. I'd spend all evening outside with the telescope mounted on its little folding wooden tripod. It might have been freezing but the cold never stopped me – I just loved it, you see.' Her eyes twinkled back at him. Now it was she who'd become caught up in her memories. 'I remember sleeping in a small room at the back of the house. Before I turned out the light, I would write down what I'd seen in a book I kept to record my sightings. One night I witnessed the most amazing meteor shower. I was so excited about seeing that. After I'd finished writing my entry, I put the notebook away in the drawer next to the bed and turned out the light. When I closed my eyes,' she said, shutting them now as she spoke, 'I replayed the scene in my head.' Her eyes remained shut – the girl still immersed in the memory. Eventually they opened again and she smiled warmly at the agent.

'It sounds to me like you had a happy childhood,' he said. 'And a good home. Why did you choose to move so far away from it and from your family?'

She gazed back at him, her smile waning – eyes narrowing again, refocussing on the present. 'I didn't choose – that's not how things work in my country. I was chosen.'

'Well, what made you accept then?' The agent sensed her discomfort.

'In Russia things are not as they are in your country, Mr Coldblow,' she said a little coldly.

He understood that he'd breached the boundaries they'd unconsciously agreed. The conversation faltered. They ate for a while without talking.

Her bowl finished, she pulled at a piece of chicken left in the pot and popped it straight into her lovely mouth. 'I'm not unhappy to be here,' she said, breaking the silence.

'Neither am I,' he said, his eyes burying themselves in hers.

Her smile returned and she laughed. 'It's getting cold. Let's have coffee inside. We can sit on cushions by the fire in one of the rooms downstairs – it'll be more comfortable.' She shot him a wicked look. 'And we won't be disturbed.'

Chapter 12

Anfa

When the agent called Dowling's office in the morning, he was told the head of station wasn't going to be in that day. Dowling had left a message for the agent asking him to call at his house instead at ten thirty. The address was in Anfa, a district in the old part of the city perched on a hill beyond the medina, to the south of the city. Befitting its tenant, the house was a suitably drab affair – a perfunctory French colonial dwelling, providing perfectly adequate accommodation for a middle-aged Englishman and his wife abroad. Their home was set in the small grounds of a tired-looking garden. Much like its occupant, the estate appeared to be hanging on to its past glory.

The agent parked the Maserati under the shade from a well-established orange tree and walked across the parched lawn to the front steps. He rang the bell. After a while Dowling appeared looking a little worse for wear.

'Morning, Dowling. Heavy night?'

'Ha, ha,' Dowling said.

'Not up for the office this morning?' the agent jibed at him.

'I'm normally off on a Thursday.'

'A good excuse then, to get sloshed midweek.'

Dowling looked a little pained. 'Why don't you come in, old boy,' he said ignoring the dig.

The agent, keeping his sunglasses on, followed Dowling through the hall and into a large, bright sitting room. He took a look around the room. 'Is your wife at home?' he asked, already suspecting what the answer might be.

'Actually, she's away at present,' Dowling said. The statement sounded rehearsed – or oft-repeated. There was something too about the room which gave the agent the impression that Mrs. Dowling had not been in residence for some time. Besides the previous evening's detritus – glasses and bottles left scattered about – the room clearly lacked any recent sign of feminine attention: a vase on the bookcase held some dead-looking flowers, the television cabinet had been pulled up to one of the armchairs and that chair's cushions were squashed completely flat into the back of it. The agent would say she'd been absent for weeks rather than days.

'I see,' he said. 'Even more reason to let your hair down then, I suppose.' His blatant lack of sensitivity seemed to heighten Dowling's obvious discomfort. The agent realised that he was bullying him and he at once checked his behaviour. 'Silly of me to say that. Sorry Dowling.'

'Oh, it's not like…' he began. Then, looking around the room himself, as if for the first time like the agent, he abandoned his protestation. Perhaps in the light of overwhelming evidence, he decided against pretence and instead said, 'Yes, well… look, why don't you come out onto the veranda and I'll fetch some drinks? It's too stuffy in the house. I keep the fans off, you see – damned noisy things.'

The painted wooden veranda ran the entire length of the house at the back – though the dismal view out towards the airfield across the uninspiring rooftops of suburban Anfa wasn't up to much. In the clear blue sky of a North African spring morning, the sun was making its presence known as the clock edged towards eleven.

'As near as good enough to midday,' Dowling declared, emerging from the house wearing a straw boater and holding a tray. 'Fancy a G&T?'

Whatever the agent's feelings might have been towards Dowling, he had to admit that the head of station made a fine gin & tonic. Served in a stubby tumbler, it was strong and, with copious amounts of squeezed lemon and plenty of ice, perfectly mixed. The drink was certainly refreshing and Dowling perked up immediately he'd taken his first mouthful – such is the way with alcoholism.

'I've got something for you,' Dowling said brightly. 'Wait there a mo, old chap,' and he disappeared back into the house, drink in hand.

When he returned, the agent noticed his host's drink was already half-drunk – Dowling would be too, shortly, if he carried on in this manner.

'Here we are,' he said, proffering the agent some papers. 'That's a list of all the scheduled flights in and out of Casablanca for the next seven days.' A magically revived Dowling seemed pleased with himself. Handing them over to the agent, Dowling finished off the remainder of his gin & tonic with a flourish in a single gulp.

'Have another?' Dowling asked, rolling comfortably along the road again, steadily gaining pace toward his inevitable destination.

'Not for me, thanks.'

Disappointment at the impending loss of a drinking partner flickered momentarily across Dowling's face. 'Well, I might just have a small top-up myself. You have a gander at those while I'm gone,' he said and then he was away again to the fridge – the surety of attraction like a tide, pulled back and forth by the moon.

The agent scanned the flight schedules for anything coming out of the Eastern bloc countries. Among the neatly typed pages, only one flight was listed that was a possible match. A commercial carrier due in from Budapest in five-days-time, it wasn't likely to be the one the agent was looking for. Budapest was hundreds of miles from the suspected origin point of the consignment he'd been asked to trace, and equally as far inland from the Star's home port of Odessa on the Black Sea. And anyway, the date was wrong.

The whine of an approaching aircraft seemed to signal Dowling's return.

'That's everything, is it?' he asked as Dowling came hurrying back out onto the veranda bearing his refill.

'Besides military traffic. Not found what you're looking for?'

The agent shrugged. 'And you've nothing on military flights?'

'Actually, yes and no,' Dowling replied cryptically. 'I've nothing concrete for you – as I said, we're not privy to that sort of gen and neither is anyone I could ask.'

The sound of the plane built as it descended towards the airfield. The agent had to raise his voice above the noise. 'And what's the *yes* part?'

As if on cue, the plane shot into view almost directly overhead. Seizing the opportunity to create a small moment of melodrama, Dowling pointed up at it. 'That,' he shouted above the roar.

The agent looked up through the tinted glass of his Aviators at the silver belly of the plane flashing through the sky above – the sun catching on the distinctive polished aluminium fuselage of the DC-3.

Dowling, waiting for the noise to diminish before continuing, stole the moment to take another gulp of his second hair of the dog.

'As you can no doubt gather, this house is directly below the final approach path for Anfa – and that can be a bloody–'

The agent had already recognised the significance of this. He cut in. 'So, you hear the night flights coming over too – the military stuff.'

Dowling looked suddenly deflated – a bit like he'd had the punchline of a joke stolen from under him. 'Yes,' he said, 'that's precisely what I was about to say.'

The agent was keen to get to the specifics. 'When?' He asked.

'Well, I hadn't really given it any thought, you understand – why should I? Living here, it's become such a normal thing for us…' he faltered. 'One never pays it any mind – other than the damned annoyance of sometimes being woken up in the middle of the blasted night…'

The agent sipped his drink while he waited for Dowling to tell him. The noise of the plane dissipated – reduced now to a whisper as it was carried off and consumed by the thickening late morning air.

'Anyway, I did think about it last night and, well I thought there may be a pattern to it – over the past few weeks at least. I'm fairly sure of it now, in fact since I've thought it all through.'

'For goodness' sake Dowling, *when?*' For the agent, patience wasn't always a trait in great evidence and his was deserting him fast.

'I'm going to tell you,' he said but perversely poured more gin into his mouth instead.

The agent groaned.

Finally, Dowling said, 'So, I think there's been something regular coming in on a Thursday evening for at least the past three, maybe four weeks – It might've been longer but… well, there's been quite a lot going on.'

'At what time?'

'Must have been at about nine thirty or ten. I know because I'm in the habit of coming onto this veranda for a nightcap at that sort of time – after the wife's gone to bed… when she was here, that is… I suppose I've rather held onto that routine.'

'And you think it must be military?'

'I couldn't say for sure but the sound is unmistakeably that of a four-engine turboprop – you get a different note entirely from it than you do from a twin prop – so it'll most probably be a heavy transport of some sort rather than anything else. And given the time of night and the fact these flights haven't come up on any of the commercial carriers' schedules – I've checked – I'd say it was almost certainly military.'

'You're sure it's always a Thursday?'

'Definite about that, old chap. It's the only night I'm at home at that time: Monday is bridge; Tuesdays I dine at the club; Wednesday–'

'Okay, I get the picture,' the agent said, quickly cutting him off.

***

Driving back to his hotel, the agent wondered whether Dowling had deliberately engineered the scene on his veranda for some personal desire to effect drama. The whole thing had felt stage-managed… as for that rubbish about keeping the fans off – it was cooler by half in the sitting room than it was out on the veranda in the blazing sun. But, would he really have gone to the trouble of arranging for the agent to be on his veranda at just the right time to witness the DC-3 overfly the house – only for the sake of this feeding his apparent need to create a show? If he had, then possibly the man was actually unhinged. The departure of his wife would explain the heavy drinking, but could the strain put upon him by it have been enough to push him over the brink?

It occurred to the agent too, that he might be imagining something that just wasn't there. But what if Dowling *had* contrived that piece of theatre – why should he care anyway? Dowling's behaviour irritated the agent in a way that he was unable to define. He realised that he was becoming obsessed with the man – why?

Chapter 13
Special Consignment

The agent had been in position since just after nightfall. He'd parked the Maserati in the dirt just off the side of the perimeter road in the best cover he was able to find – under the low branches of some stunted trees and in amongst the straggly bushes beneath them. The dry, thorny branches had scraped and scratched painfully against the bonnet and the hardtop roof of the car as, inching the Maserati into the hiding spot, the agent had reluctantly allowed the pristine Vignale coachwork to become vandalised in slow motion.

He'd climbed the bank and found himself a good spot on some higher ground just to one side of the communications tower, behind the latticed wire fence which enclosed the compound. The building gave him some protection from the spill of the airfield's lights. He lay on his stomach, his body warmed by the heat of the daytime sun still radiating from the friable earth, and waited. Whatever this 'special consignment' might be, the phrase inferred a sense of urgency. If, as he suspected, this were a replacement for the cargo which was lost aboard the Star, then the agent reasoned it was likely that it might be sent by faster means. He'd taken a punt on it coming by air.

The steady drone of the aircraft's four engines preceded the landing lights of the approaching plane as it slowly became visible in the night sky. Coming in to land, the plane taxied onto the apron in front of the control tower where an eight-wheeler flatbed truck was standing by. The plane was indeed, as Dowling had correctly surmised, a large four engine turboprop transport. The agent recognised it as a Soviet Antanov A-12 (or Cub as it was known to the Allies). The Cub was a medium-lift military cargo plane, roughly equivalent in terms of capability to a Hercules. Unusually though, when he brought the telescopic sight up to his eye, he couldn't see any markings on the aircraft to indicate sovereignty. Given the size of the truck, the Cub would have to be carrying a large payload and he guessed that unloading it wasn't going to be a quick operation.

Two Land Rovers sped onto the apron and pulled up behind the plane. Surveying the scene through the scope, the agent observed a number of well-trained men moving about efficiently around the plane. They weren't wearing uniforms but were dressed in dark-coloured, military-style clothing. It was apparent that this was a smoothly-run outfit – these soldiers weren't regular army: either they were a specialised unit or this was a private force. In command was a huge man with arms as thick as legs – and legs like tree trunks. The agent studied him for a moment. He stood among his men, his mouth contorting to form the orders which he shouted at them. At this distance, and with the noise of the Cub's engines swallowing his words, the man's larynx appeared to make no sound at all.

Now a third Land Rover arrived and the agent watched as Valentina got out with the man he'd seen with her at the villa –

who the agent could only assume to be de Sauveterre. They went over to the rear of the aircraft where the powered door had opened, dropping to the ground to form a loading ramp. In the cargo hold the payload was being prepared to be winched out onto the ramp and down onto the concrete runway apron. Ahead of it another man descended the ramp and approached them. The agent recognised this man immediately. He was the Russian – the one he'd seen at the pier – only this time he'd swapped his uncomfortable-looking civvies for something which suited him far better. The agent had been right about his military pretensions: in uniform now, he wore the light blue and gold insignia of a top brass in the Soviet Air Force. There followed an exchange between the two men, mediated by the girl who was, of course, interpreting for them. Though the agent was deprived of the benefit of hearing the conversation, from what he could see, it was clear that this was a heated exchange – body language becoming so much more eloquent when sound is absent. The Russian was pointing his finger at de Sauveterre who in turn was displaying that classic gesture intended to call for reason and calm: both hands were presented, palms open and facing outward. He dropped his hands together repeatedly in a series of short but confident strokes. De Sauveterre was standing his ground. Whatever was said by him to accompany this physical display seemed to do the trick and at last the Russian appeared to calm down, finally even taking the other man's hand and shaking it vigorously. Not a bad performance, the agent thought – and with not the easiest-looking of adversaries. This was evidently a man with a silver tongue to match his hair. But there was something else about the exchange, which the agent couldn't quite put his finger on.

The agent put down the sniper scope and, from his bag, pulled out a camera case and a short metal pole. The pole was a telescopic support leg – a sort of one-legged tripod – which he screwed onto the base of the slim camera body and, setting the foot of the thing onto the earth, extended the leg just enough for it to bring the viewfinder up to his eyelevel. The camera was a Japanese built Nikon F, a new type of design where the viewing is done – and the exposure made – through a single lens by means of a clever arrangement of mirrors and shutters. The design made for a much more compact instrument than the bulky twin lens German Rolleiflex he had used in the field previously. The model was not readily available outside of Japan but the agent had picked this one up on a recent assignment in Tokyo. With fully interchangeable lenses, the agent attached a powerful zoom and took a look through it. He rotated the focusing ring until he brought his subject into sharp relief.

The combination of the low lighting conditions afforded by the airfield's artificial lights and the deep focus that was required, dictated that a long exposure was necessary. He held the camera as steady as he could on the stick and shot off several exposures. After waiting until his subject had stopped moving, he shot off the rest of the role. Satisfied that he must have got at least a couple of good shots, he stowed the camera apparatus back in his bag and returned his eye to the sight of the sniper scope.

Whilst the agent had been snapping away, the cargo was being carefully winched down the plane's rear ramp. Slowly it emerged and the agent saw that it consisted of a number of pallets constructed from square steel section. Securely strapped to each of the pallets, and laying on their sides, were a pair of white cylindrical canisters, each about six feet long by two feet across. Each canister was banded twice along its length but was otherwise plain. The magnification of the scope was powerful enough and the area lit well enough for him to have been able to see any markings on the canisters had they been present, but here again there was nothing visible. He had no preconception about what might be coming off the plane and at first, the sight of the canisters left him none the wiser. But a thought came to him – half an idea. In truth though, he had no real clue what was inside these canisters – it could be hot air for all he knew.

Once the cargo had been winched to the foot of the ramp, the truck moved into position to be loaded using a forklift which had also now arrived on the scene. With the procedure complete, the Russian disappeared back into the belly of the Antanov. The turbo props fired up and the Cub taxied away from the apron and towards the runway. Whoever this cold-looking player was who had appeared again here, he was gone.

The load was carefully and methodically harnessed to the flatbed and canvas tarpaulins pulled over and securely tied down. With a great cloud of black exhaust smoke, the diesel engine started up and the truck moved out across the airfield's concrete apron in a wide arc towards the perimeter gates. Time for him to get moving too. Quickly, the agent stowed the scope and ran back down the bank towards the spot where he'd left the car. Roughly pulling the vegetation aside, he jumped in and, with headlamps off – the light from the fingernail moon would have to suffice – started the engine and engaged first gear. The thorns dragging against the paintwork emitted a punishing squeal as he shot out from the undergrowth, up the gravel verge and onto the airfield perimeter road.

Passing the main gates, he soon caught up with the truck, now flanked front and rear by the Land Rovers. To warrant the escort, whatever was being transported was either extremely valuable or sensitive – likely it was both. The convoy was travelling slowly and the agent hung well back. Keeping the headlights off, he maintained a safe distance: just able to keep sight of the tail lights but nothing more. The convoy turned onto the main east –west road. This was an altogether different sort of pursuit to the one he'd enjoyed that afternoon. Crawling along at barely thirty miles per hour, he fell into thought as he followed the lights of the convoy.

What was it about Dowling that agitated him so? The drinking primarily. It was why he didn't want to let the man in on his investigation any further than needed. He couldn't trust him – not fully. You can't really rely on a man who drinks like that – so heavily and consistently. But it was more than just that. The man disgusted him if the truth were told. It wasn't his fault though – in fact, it had very little to do with him at all. It was what he represented that horrified the agent. For, if he saw his father in the chief, to some degree he saw himself in this man – the future self which he was destined for if he wasn't too careful about things. The idea appalled him.

The agent drove steadily behind the convoy for nearly three hours before he saw it make a sharp turn to the left toward the High Atlas mountain range. He felt sure now about what it was heading for and, following, turned onto the unmade stony track. Ahead, he could see from the lights that the convoy was moving onto higher ground. Now he could hear the strain of the climb in the note from the large diesel engine of the truck. The way became stony and rutted and was littered with sizable rocks. The Maserati was a touring sports car and it was built for driving on the smooth tarmacadamed roads of Europe. It certainly had the power to make the hill climb but the chassis was low to the ground and the car was not designed to cope with this terrain. He had to slow and, by only the limited light of the young moon, pick his way carefully between the obstacles along the increasingly uneven surface. The lights ahead dimmed as the convoy began to put some distance between it and the agent. It wouldn't be possible to keep this up if the going got any worse.

Then, mercifully, the lights ahead grew bigger and brighter – had the convoy slowed too? The lights were hypnotic. An awful sound of sheering metal coming from below the floor of the car broke the trance. Distracted by the lights and by trying to gauge the distance between himself and the convoy, he had finally driven over something too big. The car came to an abrupt halt with the engine still revving – he'd beached the damn thing. He cut the motor and got out to have a look underneath but it was too dark to see. Up ahead the lights were static – the convoy had stopped. He could just make out the outline of a narrow, steep-walled gorge immediately up ahead of it. Thankfully, he could still hear the drone of the truck's diesel engine idling – if they'd cut it, they would have heard the noise of tearing metal being carried up the valley. He reasoned that with the truck's engine still running this wasn't the convoy's final destination – more like a stop for a smoke and a call of nature before pressing on up through the gorge and into the mountains.

Well, there wasn't a cat in hell's chance of him getting the car off the rock quickly enough to keep going. He could have tried gunning the engine but even if that had worked, it would have made far too much noise – it was out of the question and anyway the off-road sojourn into the desert had already proved too much for the car. Damn the bloody thing. Angry now, he delivered his foot sharply onto the side of the driver's door. The agent imagined the paintwork, already scratched and no doubt chipped from all the stones thrown up from the track, cracking now around the dent he made with the pointed toecap of his brogue as it contacted the thin sheet steel of the door panel.

There was nothing else for it. He would never be able to keep up with the convoy on foot – he needed to get aboard. There wasn't time to hatch a plan – they could be moving off at any moment. He'd have to wing it. He set off immediately, running up the track towards the lights and keeping his eyes on the ground ahead. As he got closer he needed to move quickly but quietly enough not to be heard above the noise of the diesel. He lessened his pace a touch and concentrated on controlling his breathing. He was almost on top of the convoy now and voices floated towards him above the drone of the idling engine. Nothing discernible but the speech was delivered in hard, stressed syllables. He recognised the language without needing to hear words.

In the half-light, he could see the men standing about as he'd imagined – smoking and kicking at the stony ground with their heavy boots. It wasn't raucous, this was a disciplined group of men. He kept low now. To his left, the ground sloped away and he could make out the darker silhouettes of some patches of indistinct vegetation. He moved down towards them for cover. The thin line of wiry bushes ran along close to where the truck was parked. He crouched behind the bushes and carefully made his way towards it. He was out of sight here. He reached the truck and felt for the edge of the tarpaulin – there should be enough space for him underneath it, next to the cargo. But the tarp had been roped up tightly and was quite taught against the body of the flatbed. No way in there – it might have been possible from the other side perhaps but he'd be seen – forget that. Unlike the hopelessly unsuitable Maserati, the chassis of the truck was set high and afforded excellent ground clearance. There might be room for him to squeeze himself in underneath the flatbed, between the rear axles. It would be a bumpy trip but if he could get a good enough hold, he'd be alright there. In a moment he was in place, his body wedged between two mighty axle housings. It wasn't first class but it would do.

The agent heard the sound of the cab doors being slammed shut and then the revving of the diesel engine as the truck took off and, as he'd expected it to, head straight ahead towards the mouth of the gorge. The pounding reverberation of the diesel, set up by the vertical valley walls, told him they were inside. From his position underneath the chassis, his sense of the topography came mostly from the variance of the noise level from the engine as the truck climbed steadily up along the valley floor of the gorge. Gaining altitude through the steeper sections, the motor roared and, as the gorge narrowed, the noise built in intensity as it was bounced back by the canyon walls almost immediately. It thundered in his ears. After a while the cacophony eased and he felt the truck slow, then lurch from side to side.

He could see very little, only the headlamps of the Land Rover behind which occasionally flashed underneath the truck, momentarily illuminating the ground a couple of feet below him. Here, these precious bursts of light revealed the rocks and boulders to be smoothed. In darkness again, he felt the spray of cold water against his legs and he remembered something: the gorge contained a stream and the truck was driving across it. Above the racket of the diesel engine, he could hear water sloshing about as the huge tires splashed through the stream. Soon they were through it and across to the other bank. The reverberation from the engines lessened, telling him the convoy was passing through a more open section of the valley.

The lorry lurched forward and again the spray hit him. This time it showered his legs with ice-cold mountain water, leaving him soaked up to the groin. They were crossing the stream again but with the spring melt, it was more like a river. The convoy must be zigzagging across it as it ascended the gorge. How much of this was he in for and would it get any deeper? The truck had a high draft for this kind of thing. He could hear the sound of the engine change – they were closer to the side of the gorge again, away from the stream. A few minutes later though, the truck was moving back towards it. He heard the lorry hit the water again and it sounded deeper here. Bracing himself, he took a quick, deep breath and held it – just in case. It was as well he did, for in a moment he was fully immersed. The water screamed in his ears. He wouldn't be able to move from his position – he'd have to hang on until they were out the other side – it shouldn't be long. He'd just have to hold his breath and hang on.

A peculiar, deep groaning pitch was lent to the sound of metal grating on rock as it was transmitted through the water – one of the axles had hit a submerged boulder and it sounded almost as if the collision were slowed down. The agent felt a heavy jolt as the truck came to sudden stop. Good God, not again. He held his breath – what now? He'd have to get out or he'd drown here. Letting go of his hold on the chassis, he felt about him underwater in the blackness. His hand grazed a rock and then the current of the stream got hold of him and swept him out from under the truck, smacking his head hard against metal on the way. He got his face out the water and took a precious gulp of air.

Thrashing his limbs against the boulders, he swam blindly until he got himself into shallower, slower-moving water and then, putting his feet down, he was able to stand. The stream was lit only by the thin sliver of moon. He could just make out the bank and he trudged towards it then perched himself on a boulder to catch his breath. The current had pulled him downstream from the truck and, at first, he could hear the engine screaming up ahead of him as the driver attempted to manoeuvre the great flatbed clear of the obstacle. Finally, with a great jolt it moved and, in the headlamps of the trailing Land Rover, he could see it pulling away from the river. Damn, he should have held tight. The convoy went on, further up into the gorge and his view of it disappeared into the gloom.

He could still hear the noise of the truck's diesel cannoning down the steep walls of the gorge. He knew there would be no chance of him catching up with it on foot at night on this terrain, but he could follow the trail up through the gorge to see where it led. With the convoy gone, it was safe now for him to get his torch out. The Eveready Hydro-Lite was a new type of waterproof pocket torch. He pressed the rubber grommet switch on the side of the plastic body. The seals had done their job at keeping the water out and the light came on. Keeping the beam low to the ground, he surveyed his surroundings. The gorge was narrow here which would account for the sudden deep water caused by the natural bottleneck. Beyond this, the way opened out a little.

The highest peaks at the centre of the Atlas mountain range were snow covered in winter. In March, when the snow and ice first began to melt, he imagined the stream would have filled the width of the gorge and run in a torrent. Now, with a good deal of the snow gone, there appeared to be some sections of dry riverbank up ahead. He might avoid another bath but, in his sodden clothes he was shivering and he must keep moving or he'd freeze.

The valley floor was strewn with rocks and some fairly large ones at that. He picked his way through, listening for the noise of the diesel which, already fading, now abruptly stopped altogether. He imagined the gorge must form some sort of pass into a corner of the mountainous interior. The convoy would have gone through the head of it and out the other side – either that or it had stopped. He carried on for about half an hour until the valley narrowed again and he had no choice but to wade through the stream. The noise of the rushing water intensified here and, as he rounded a bend, it became a crashing thunder. He directed the beam of his torch upward to see what lay ahead. What he saw stopped him dead.

Ahead, the trail was barred by a sheer vertical cliff rising up thirty feet or so above him. Water cascaded down it in a spectacular waterfall. He swung the torch around looking for another way forward. There wasn't one. His mouth dropped open. This wasn't possible – what had happened to the convoy? There must be another route, a fork he'd missed further back – he'd only been concentrating on following the stream, damn it – he'd have to track back to it. But would he not have noticed if that were the case? The gorge would need to have divided into two to make a fork large enough for the vehicles to pass through – no, that couldn't be right. The convoy had simply disappeared into thin air. He shone the beam on the waterfall again and starred at it in disbelief. And then he remembered.

He switched the torch off – but he carried on looking at the waterfall. Slowly his pupils dilated, adjusting to the darkness. The canyon was deep at this point and what little light the moon had provided earlier didn't reach down here. Despite this, he started to make out the waterfall – or at least a part of it. At its base the water shimmered and gently glowed in roughly a semicircle – the waterfall appeared to be illuminated. This was no trick of the eye – the water was being lit from behind. He skirted around to the edge of the fall, where the volume of water wasn't so great. Here he thought he could make out the flicker of artificial light shining through the stream of water. Pieces of the puzzle started to assemble in his mind. And then he knew. He took a few steps backwards then ran towards the fall, leaping into the thick ropes of water uncoiling from above. The tumbling water screamed in his ears as he jumped clear through the waterfall and landed beyond it onto a flat, smooth surface.

The convoy hadn't disappeared. It had simply driven through the waterfall at the head of the gorge and into the hidden tunnel, carved out through the mountain. The arching tunnel walls were hewn from the solid rock but the floor had been paved with concrete. Sodium-vapour lights were attached at regular intervals to the dripping stone walls, lighting the subterranean passage. The tunnel continued on for about fifty feet until it was barred by a very solid-looking set of steel gates. From either side of the gates, two enormous metal pipes – each maybe three feet in diameter – emerged and ran back along the sides of the roadway towards the entrance where they rose up, supported by heavy steelwork, in a gentle arc as they approached the waterfall. Here he could see that the pipework had been split off into several smaller diameter sections which were suspended from the ceiling by a series of substantial metal cradles. From their ends they disgorged the water which was running through them to create the artificial waterfall.

The agent put everything together now. That delicate blue line on the architect's survey map traced over in ink pen described a route up the valley that appeared to go nowhere – but which the agent had now just followed. And that business about water being diverted from the mountain streams which Dowling had bored him with earlier… this was the entrance to a secret subterranean labyrinth. The agent had been led to de Sauveterre's lair – and whatever was on that truck was now inside the mountain. But why would de Sauveterre have gone to such extreme lengths to conceal the entrance and moreover, what the hell was in those canisters which had been transported up here in the dead of night? With his mind racing as he took it all in, the lights were suddenly extinguished and he was left in complete darkness. It was time for him to move out. He must get word of it to London – and urgently. The agent switched his torch back on, ran back down the tunnel and took a running jump into the waterfall.

Chapter 14
Bed & Breakfast

The deafening noise emitted from the fractured pipes of the Maserati blasted out into the night as the agent gunned the car back along the highway into Casablanca at high speed. He'd forced it off the rocks where it had beached using the brute force of the engine in a series of churning alternate forward and reverse thrusts, and the exhaust system had been cut to ribbons in the process. He pulled up at the British Consulate in the early hours of Friday morning. The racket from the car must have woken half the neighbourhood but he couldn't have cared less about that, nor about the car or the damned Italians – and neither would his chief once he'd read the report he was about to hammer out to London. Pennycook was the duty officer on call and when the nightguard telephoned he came in straightaway and, though it was quite unnecessary, he insisted on sending the agent's communication through to London himself. Exhausted, the agent had chosen not to bother returning to his hotel after he'd written his report but instead to remain at the Consulate and get a couple of hours sleep on the cot which Pennycook had kindly made up for him in one of the station offices – the man had even managed somehow to procure pyjamas for him too. He fell asleep quickly but slept badly. There were nightmares of an apocalypse.

He was woken by Pennycook at nine with clean clothes and a cup of bitter-looking black coffee. While he was laying on the cot deciding whether to drink it or not, Dowling came in.

'I hope you managed to get some sleep on that thing,' he said, vaguely gesturing towards the cot. But Dowling's words sounded hollow and the agent sensed a black cloud hanging over the head of station this morning.

'It wasn't quite up to the Dorchester but it sufficed, thank you.' The agent pondered the coffee, took a mouthful and lit his first cigarette of the day. The packet he'd had in his pocket the previous night, his own brand, were ruined. Now he was down to smoking the Camels – retrieved from the floor of the car's footwell – until he could get back to his hotel and pick up more Morleys.

Pennycook came back in again. 'Just got this for you Sir, from London,' he said, addressing the agent, and handing the telegram to him. 'And the photographer has developed your negatives – he says he'll have the prints done by lunchtime. Oh, and will you be needing the car today Sir? Because, if you do, I think it may require some attention first–'

Dowling exploded. 'That's a joke. The parts alone will take a month or more to arrive from Italy. I'm afraid, old boy, that you have rather dropped me in it with the Italians. You've only had that bloody car for about five minutes and now it looks like it's been driven over a ruddy minefield. Pennycook tells me it wouldn't even start this morning. He says there's a damn great hole in the radiator that's run it dry – he thinks the engine's overheated and seized.'

But the agent wasn't listening to him – he was already reading the telegram:

```
INFORMATION AS REQUESTED: M.
ARISTIDE DE SAUVETERRE. FRENCH
NATIONAL AGED 55. PUBLISHED
PROFESSOR OF PHYSICS. REGISTERED
DIRECTORSHIPS WITH COMPANIES IN
FRANCE GERMANY ITALY AND UNITED
STATES. POSSIBLY OTHERS. PRINCIPLE
CONCERN IS MANUFACTURE OF
SCIENTIFIC AND OTHER INSTRUMENTS.
NO RECORD OF CRIMINAL ACTIVITY OR
ASSOCIATION IN ENGLAND FRANCE OR
USA. REGISTERED RESIDENCES IN
FRANCE MOROCCO AND HAWAII.
```

The coffee wasn't good but he took another mouthful and drew deeply on the cigarette. He turned to Pennycook. 'When those prints come back, I want you to check the faces in them against those you have on file for the other side. If you find any matches, then let me know immediately what information you have on them. Now Pennycook, judging by the way you managed to get hold of all that scuba equipment for me so damn quickly the other night, I would trust that if anyone could get that car fixed, then you'd be the man to make it happen–'

'Thank you, Sir. I'll get on to it right away.'

'No, don't worry about it for now – get it repaired properly later and have it returned to the Italian Consulate with my sincere apologies. The roads here really take it out on a car like that – I'm going to need something better suited to the terrain. And I'll need survey maps of the area around Beni Tajjit – that's near the border with Algeria. Can you organise all that for me, do you think?'

Two words later, and Dowling's surprisingly efficient duty officer had left the room.

Now he'd got it out of his system about the bloody car, Dowling's curiosity got the better of him. 'What's all this about survey maps – care to fill me in?'

The agent swung his legs off the cot and got to his feet, 'Fancy some breakfast, Dowling? I know a great little cafe on the Rue Soumania – I can vouch that the coffee's a lot better there.'

While he had a rudimentary wash at the basin in the cloakroom, he thought about a way in. He wasn't going to attempt going in through the front door, that was for sure – those heavy steel doors would not only be securely locked but also, they would likely be guarded inside. He remembered the ventilation shafts that he'd noticed on the architect's model. They must each be several feet in diameter. He could easily lower himself down one of them on a rope. But how deep were they? He remembered the shafts looking fairly sizeable and so it would need plenty of length – he couldn't afford to be left short when it came to descending them. He'd have to climb to the ridge first to get to them and there was a limit on how much equipment he'd be able to carry up there on his own. How much rope could he sensibly manage on a sheer ascent – a hundred and fifty feet? It would be a bugger to haul the weight of all that rope up the mountain with him. Could he get away with a hundred – would that be enough?

On his way out of the Consulate compound, he stopped at

the battered and now useless Maserati. He wanted something from the glovebox. The information on de Sauveterre he'd received from London wasn't enough for him to go on – he needed to know more.

At the cafe, he discussed his plan to get inside de Sauveterre's lair with Dowling over a good Moroccan breakfast of homemade breads with cheese, fresh dates and pancakes dipped in olive oil, honey and jam. The agent could hardly remember when he'd last eaten and he made up for it. The breakfast came with nearly a whole squadron of wasps, and when a pair of hornets turned up to join in the melee, Dowling had had enough. He called it a day and had the waiter remove what was left of the morning's feast and bring more coffee. With a decent cup now inside him already, the agent made use of Dowling's keen interest in geography by getting him to look over the survey maps of the area.

They decided that he would be best to make his approach from some way north of the gorge. This was higher ground and the route would cover some fairly difficult terrain. He'd only be able to get so far by vehicle along the unmade-up roads and tracks of the mountainous interior. From there, he'd have to make his way on foot for the last few miles to the base of the ridge.

'I'll need Pennycook to get hold of some reasonable climbing gear for me,' the agent said. 'A hundred feet of rope should just about do it, carabiners and a decent set of pitons – I don't care too much about any particular style, just a good selection of whatever shapes he can lay his hands on – but ask him to make sure they're good and sharp, will you?' He'd given him plenty to get on with and as soon as he'd finished his coffee, Dowling left, keen to get his DO started on assembling the equipment. The agent looked at his watch – after the long breakfast it wasn't far off midday. He ordered another coffee.

She was several minutes later today. At first the agent worried that perhaps she wouldn't show, but he had Valentina down as a woman with a routine and so he hung on for her to make an appearance – which she did at just after a quarter past twelve. He watched her cross the busy thoroughfare, coming straight over in the direction of the café. She smiled as she approached his table.

'Hello,' he said. 'How did you know I'd be here?'

'I didn't. I just came to get cigarettes,' she said brightly.

'Don't tell me you have to rush off again this lunchtime?'

'No. I'm all yours today.' Her voice was warm.

This might prove to be even easier than he'd thought. 'Then I wonder if you might enjoy going for a spin?'

'How charming – in one of your sports cars?'

'Actually no. You see I had a bit of a prang last night and so my car's with the garage today, but we could go in yours – if you've a car?' He hoped the citrus and bergamot top notes of the Italian cologne he'd taken from the Maserati's glovebox were sufficient to mask the smell of a body which had spent half the night in dirty, wet clothes. 'You see, there's something I want to show you – back at my hotel – and I've something to ask too.'

'I see,' she said, narrowing her eyes as she considered the overt invitation.

'And then perhaps you might want to swim afterwards? I'll drive of course,' he added for good measure.

'Okay,' she said finally, 'but I have to be back at work this afternoon – so you'd better not have another accident.'

'Don't worry, it only happened because I'd had too much to drink. I'll have you back at your desk by two thirty at the latest. Now, where are you parked?'

The agent liked the Berlinetta and he enjoyed racing the little car along the boulevards towards the hotel. Valentina seemed relaxed in the passenger seat. She lit a cigarette and talked to him about matters celestial. The latest coup for the Soviets in the space race was still very much in the news now that Gagarin's flight had been confirmed by various international science agencies – including Britain's own Jodrell Bank Observatory which, with its radio telescope, had apparently picked up and monitored the Vostok craft as it made its single orbit around the Earth.

'Did you know that Vostok is the Russian word for east?' she asked him (the agent admitted that he did not).

The girl took a final pull on her cigarette before offering it up to the open window – but toying with it first, holding on to the filter for a moment before finally letting the wind take it – abandoning it to the gale and then onwards to collide with the tarmac. Sparks flew as it hit the ground and then, still unextinguished but no longer visible to the agent in the conical-shaped, chromed wing mirrors, he witnessed the drama of its demise end in anonymity.

There was an undeniable chemistry. It was just there, between them. And in a similar way to that in which elements crash violently together in the hearts of stars to form new suns, the agent knew that he and this girl, Valentina, would come together too. But what would their collision create?

***

The agent admired her body as she lay on the bed in her underwear. Her skin was flawless. Her long, tanned legs emerged from under pink lace bikini briefs with a sheer panel at the front, revealing the shape of the dark bush of pubic hair covering her mons pubis. Above, her stomach was flat and her breasts were also half-visible beneath a matching brassiere. Her shoulders were well defined, the hollows at their fronts seducing him as they trembled slightly while he looked on her with intent. He pulled out his belt and went to her. Manfully, he took hold of both her slender forearms and lifted them up and behind her to the head of the bed. She looked at him quizzically for a moment before she seemed to understand. Then she took a short, trembling breath. The sound of it stirred the agent further, hastening him as he worked the belt around her wrists and then the metal frame of the bedhead. He tied it tightly enough to cause the girl to wince. Her eyes narrowed and shot him a look of utter seriousness. The agent loosened his tie and, yanking it off, went to the foot of the bed. Her legs squirmed as she played idly at fighting his grip on her ankle. And then, finally, she abandoned herself fully to him and let him, without any protest, tie the other leg – her last remaining untethered limb – to the bed, using the cord of his dressing gown. Her body was now spread before him, slowly writhing in anticipation. She moaned softly. Her eyes maintained their look.

This was a serious business. The agent struggled to control his desire for the girl's body. Neither of them had said a word since they'd arrived at his hotel room. Now he spoke to her. 'I'm afraid this isn't what you think, Valentina.'

Her look faltered but it wasn't yet entirely lost.

'I need you to answer some questions for me.' His words felt like a betrayal. 'You can start by telling me everything you know about the pyramid and what exactly it is that your French boyfriend is up to there. And then I'd like to know what part Russia is playing in it.'

For the girl, the transition from sexual longing to fear appeared to take time. The agent waited before he said simply, 'Talk.'

The look was gone completely but the girl remained silent. She appeared horror-struck, her body trembling – now for an entirely different reason.

'Okay Valentina, as you please.' The agent noticed her testing the bindings which held her captive. Unperturbed, he walked over to the wardrobe and extracted his attaché case. Calmly, he brought it over to the bed, opened it and pulled out the silencer. Then, pulling the Beretta from its shoulder holster he proceeded to screw the silencer onto the barrel. Better to do it like this than in plain view out on the street – resorting to having the gun in his pocket, poking into her side.

Talking of views, he let his eyes slowly crawl across her body – she was exquisite. Her neck was flushed now and her chest heaved in distress. The sight of the firearm did the trick of course and she started talking at once. She had been recruited to act as an interpreter for her senior's dealings with de Sauveterre, who had indeed built the pyramid in the desert. Her country had made an agreement with him to provide certain equipment which would assist him in his scientific activities. The agent asked her what activities these were and about the nature of the equipment. She said she didn't know exactly what the pyramid was for. She knew that he had spent a lot of time mapping the desert and understanding the geology of it. But he wasn't a geologist and, while he was immensely knowledgeable on the subject, he was in fact a physicist. As far as the equipment was concerned, she had been told nothing about the detail of it beyond knowing that a great deal of it was coming from Russia – it had been arriving both by sea and air for weeks now, she told him. It seemed as though there was to be some kind of test very soon, she thought – she'd heard some talk about the 'land test' and the 'sea test' but it meant nothing to her.

'What happened to the Star of Odessa?' he asked her.

'It was the final shipment but there was an accident on board while it was being unloaded and the consignment was lost. That is all they told me. A new consignment was sent by air instead. It arrived last night.'

'I know.'

The girl's eyes widened. 'I realise that you're not a car salesman. Who are you?'

'Never mind that. Who was the Russian brass I saw you with – the one who flew in last night?'

'He is the polkovnik, the colonel.'

'And what was the argument about he had with de Sauveterre?'

'How could you know about–?'

'Just tell me.'

'It was a misunderstanding, I think. You see, the interior minister was dealing with the procurement side of things here – until he disappeared that is. Well, shortly before he went missing, he contacted the colonel through a telephone call which was put through to me. The minister was keen for me to set up a meeting with him as a matter of some urgency. Well, the colonel had returned to Moscow when the call came in and so I asked the minister what the nature of the emergency was. He said that he had acquired some information concerning de Sauveterre which he felt the colonel should be made aware of as soon as possible – one of his staff had unearthed something at his office, something fishy. It concerned land permits purchased several years ago in de Sauveterre's name and it looked as though the deal had deliberately been kept hidden – likely, it was buried with a big bribe going to someone in the department. This wasn't about the land on which the pyramid had been built, but the desert plain – vast tracts of it too, in and beyond the Erg Chebbi. He felt it might signal that something untoward could be going on out there. That's all he said. And then he disappeared.'

'And so, your colonel was having it out with de Sauveterre over this then?'

'Yes, he came straight back on the plane from Moscow to see him. I don't really understand the significance of it but I know that he was concerned. He became paranoid and accused de Sauveterre of plotting to betray the Soviet Union.'

'And what was said? What happened?'

'The colonel accused him of planning to subvert the rightful use of Soviet equipment – which had been placed in his care – to suit his own interests.'

'And de Sauveterre talked him down?'

'Yes. He said it had nothing to do with their agreement – that what he was doing with that land wouldn't affect the plans he had in place with the Soviet Union. It was all fine in the end.'

'And what do *you* think – about what he's up to?'

'I think…' She trailed off.

'Go on,' he said, flicking the gun towards her to remind her of its presence. The girl was becoming a little too relaxed.

She flinched appropriately. The agent was confident that Valentina would tell him everything she knew without him having to resort to any of the unpleasantness he'd been forced to meter out on the architect.

'I think that he plans to take something from the desert,' she answered, without any hesitation now.

'You mean extraction?'

'Yes, I suppose so.'

The agent thought about the geological surveys he'd seen in de Sauveterre's study. So that was it then? It made sense to him now – at least to a degree. Oil, then? It must be – what else comes out from under the sand but oil?

'And what about you, Valentina? You're more than simply an interpreter in all this. What is de Sauveterre to you?'

'I… I was told to watch him, to get close to him and… well, we've become friendly.'

'Yes, I see you have. I've been watching you, Valentina.'

'It's not like that,' she protested angrily. For a moment the girl seemed to have forgotten her predicament – trussed up on the bed like a chicken.

'How is it then?'

The telephone rang. It was Pennycook. He'd matched the Russian in the prints to another photograph held in the station's file, named as Polkovnik Polyakov. (The girl had probably told him the truth about the rest of it too – after a while in the game you got to know these things.) Polyakov was attached to Yangel who headed one of the design groups which Khrushchev was so keen on, Pennycook told him. As he listened to Pennycook, the agent watched the girl's body slowly writhing on the bed, her back arching away from the mattress as she strained determinedly at her bindings. The thought of undoing her, in quite another way, was a difficult one for him to ignore.

Part Two

Atlas

Chapter 15

The Mountain

The telephone rang again sometime later. This time it was Dowling – everything was ready and the agent was to be picked up in half an hour from the hotel lobby. Methodically, he put his things together. The girl lay very still on the bed – she wouldn't make a sound now. Absently, he pulled a sheet over her body to protect her modesty and left the room, hanging the *Do Not Disturb* sign over the door handle – it should give him until the next morning before the girl was discovered by the chambermaids.

Dowling arrived in an old four-wheel-drive Willys American Army jeep which, he told him, Pennycook had got hold of from his opposite number at the US Embassy. 'I'm driving this time,' he said firmly to the agent. 'I'm not getting caught up in another of your bloody scrapes.'

They drove east, skirting the southern extent of the High Atlas mountain range and continued on as far as Ksar Tazougart where the road stopped. Ahead, the desert loomed. The date palm plantations, demarcating the edge of the desert steppe, had finished just beyond the last town and there was no real road to speak of – now only tyre tracks in the sand indicated the way. They pressed on through featureless flat terrain for another hour.

Dowling brought up the subject of the mountain water run off – which had clearly been diverted to meet de Sauveterre's need for secrecy – and then, as only an Englishman could, he steered the conversation neatly along to talk again about the weather. '…And you see, beyond here, away from the High Atlas to the south and east there's no irrigation whatsoever. Rainfall in this region is of course uncommon and only ever brief, but apparently desert nomads *have* witnessed extremely rare, freak weather events – would you believe that even snow flurries are claimed to have fallen in the desert near here?'

The agent stared out at the parched sands and pondered how the desert might look if such a freak of nature were ever repeated. He couldn't imagine it. As much as anything to relieve the monotony of Dowling blathering on, he interrupted the lesson in meteorology to ask what he knew about fuels extraction in the region.

'You're talking about oil. There's a bit of shale oil being pulled out in the north near Tangier is all, but that's not going to make anyone rich beyond their wildest dreams. Other than that, there's nothing doing. I doubt there's any oil under the Moroccan Sahara, old boy – unless that is, you've been given a rare tipoff. As far as the oil companies are concerned, it's all in Algeria – I don't think there's a damned thing under this particular, godforsaken slice of the pie.

Dowling's apparent knowledge on the subject of geography had already been keenly demonstrated to the agent. Putting aside the fact the man was a drunkard, he decided – for better or worse – to take Dowling into his confidence. 'I think de Sauveterre has bought up extraction permits – but I don't know what they're for.'

'I see – well it won't be oil. If those prospector johnnies had smelt even the faintest whiff of the stuff, then you can bet that the government would have sold the oil companies their permits long ago, along with their right arms – and their left ones too most likely. You see, all the North African countries have fairly pitiful economies. Morocco's a piss-poor kingdom and if there were any gain to be made from selling drilling permits, the King would already have done so – and then, of course, it would have gone the way Algeria is going now, with all the big players jumping aboard the bandwa–'

'All right Dowling, save me the lecture will you. Not oil then, but something else – minerals perhaps.'

'Gold is it eh? No, that's all down in West Africa: Guinea, Ghana, the Upper Volta, a bit in Mali, Liberia – there's diamonds too in Liberia and Sierra Leone. There's none of that up here though. Unless maybe it's coal he's after – there could be some anthracite seams here and there I suppose.'

'No one would go to the trouble and expense to so elaborately conceal the entrance to a blasted coal mine,' the agent snapped at him. 'It has to be something of significant value.'

'Well there's nothing else... besides hundreds and thousands of square miles of stones, gravel and sand.' As if to illustrate Dowling's point, the Erg Chebbi dunes reared up ahead like a heavy sea threatening to engulf them. 'You know that if you walk into the Erg Chebbi, you'll quickly find yourself disorientated – and then you'll become completely lost. Without water or shelter from the sun, you wouldn't last twenty-four hours,' Dowling said cheerfully as, at a barely discernible fork in the tracks, he steered the Jeep to the left over the sands,

'In that case, I hope you know which way you're going,' the agent remarked, dryly.

'These mining permits, or drilling permits, whatever they are of yours. Now, unless we're talking about privately owned land, which most probably we're not because the Kingdom has sovereign ownership of pretty much all of the Moroccan Sahara, then the state will have sold them to him. If it's of any use, then I can look into it – see if I can drag up anything more on it. Do you have any idea when your man obtained them?'

'I understand it to have been sometime towards the end of the fifties, but I have a feeling the records showing their purchase may well have been…lost.'

'I see, well another thing that's just occurred to me is that there may also be a logistical obstacle in my obtaining the gen at the mo.'

'And what's that?'

'Well, you see, what we're talking about: land extraction permits, now that's something that would normally be dealt with by the Ministry for the Interior. And that particular department of government may be feeling rather short staffed at present. I am of course referring to their captain – you know, the minister. Meant to tell you about this earlier – I was looking forward to telling you but it completely slipped my mind what with all the excitement of this carry on.'

'You've news on that, have you?'

'I'll say. Had a call from my old pal at the Sûreté about it earlier while you were off packing your suitcase and whatnot. Anyway, it appears that our man nicked himself shaving before he went for his swim. From the account I was given, when the body was fished out of the soup yesterday, it was all bloated and grey like a great cod…' Dowling grabbed the agent's attention for a moment and made a gesture with his finger, 'and with a deep slit across his neck, flapping open to resemble the gills.'

The agent raised an eyebrow at the colourful metaphor. Dowling certainly did have a particular way with words – and he was clearly loving all of this too. The agent's hunch about this having been foul play had been right though.

Gradually the sand gave way to stonier ground and they picked up something more recognisable as a track. 'The roads here simply peter out when they hit the desert,' Dowling explained. 'We're heading away from it now though and up into the foothills. It's about another hour's drive from here to your drop off point. Any chance, do you think, that you'll be expected?'

The agent thought about the girl. She wasn't the first he'd had in his hotel room since his arrival in the country, but he'd left Valentina in an altogether different state to the girls he'd left dozing the other morning. 'None,' he said, firmly.

After having had their bones shaken to pieces on the potholed excuses for roads, Dowling finally brought the jeep to a stop and consulted the map. 'This should do you well enough,' he said. 'Now, I won't hang around. I'm sure you're keen enough to get moving. And I've a prior engagement this evening so I need to turn this thing around and get back to town fairly pronto.'

'You get along. And Clyde,' the agent said, offering his hand, 'Thank you for all your help.'

'My pleasure, old man,' Dowling replied somewhat awkwardly, probably taken aback by the agent's sudden and uncharacteristic warmth towards him. They shook hands and, with Dowling wishing him good luck, the agent climbed out of the jeep, hauled the Bergen out from the back seat and hoisted it over his shoulders. After a poorly executed three-point turn, Dowling was gone.

The agent set off on foot with enough time to get to the ridge while there was still daylight. Besides the rope and the various items of climbing gear which he had strapped to the outside of his Bergen, he took with him a minimum of equipment – he had to keep the weight down if he was to manoeuvre with any kind of stealth. By way of ordinance, he had a couple of hand grenades in the knapsack and the lightweight Beretta. The little gun was perfect and for this type of operation he favoured packing it in the ankle holster. In addition to this he carried a Victorinox Swiss Army Officers' knife, a compass and a torch. For nourishment he took a good-sized piece of cured sausage and a small flask of hot coffee, a small canteen of water and a separate hip flask filled with whisky. In his pocket were a full packet of twenty of his own brand of cigarettes and the Ronson. That was all.

He walked for about two hours, making steady progress up the gently sloped incline of the north face of the mountain toward the ridge. He had to pick his way between the larger boulders and negotiate a few dry, rocky stream beds but, on the whole, the going was fairly good. These lower slopes were made up mostly of loose shale and were without much in the way of vegetation to hamper progress apart from a bit of low ground cover and the occasional thorny bush in the way. The environment was a pure wilderness and there couldn't have been a soul up there to see him but still he tracked his surroundings constantly, avoiding any paths and keeping away from the skyline. These practices were so ingrained in him from the gruelling training he'd undergone on Pen y Fan in years past that it meant he was quite unable to do otherwise. If, while off-duty, he took himself off to the Brecon Beacons for some time alone in that landscape walking for pleasure, rather than following the path, he'd find himself trampling his way through the gorse.

His inexplicably sincere farewell with the head of station had taken the agent by surprise as much as it had seemed to have done with Dowling. Had he said it because he knew that his mission was perhaps suicidal – after all, had he not seen a small army disappear inside the mountain he was now planning, single-handedly, to storm? Though the circumstances were far from unusual for him to be in, he couldn't recall ever allowing sentimentality to overcome him in a similar situation. Was it something else then?

As he walked, the agent considered his feelings towards Dowling – hating him really for being the man he feared he may himself one day become. To the agent, Dowling seemed somehow to represent the end of the line – to embody the inescapable horror of where the service would surely one day take him: put out to grass in a desert outpost where excitement had to be manufactured out of a dead man being pulled from the water or from a plane flying over the house on cue. Only the possibility of a violent death could stand in the way of it all happening to him. Without being conscious of it though, he'd rationalised that the way he'd felt about Dowling wasn't justified and that, in fact, he had no legitimate reason to be fearful either. The agent wasn't like Dowling in any way and he never would be – and so he should have no cause to despise him… and then he realised that, in fact, he no longer did.

He stopped at the foot of a vertical cliff face. There he found a bare slab of rock which sat up from the loose shale all around it like a little stage. It was a good spot: in the lea of the ridge, he was both out of sight from above but also had a clear view back down the lower slopes he'd climbed. He pulled the Bergen off, set it down on the rock and sat down beside it. It was early evening now and he had only about an hour or so of good light – the sun was already starting to dip down behind the mountains to the west. He pulled out his picnic and used his penknife to cut the sausage. He shouldn't stay too long here – the sky was already starting to colour a little and he wouldn't want to find himself only halfway up the cliff, losing the light. As he ate, he watched the sun disappear behind a far peak and, with the warmth of it gone, he felt the first chill of the approaching night. Even at this latitude it was cold in the mountains once the sun had set.

He poured himself some coffee from the flask and lit a cigarette. The coffee was good and strong – and it was still hot. He looked up. With the daylight fading, the stars were coming out. He thought about Gagarin up there only a few days before in the little Vostok capsule going around the Earth. He'd read in *Le Monde* that the accommodation was probably only the size of a dog kennel. The agent felt the comparison was particularly apt since the occupant of the previous Soviet rocket ship was of course a dog. Gagarin had been entirely alone in the command module, bolted inside a sealed metal coffin in an alien wilderness. The agent tried to imagine how he might have felt, with no one else there to help him – no one to save him, had things gone wrong.

He poured himself a second cup of coffee and lit another cigarette. Russia was an enigma. This was a nation so advanced that it could launch a man into space – to stretch what is possible for human beings to accomplish and to make such a rare achievement for mankind. And yet, at the same time Soviet Russia suppressed its own people under a vile totalitarian system of governance that also displayed a hostility and arrogance towards the rest of the world. The Soviets were heavily involved in whatever was going on inside the mountain, he knew that. The soldiers he'd seen last night in the convoy from Anfa were no private force. Despite the lack of uniform, he was confident they were a covert division of the Russian Army and, judging by the highly competent way in which they'd carried out that little operation, for his money they were Spetsnaz: Soviet Special Ops – his opposite numbers. He considered again the thought which Dowling had put to him: that his assault on the mountain might somehow be anticipated. He reasoned that, even were this a possibility, he wouldn't be expected to be coming in from above.

The sky to the west was showing various shades of the red spectrum – time for him to quit his musings, stow his things away in the Bergen and hide the empty flask and the cigarette butts in the bushes. The sustenance and the brief rest had restored him. He uncoiled the rope and slung the rucksack onto his back, checking that the climbing tackle – attached by various loops and buckles to the sides – was all close at hand. He had planned his timing for the climb carefully – he certainly hadn't wanted to arrive in broad daylight on the top of the ridge where he would be exposed. Now it was time to move if he were to reach the ridge's summit at dusk, as he hoped. Soon he was going to find out the answer to the puzzle contained within the mountain.

***

The wind had picked up and it whipped at him as he worked the rope. Now the air was full of sand, sucked up from the desert to the south. It stung his eyes and hampered his progress. The challenge of negotiating an overhanging section of the rock face had suddenly become greater. But the agent worked calmly, hammering in the pitons, securing the rope and then methodically inching his way further up the cliff toward the top of the ridge. He was close now and could see the final section just above him. As he neared it, his expectation piqued and for a moment his concentration was compromised – he moved too quickly and his hand came away from the rock face empty.

His body momentarily flailed backward but instinctively he was able to flatten himself to the mountain. He regained a handhold and took a breath. Lifting his head up, he found a better hold and pressed on. He moved his left foot up a little and found a meagre grip on a little rock spur. The wind suddenly gusted heavily and he lost the better footing of his right foot. His body lurched to his left but it hadn't sufficient support there and in a split second he fell. Under the weight of his falling body, the first piton flew clean out from its fixing and the rope immediately went slack again. The fixing of the next piton was better – it held the rope and arrested his fall. Stopped dead by the sudden torsion of the rope, he was slammed face first into the side of the mountain. He hung there, bleeding and lifeless, like a slaughtered bull.

At the end of the rope, the still body spun slowly in the wind. The limbs were limp, the eyes closed. Minutes passed. Something stirred. An eyelid opened – all was not quite lost. Survival had kicked in and slowly life came back to the agent. He was suspended below the overhang, about six feet away from the rock face. As he spun he faced the rock and could see his blood on it like the aftermath of a sacrifice. Looking up he saw he'd dropped about twenty feet. He moved his arms, and then his legs. Nothing was broken, thank God. He needed to get back onto the mountain. Moving his body, he used it to generate a gentle momentum, swinging away and towards the rock face like a human pendulum – building-up the depth of swing slowly in order to get close enough to the mountain to grab a hold.

Suddenly the rope gave and fragments of rock fell on him from above. The already-strained piton was being put under too much pressure from the movement. It was losing its hold in the rock and could fail at any moment. The agent acted decisively – he had no choice but to risk it all on one single chance to get back onto the mountain. Throwing all his weight backward to increase the arc of his swing, he pitched himself one last time outwards from the cliff. He sailed well away from the mountainside to the point of apogee, and then back again towards the rock. This time it came to him – just, and he clawed at it with his fingertips.

Gaining a little purchase, he pulled his body to it, flattening himself to the near vertical cliff face. Above him, the piton finally came away from the rock and the heavy rope fell away, the pull from it nearly causing him to lose his fragile hold. Desperately, he clung to the rock with everything he had. If he lost his grip, he'd be dead.

Carefully, he shifted his weight about and found a better hold with his feet. Tentatively, he moved his left hand up a little and transferred some of his weight onto it. Now he reached up with his right and getting a good grasp on a jutting piece of rock, he drew himself up a little. He improved his holds further and located a fissure in the rock to his side. Reaching behind him to his Bergen, he took out the little hammer from its buckled canvas loop and a piton from the side pocket. The agent drove the peg into the rock with the care and dexterity of a surgeon. Without delay, he clipped the rope to it and hammered a second peg into the rock on the other side of him. Looping the rope through this fixing too, he made himself secure once more. It had been a close call. After a couple of minutes rest, he plotted a course up the cliff from his new position.

Dusk had come. Hold by hold, he made his way steadily up the face of the ridge, driving in pitons as he went until the incline began to fall away and at last he had reached the summit. As the light finally faded, he collapsed exhausted. Slowly, methodically, he went about pulling the rope up after him. He could feel the blood clotted on his face – he'd hit the side of the cliff hard – it must look a mess. Pulling out the hipflask with the whisky, he took a large gulp and dabbed a little of the liquor where he could feel his face had been cut. The agent shook his head to clear the horror of the incident and took another long swig before replacing the flask back into the bag.

The ridge sloped upward from his position and some way along it, up above him, he could see the pyramid lit up from within – an inverted prism, glowing white. He shouldn't have risked the light from a cigarette up here but he needed it after what had just happened and he lit one anyway. He ducked his head and brought his shoulder round to mask the flicker of the Ronson. Together with the whisky, the cigarette pulled him back together. Afterwards, he carefully coiled the rope and attached it back onto the front of the Bergen. The agent took out the Beretta and emptied the chamber into his hand. It was nearly dark now and the light from the young moon only provided limited visibility – but he was quite capable of doing this by feel. He checked the mechanism and, satisfied with the operation, returned the live round to the chamber and holstered the gun. With clear skies, he didn't need to use the compass to get a bearing and, once again, he located Polaris to determine his position.

He was about to set off when, from the southwest, there came a faint glimmer of light and then another. He strained his eyes to see more. Directly from above, a small streak of light fizzed for only a moment. He knew that it was a comet, a giant rock of ice hurtling through space at around thirty miles per second, leaving its distinctive trail of vaporised ice particles in its wake. It was followed by an explosion of tiny, glittering white tails brightly arcing directly overhead. A comet shower, caused by smaller chunks of meteoroid debris being vaporised as they entered the Earth's upper atmosphere. Now, fainter lights were visible streaking towards the southern horizon. The agent carried on starring up into the night sky, craning his neck waiting; wondering if there would be more – but the display was over.

Setting off across the gently rounded summit of the ridge, he was mindful of being exposed against the skyline and so kept his body low to the ground, feeling his way with caution along the rock to where he estimated the shafts to be. There was nothing. He took out his compass to get a more accurate bearing. The luminous green dial suggested he may have strayed too far to his left. He backtracked a little, took another bearing and then edged forward on the corrected line. Nothing again. Based purely on his memory of the architect's models, it was like trying to find a needle in a haystack.

He thought that perhaps he'd missed them again and considered backtracking once more but then he made out the subtle tonal variation of one of the openings – a darker void amid the general gloom surrounding it. He moved forward and took off the Bergen, unbuckled the rope coil and attached the compact grappling hook he'd brought. A natural fissure in a protruding rock at the mouth of the shaft provided the perfect hitching point for the grapple. He wedged it into the fissure and gave it a good pull – it was secure. Using a crampon, he clipped the end of the rope onto the grapple and held the rope coil out over the chasm. He let it drop. It fell silently down into the shaft below. He took out his gloves, put them on and hitched the bag securely onto his back. Gripping the suspended rope in his gloved hands, he carefully let himself out on it, walking backwards out over the lip of the shaft. Leaving the stars behind, he inched himself down into the void.

***

He lowered himself once more down the rope – surely, he must come to the base of the shaft soon. Repeating the sequence yet again, he held the rope firmly between his ankles and eased the grip he had with his hands, allowing the rope to slide slowly through them. Now, holding the rope tightly in his hands, he lowered his legs, letting the rope pass between his crossed ankles. To his sudden alarm the rope was gone. Instinctively he reversed the manoeuvre and regained his ankle grip. Supporting his weight with his ankles, he moved his hands back up the rope to gain a better holding position. He was in trouble. The rope had run out and yet he hadn't reached the foot of the shaft. Silently he cursed himself for taking his chances with only a hundred feet of rope. His hands and arms ached with the prolonged strain of supporting his body.

This was a perilous situation. He wondered how far he could drop without breaking his bones so badly that he wouldn't then be able to defend himself. Onto a hard surface, perhaps twenty feet if he was lucky – but he would have to land well and he couldn't do that unless he knew when he was about to hit the ground. Though his torch was at hand, he couldn't risk using it. Instead, he reached into his pocket and pulled out a stone from the handful of small shale pieces he'd put there earlier for such a situation. He let the stone drop. It produced a metallic jangle as it bounced off something immediately below him – what was it? The stone continued to drop for a moment or two, before he heard it make contact with the base of the shaft. He calculated that it must still be a good thirty feet to the ground – too far for him to drop without risk of serious injury.

Composing himself, he thought that if he were able to get a foothold on the wall of the shaft, then perhaps he could free climb down it to the bottom. First, he would need to descend as far as possible – use as much of the rope as he could. He lowered himself once more, his feet letting go of the rope and dangling freely below it. Now he was suspended only by his hands. Taking his weight with his lower hand alone, he let go of the other and quickly took hold of the rope again below it, repeating the process until his hands were at the very end of the rope. He hung there, his body tested to the limit. As he had done before, he used his body to propel him from side to side – but the swing also produced a rotation and suddenly he found himself spinning wildly. Trying to control the spin only made it worse. Feeling nauseous now, his hands were becoming numb and he was near to losing his grip. He was desperate.

The agent had run out of options and the only possibility he could see was to drop to the ground and take his chances. But, with a clang, the heel of his shoe glanced across something solid. The shock of it nearly caused him to lose his hold on the rope there and then. His legs flailed out into the void below as he tried to locate the thing again – whatever this was, it offered him the only chance of breaking his fall. As he made contact with it for a second time, he let go of the rope and launched himself in the general direction of it. He fell, lunging in the darkness at it and his body hit something hard. Momentarily arresting his fall, he fought for a grip on it – but he was still under the control of gravity and he sailed on past. His head caught a blow on something else and his flailing ceased as the agent completed his descent. He was only half conscious when his limp body hit the ground, impacting the concrete floor with a sickening thud and triggering the movement sensors. The lights came on and an alarm sounded.

***

The agent came to, lying prostrate, on the cold concrete. He realised he had blacked out for a moment. His head throbbed with pain. He tried opening his eyes. The right eye didn't register much and may as well have remained closed – it felt as though it were on fire where he'd hit it on the way down. Through his other, he could see blood pooling in front of him on the smooth concrete. He tried to move but was in too much pain and instead let out a soft groan. Attempting to lift his head, he discovered that his back wasn't broken at least. He looked up at the shaft, lit now by harsh floodlights arranged in stages around its circumference. Through his one good eye, he focused on the empty rope hanging motionless above him, then on what it was that had broken his fall. What he saw made him shiver. He heard a door burst open before losing consciousness again.

Chapter 16

Morphine

There was a television on in the corner of the room. The grainy picture showed a man in what looked rather like a deep-sea diver's suit moving about on a grey expanse of, presumably, the seabed. The bulky arms and legs of the occupant moved slowly underwater but the scene looked odd somehow – what was wrong about it? Inside the great fishbowl helmet, the face of the diver, busy at some task, was hidden behind extraordinary, gold-tinted glass. Dowling was blathering on at him as usual while he was trying to watch. But there was something odd too about what he was saying – or rather about the way in which he was saying it. He wasn't speaking in English. He was talking to him in another language and though it sounded familiar, the agent couldn't understand a word of it.

The submarine in the background of the picture looked like no submersible the agent had ever seen. A great metal orb supported on four telescopic legs and with all kinds of ancillary equipment strapped to the body. The agent watched the diver with curiosity as he went about setting something up on the seabed – he'd unfurled a large red cloth, swaying gently in the deep, still water – it dawned on him what it was. Against the red, there was the yellow star and the hammer and sickle of the Soviet Union. Of course, Dowling was talking in Russian. Was this normal? The agent drifted.

He could hear the buzzing of an insect – a bee or a wasp, he wasn't sure. It was getting very loud – it must be right beside his ear. He opened his eyes and saw that it was, in fact, flying slowly around in front of him. But this must be a hornet, it was so big. Though surely even a hornet couldn't possibly grow to be so large, even here – even in the tropics – the thing must have been a good foot long. The hornet flew around to face him and hovered a few feet away, above the bed. The agent recoiled suddenly with alarm as he looked at the insect's head. It wasn't that of a hornet. It was human – and it had the face of de Sauveterre. The agent closed his eyes. When he opened them again, the monstrous thing had gone. He closed his eyes once more and drifted back to sleep.

The first thing he became aware of was the pain. His head was throbbing badly but there was pain throughout his body too. The second thing was that he wasn't alone. He could hear them talking. They spoke quietly though and, with the fury going on in his head, he couldn't hear what they were saying clearly – but, he thought he could discern a man's and a woman's voice. Somehow, he had a sense they were talking about him. He felt the cool sheet on his naked body. He was in bed. He must be in a hospital – yes, that was it – and a doctor was discussing his patient with the nurse. But their words were strangled – they sounded to the agent like the abstract noises made by an infant. And then a part of their dialogue separated itself from the rest, though he wasn't sure if what he thought he'd heard was right or not.

'Not everything is as it might seem,' the doctor seemed to be saying.

'Don't you think I don't know that already? the nurse responded. 'My heart and my home – how can I be loyal to both? It's not possible now. I don't know any more what I should do – and now this.'

'Don't worry about him,' the doctor said. 'A fly in the ointment, that is all. He won't cause us any trouble now, my love.'

This was a strange conversation for medics to be having. It was more like a scene from a romantic film than a doctor's rounds on a hospital ward. Or was it that they *were* actors – was it in fact a film? He felt sure that he knew her voice – she must be a very famous actress. The doctor said her name, but was it *her* name or was it the name of the character she was playing? It was all very confusing. Another word, a single word, one which he recognised. It filtered down through the morass of noises and into the agent's fragile and fleeting consciousness. Was it really what he'd heard the doctor say? But why would a doctor be concerned with the stars? Or was it *film stars* that he meant? He thought about her and he drifted again.

He came to again but not fully – he was in and out – floating, drifting along. The throbbing in his head had subsided but his left eye still felt as if it were on fire. The voices were gone but now there was something else. Movement, and then familiar sounds: the softest rustle of fabric, a zipper, silk quietly pooling onto the floor. More movement, closer – much closer. He felt the sheet being pulled up away from him and then being drawn back down again. Someone else had just got into the bed with him.

The body moved over towards him until it was touching – soft skin up against his own. A woman. She turned onto her side and pressed her crotch to his hip. Under the sheet, her hand explored him. She ran it up his chest, over his shoulder and down the injured arm. It felt the bandage which started at the wrist and entirely covered his broken hand. She held it through the bandage and squeezed. He let out a moan. She began to gently rotate her pelvis. He drifted.

She squeezed his hand more tightly and he stirred again – pain stole through the bandage protecting it. She let go of his hand and with hers, began rooting out his other injuries. With some, she merely caressed the dressings but with others her nails pulled at the surgical tape holding the gauzes in place, peeling them back to expose the wound – then pushing a nail right inside him. He felt it all but the drug in him numbed the pain, protected him from the brutality of it. Now her other hand was elsewhere. He could feel it against his side, busy under the sheet. Inside her knickers, the back of her hand rubbed against the silk as she penetrated her own body. She only reached for him at the very end, cupping his limp penis in her bloody, sticky fingers and squeezing it hard as she shuddered.

Afterwards, he thought she might be about to kiss him but she had only put her mouth close to his face to speak. She said something to him. What was it? Something about change, something about how funny it was. It didn't seem funny to him though. It was over – she got out of the bed and he listened to the sounds she made getting dressed. The sheet now stuck to his body, mapping out her interventions in a bloody trail. The agent heard her let herself out of the room and lock the door behind her.

In and out, drifting.

Dowling again, this time with the captain – the one with the bortsch – they were sitting around his table in the captain's cabin aboard The Star. And his chief was there too. He had come to visit the agent aboard the ship. How was he feeling, the old man asked him? As he spoke, bubbles issued from his chief's mouth. Of course, they were underwater. The soup wouldn't stay in the bowls – it was going everywhere.

The agent tried to find the words but the water smothered them – and then he didn't know anymore. What was it that his chief had just asked him? Wasn't there something he had to do here, something important? Was it to do with the ship… or was it another thing? There *was* something else though. The girl, she was here too. Was it to do with the girl?

And there was someone else with her, the other captain, the one with the Sûreté. But there was something odd about the man. His throat was slit open and when he spoke, his voice emerged from the wound. The agent realised there was something funny about the captain's head too. It wasn't his. It wasn't human even. It was the head of a fish – a great cod. It wasn't the captain at all.

***

The agent guessed he'd been given a painkiller, a powerful painkiller – his mind had been curdled – most likely it was morphine. He found that he was now able to open both his eyes. His right felt swollen and his vision through it was blurred and restricted – but he wasn't blinded. There was a low, ambient light. Looking around him, he discovered he was in a small, windowless room. The floor looked like it might be concrete but the walls and ceiling were of roughly-hewn granite. The realisation came to him that he was inside the mountain. He remembered falling... how long had he been out? He moved his left arm and felt the reassuring weight of his Rolex Submariner wristwatch. The agent tried to focus on the watch face but, despite the luminous dial, he found that he couldn't read the time.

He analysed his injuries. His face throbbed and would, no doubt, be cut and bruised. He went to move his arm up to it but moving it was painful and he stopped – could he have broken it? He tried his other arm. It was fine. He brought it up above the sheet and felt a large dressing which had been applied over his cheek. No matter. Running the good arm back under the sheet, over his legs and torso, he felt the tenderness of bruising and more dressings. He must have been writhing around in some drug-induced state, for many of the dressings seemed to have been pulled away by his tossing and turning. Going by the position of his wounds, he'd fallen on his right side. The question was whether or not his injuries were merely superficial. He tried bending his legs and rotating his ankles. First the left – it was fine. Now for the right leg – he needed some luck here. It bent at the knee though not without some pain. He extended it and then tried rotating his ankle. This was painful too but it was only bruised. Nothing broken, thank God – he'd been lucky. Back to the other arm. It certainly felt restricted when he tried again to move it. This wasn't good news. He went to rotate his wrist and wished he hadn't. Hot daggers stabbed at it and sent fire up through the arm in a message to his brain to stop. Gingerly he explored the extent of the damage with his other hand. His right hand was splinted and, together with his wrist, had been securely bandaged. Maybe not so lucky after all.

He swung himself off the bed and, lowering his bare feet onto the cold floor, sat on the edge of it to inspect his injuries as best he could with his impaired vision. The finger splint protruding from the bandage on his hand indicated that in addition to the wrist, he'd suffered a broken digit. Why could it not have been his left instead? With control, he quietly uttered an obscenity.

At least his legs seemed okay – he should be able to stand. Carefully he attempted it, holding onto the bedside with his good arm. Yes, that was fine – he wasn't a broken man just yet. Cautiously he took a step and then another – he could walk. He'd be alright. The agent padded slowly over to the door. It was a heavy metal-lined affair with a modern, spherical polished steel knob. Though he realised he was stark naked, he needed to understand his situation. He reached out and turned the door knob. It rotated a few degrees but then the lock denied any further movement. Returning to the bed, he sat down and weighed up his situation. After falling twenty or thirty feet onto concrete, it was remarkable he wasn't seriously injured. Also, in his favour, the fact that he'd been given medical attention meant it was unlikely for him subsequently to be killed by the Russians or on the orders of de Sauveterre whose subterranean lair he'd dropped into uninvited. Against these things, he found himself locked in a room behind a heavily constructed door with no visible means of escape. In addition, he had been disarmed, had no clothes nor equipment.

He rested on the bed for a while and then got back into it and slept – this time thankfully, without the fantastical drug-induced nightmares. When he woke, he felt much better and his sight had improved somewhat. His clothes had appeared, freshly laundered and folded in a neat pile on a chair. He got out of bed and went over to inspect. All of his things were there with the exception of his shirt. In its place was a replacement in white linen. On top of the pile of clothing was, bizarrely, his empty ankle holster. His shoes had been placed below the chair, newly polished. Someone had been to more than a little trouble on his account. What the hell was this about?

He pulled on his underwear and slid the trousers on over his lacerated legs. He noticed it immediately. Whoever had checked his pockets hadn't done nearly a thorough enough job – the thing may have been thin but how in God's name could it have been missed? The trousers had even been ironed for heaven's sake. He dug his good hand into the deep pocket of his tropical worsted trousers and, pulling out the piton, held it up to his face in disbelief. Either there was a God after all or someone more secular was looking out for him. He felt the point. The pin was fairly sharp – not as sharp as he would have liked but in the absence of a knife it would serve him adequately.

The agent put on the shirt easily enough (being a size too large for him helped) but he struggled with his socks. If he needed to fight, then how the blazes could he in this condition? Leaving the shoes off for the time being so as not to make any noise, he slid them over next to the door. He tried the door knob again. Still locked. He took the pin out of his pocket and tried it for size against the gap between the door and the door frame. It wouldn't do: the pin was too wide for the job – he needed something thinner to slide the latch open. Looking around him, the room was empty save for the chair and a simple nightstand on which stood a Dixie cup of water. He could try tearing open the paper cup then flattening and folding it. Then he had a better idea. He unwound the bandage from his hand and threw it on the bed. The fall had made a proper mess here – his wrist was heavily bruised and swollen. His index finger had swollen to almost twice its normal size and was obviously broken. It had been dressed with another strip of lint wound around a wooden splint. Carefully he unwound the dressing and took out the splint. It would make the perfect tool.

The agent wound the lint back over the broken finger and middle finger, using the neighbouring digit as a brace in the absence of the splint and not bothering to replace the bandage which shouldn't be needed if he were careful. He reviewed his situation. He had a lean equipment inventory: a sharpish climbing pin, a few pebbles – also overlooked and left in his trousers pocket – the empty holster and a finger splint. His injuries consisted of impaired vision through his swollen eye and a severe reduction in the usefulness of his right arm. Even the carefully restrained use of his hand to dress himself had hurt like hell – he'd better learn to use his left in double-quick time.

Now he returned his attention to opening the door. Taking the splint, he eased it into the gap between the door and the frame. He ran it up and down until he located the latch. Gently, he pulled the splint out and then reinserted it exactly where he had felt the latch. The splint made contact with it and pushed against the sprung latch. Now he pushed the splint towards the door frame to provide leverage. He had to exert enough pressure on the splint to compress the spring inside the latch but not so much as to cause the splint to snap. Patiently he worked the splint until, with satisfaction, he felt the latch depress. The door was open. He slid his shoes on and stepped out into a passageway.

He'd half expected there to be a guard posted outside but he looked up and down the empty passage which ran for about thirty feet in each direction. There was no sign of life. How very rum. Which way though? He heard the noise of footsteps approaching from the right and quickly stepped through the doorway back into the room. Hurriedly, he inserted the splint over the latch again as he closed the door to keep it unlocked while he waited for the footsteps to pass. He waited a full minute before opening the door again, stepping out and then closing it quietly behind him. He'd heard the footsteps fall away to his left. If whoever it was who'd passed by were planning on coming back again anytime soon, then he wouldn't want to bump into them on their return journey – he set off down the passage in the opposite direction.

Like the room, the passage had been tunnelled out from the mountain and the curved walls and ceiling were a jagged array of incised rock – this must have been some excavation job. The passageway curved around to the left and then, a little further on, was barred by a heavy steel door. There was no handle but next to it on the wall was a small control panel with an illuminated key pad. His eye was still causing him problems but he could see that the buttons had numbers on. He'd come across this type of high security entry system before. It was likely there would be other doors protected in the same way and they would probably all work using a single code.

These codes were typically made up of four digits. He thought for a moment. A year would make a handy four-digit cypher but the current one was too obvious. What else? De Sauveterre was fifty-five which meant that he would have been born in 1906. Would he be so egotistical as to use the year of his birth? Quite possibly the man was a megalomaniac but the agent had no idea of his character – after all, he didn't know him from Adam. Try another tack. This was a large installation and there would need to be a good few people working here to run it and so, assuming the code was a year, it would have to be a year that was memorable to everyone. But which could it be? *Think,* damn it. He racked his brain for a noteworthy year but nothing relevant came to him. Guessing the code was impossible.

The agent tried another approach. What did he know about this place beyond his own certainty that it had been built by de Sauveterre? Regardless of whoever's name all this was in, he also knew for a fact that the Soviets had a stake in it – and so they probably had their people working here. Any likely years there? He thought about it. The communist system required complete devotion to its leader… Khrushchev came to power three years ago in fifty-eight. 1958 – that could be it. But the duty of your average Russian towards their leader went way beyond mere respect. It's devotion and it's personal – it's more like adoration… He couldn't afford to spend any more time thinking about it – someone else may come along at any moment and he had to evade being caught again. If he could at least find somewhere to lie low for a moment, then he could take stock, formulate a new strategy in the light of his predicament. Without hesitation he tapped out the number sequence he'd thought of onto the keypad. Nothing happened. His heart sank. But then there was a click and the door was unlocked. Clever boy. He pushed it open an inch and peered through the crack.

A short distance away were piles of neatly stacked, steel pallets like those he'd seen being transported up here from the airfield with the canisters strapped to them. Inching the door open a little further, he looked quickly about the space. There were several people in here but they were all busily engaged in whatever it was they were doing. Satisfied that no one would see him if he were quick, he darted over to the cover of the pallets and crouched down behind the wall of steel – there must have been over a hundred pallets here. The agent waited for a moment before easing his head over the parapet to take a proper look at the space in which he found himself. What he saw was quite extraordinary.

The chamber was a vast natural cavern rising seventy or eighty feet at the midpoint, by perhaps five times that figure in length. Big spaces are often described in hyperbolic terms as being 'cathedral-like' and certainly the enormity of this space was vast – the proportions not that far off the interior of St. Pauls. In ostentatious contrast to the rough rock surfaces of the walls, the cement floor of the chamber was utterly flat and polished. A majestic fusion of nature and the art and will of man: the chamber couldn't escape having a spiritual feel. But the agent recognised there to be another quality present and that quality had little to do with worship. The place had a feeling about it of evil.

Looking up, roughly in the centre of the space and at around a hundred or so feet apart, were the pair of ventilation shafts set into the roof of the cavern – he'd made his botched entrance down one of these. Staged around the openings of the shafts were a series of three-foot-thick-steel, revolving blast gates fitted with powerful hydraulic rams. At the moment, the gates were open. Beyond these, and positioned directly below each of the shafts, were enormous latticed steel gantries, rising up inside them. Housed within these structures and disappearing up into the narrowing shafts, were a pair of giant metallic tubes. The dull green-grey of the cold steel was emblazoned with the red star of the Soviet Union. At their bases were the unmistakable bell-shaped forms of multiple rocket engine assemblies. Naturally formed or otherwise, the ventilation shafts were, in fact, rocket silos.

The agent looked around the rest of the space. Opposite him were another set of thick, solid metal gates. These must be what he'd seen barring his way in the tunnel, the access point from the gorge. Over on the far side of the cavern there were at least two other unassembled missiles, laying horizontally in sections on great steel-framed supports. A number of people were working on the missiles, dressed in white, full-body hazard outfits. Some wore full-face shields but of those who didn't, it was clear to the agent that, though the faces had the hard-looking features of Soviet stock about them, these men were not soldiers. They were engineers and technicians, no doubt highly trained men. This would be the team of rocket scientists and ballistics experts from Moscow. There were figures also moving about on the high-level gantries surrounding both the rockets. A panel had been removed from the side of one of the missiles and a small team were working on something inside it. Above them, working from an even higher-level gantry on the other missile, another pair of technicians had a part of the nose cone off.

The agent knew this could mean only one thing. The missile was being armed. He swore silently.

Even more pallets were over by the missiles with their canisters still secured. The worrying hunch he'd had about what might be in these had been right. Beside the canisters were two technicians, both of them were not only kitted out with full-face shields but also with self-contained breathing apparatus. They were engaged in pumping what must be liquid propellant – rocket fuel – from the canisters through what appeared to be a cooling system and into the fuel tanks of one of the missiles. No wonder the whole bloody pier had gone up when canisters of rocket fuel had exploded there. The special consignment will have replaced that lost one. Over the bulky respirators, the men looked out through the yellow-tinted Perspex of the face shields. Cleary concentrating on the job at hand, they weren't looking in the agent's direction and he hadn't been spotted. Wanting it to remain that way, he backed out silently through the door to the passageway. He'd seen enough.

These were big missiles: intercontinental. The installation amounted to a strategic missile base near enough to the Atlantic coast to have the capacity to strike the eastern seaboard of the United States – a range just not possible for the Soviets to achieve from their bases in mainland Russia. Was this then about the balance of power? Addressing the missile gap caused by the United States' deployment of the Thor missiles at home in Feltwell and now the Jupiter missiles based in Italy. These medium-range ballistic missiles were positioned right next door to the Soviet Union and up until now Russia had no way to counter the threat. But with their own missiles sited here in Morocco, they could now be capable of matching America's arsenal.

There was no escaping the fact that the missiles were being armed but surely this wasn't about starting a war. The agent remembered the girl having said something about there being a test – at the time it had made little sense to him, but now it did. A live test-firing then or might it be more than that? It seemed like a lot of propellant just to achieve a test-fire of a few hundred miles deeper into the Sahara or out over the coast into the open waters of the Atlantic. The amount of fuel alone would be enough to blow any test target site to Timbuktu. No, it didn't add up to being a local test – this had to be a sub-orbital flight. And the thing about intercontinental ballistic missiles was that the liquid propellant used to fuel the rocket engines couldn't ever be kept in the fuel tanks for long once it had been pumped in. If a missile was being fuelled then this meant it would be fired imminently, and both these missiles were being fuelled and armed – the other technicians he'd seen on the lower gantry were probably spinning the gyros in preparation for the firing. Whichever way it was, the launching of an enemy missile perhaps armed with a nuclear warhead was bad news.

Following the passageway back past his cell, he came to another steel door. He tapped out the same four digits onto the keypad beside it and the single, wide door slid away to one side, retracting itself into a slot hewn in the stone. Stepping over the threshold, he entered a small room with walls lined out in stainless steel. On the wall to his right was another keypad. The agent knew what this room was. He put in the combination again. A mechanism clicked and then the motor began to whine quietly as the lift moved upwards.

Chapter 17
Bollinger and Kubanskaya

The lift slowed its ascent, came to a stop and the door opened onto a second cavernous space. Whatever the agent might reasonably have expected to see here, it was not this. Instead of rockets and technicians, well-dressed guests were standing about drinking champagne. The absurdity of the scene, a drinks party inside this hollowed-out mountain on the edge of the desert, momentarily halted the agent. He looked around the space. There were around a hundred people, mostly men but there were a few women present too – perhaps for balance. It was a black-tie event and the ladies in evidence wore glamourous gowns, some wearing elbow-length white gloves.

Holding court at the centre of one group was de Sauveterre. At his side – dressed impeccably in a flowing black gown, her hair artfully piled and a diamond choker around her neck – was Valentina Primakova. Her eyes caught his. He smiled warmly at her but his act of friendship wasn't reciprocated – though it wasn't met with any trace of anxiety or fear either – instead she held his gaze for a few moments before casually leaning in to de Sauveterre and whispering something in his ear. De Sauveterre, listening to what the girl was telling him, didn't trouble himself to look over to the agent. Instead, he simply carried on his discourse with his guests.

Unsure of his next move, the agent stopped one of the waiters, helping himself to a glass from the tray. He took a large mouthful – this was the first drink he'd had since arriving to de Sauveterre's lair. Though he couldn't really have cared less about it in the circumstances, he couldn't help but notice that it was an excellent wine. Its toasty, mineral flavours produced a complex, firm and rich taste. While he looked about at the assembled guests, a part of his mind was automatically, almost unconsciously, also concerned with speculating on the vineyard and possible vintage of the champagne. Most likely it was Bollinger, probably a fifty-five – one of only two exceptional vintages for this producer from the past decade, the other being the fifty-two. The fifty-five had only just been released, and to have secured such a wine for his event would surely appeal to a man such as de Sauveterre. The agent would put money on it being the fifty-five.

Scanning the room, he speculated as to who all these people were. They looked like they were made up of the usual mix of high-rolling businessmen and politicians who would grace an event such as this, but there were some uniforms too – high-ranking members of the Moroccan military and Royal Gendarmerie. They were most likely either from Casablanca or from the capital, with the notable exception of a sizeable Russian contingent who, the agent observed, were almost exclusively uniformed. Despite there being only a smattering of women among them, everyone seemed to be in good spirits – even the Russians.

Amongst the faces, the agent recognised all three of the men he'd seen on the pier the day he'd arrived and he thought he might have remembered another as being a member of the Moroccan Cabinet. What was going on here exactly? He decided to find out and walked confidently over to join de Sauveterre's group.

As the agent approached, de Sauveterre looked up and called out to him in a jovial manner, 'Ah, there you are my good fellow – up on your feet again already I see. How does the expression go? You can't keep a good dog down.'

French, privately educated, aristocratic – de Sauveterre came over to greet him. The healthy-looking sunburn was set off by his choice of outfit: a white silk suit with a plain white silk shirt, a matching white knitted wool tie and pristine white leather shoes over white socks. Dressed entirely in white like this and with his long white hair, now tied back in a neat ponytail, the overall effect was as startling as the architecture. He looked like a man who could save the world – or perhaps condemn it.

'I understand you suffered an unfortunate accident,' he said casually, as if the agent's presence here was of the least concern to him.

'It appears I took a wrong turning,' the agent replied just as lightly, but looking to see if the man believed him.

'My name is Aristide de Sauveterre and you are Mr Jenson Coldblow. We took the liberty of looking through your belongings while you were indisposed and found your card in your coat pocket. My doctor had to cut your shirt off you, I'm afraid. I do hope you approve of the replacement – it's one of my own.'

'I'm sure it'll do.'

'Now,' de Sauveterre said, turning to Valentina who had been looking on coolly at the exchange, 'let me introduce you to this most adorable girl. May I present, Miss Valentina Primakova.'

The agent turned to face the girl. 'It's a pleasure to meet you, Miss Primakova,' he said. 'And what brings you to Morocco, I wonder?'

This seemed to test the girl's cool and her eyes drilled into the agent's before she answered him.

'I am here at Monsieur de Sauveterre's pleasure,' she said, ice cold.

'Well, this all seems terribly jolly – what's the occasion?'

The girl said nothing. De Sauveterre managed a tired smile before politely asking his other guests if they would excuse him. Understanding him at once, they quietly melted away to circulate elsewhere. Only the three of them remained now and it appeared that the gloves might be off.

'Mr Coldblow, you were found in a heap at the foot of a shaft which you were attempting to lower yourself down by means of a rope. May I ask why you were thus engaged?'

Though flimsy, the agent had nothing to lose by trying out his cover story, hastily put together as it was under the pretext of an innocent out of his depth, caught up in something he knew nothing about and didn't understand. 'I climb for sport,' he said. 'The shaft presented itself as a challenge for me to descend–'

'You enjoy challenges do you, Mr Coldblow?' the girl, interrupting, asked him sharply.

'That rather depends on the situation.'

'It must feel very good to conquer something with your body, with your strength alone,' she said.

'Actually, I think that climbing mountains is as much about mental strength as it is about physical prowess.'

She laughed but there was no warmth. Instead, it was a cold dismissal. 'And do you apply the same maxim to all things, or is not simply brute force responsible for mastering your conquests?'

'I'm not sure to what you can be referring, Miss Primakova,' he said, gambling.

De Sauveterre had been studying the pair with interest during their exchange and must have noticed the tension in her voice. 'What is it that you mean, my love?' he asked her.

The sound of de Sauveterre's voice appeared to break her mood. 'I'm sorry darling,' she said. 'I've probably had too much to drink. I'm not sure if I know myself what I mean, my words were running away from me.'

'Will you forgive me, Mr Coldblow?' she said calmly, though the discipline she required to say it was almost tangible.

'Of course, and I hope that you will forgive me too, Miss Primakova.'

It was as if she hadn't heard him. This wasn't exactly a love triangle.

De Sauveterre looked quizzically at the agent. 'You were telling us about your climbing escapades, Mr Coldblow, before Valentina here took you off… somewhere else.'

'Well, the fact of the matter is that I lost my grip. I suppose I must have had a nasty fall.' The agent felt it prudent to keep his explanations short and as simple as possible.

'I see.' De Sauveterre smiled knowingly, as if to dismiss his story.

The agent knew full well that he hadn't believed a word of it and wasn't about to be fooled – especially after Valentina's telling performance – but nonetheless, was clearly intrigued and enjoying the pantomime.

'I'm sure you could do with a real drink,' de Sauveterre said.

'Actually, I have had quite a time of it,' the agent said. If de Sauveterre was happy enough to play along with the awful, concocted story, then he was just as happy to as well.

'What's your poison?' de Sauveterre asked him.

'Vodka. I'm sure you'll have something Russian – and with plenty of ice.'

'Please, come with me. We'll get you your vodka on the rocks and I can show you around.'

As the agent was directed away, he turned back to see the girl had been left standing alone. In the moment before she had been able to recover herself, anxiety and discomfort marred her looks. That moment, however, was perceptible to the agent – and also very probably to de Sauveterre who, noticing that the agent's head had apparently been turned by the girl, turned his own toward her again too.

'But do come along with us my love,' he said, addressing her. 'Let us show our dear Mr Coldblow the view.' (Hurrying forward, the girl only vaguely managed to conceal her relief at not being excluded.) 'As a matter of fact,' he said, speaking now to the agent again, 'I think we have a bottle of Kubanskaya, an excellent brand produced by the Kristall factory in Moscow. If you're up on your vodkas, you'll have known that already of course. And I can assure you,' he concluded with a peculiar smile, 'we will have no shortage of ice.'

With de Sauveterre leading the way, the trio walked towards

a high-sloping face at the far end of the cavern. Here they stopped at the drinks table, set up in front of an enormous expanse of glass set into an impossibly deep recess in the solid rock. From this position, high up on the southern face of the ridge, the view was spellbinding. Here, the mountains of the High Atlas range came to an abrupt halt at an ocean of orange sand. Far below and in miniature, the agent could see plantations of date palm hugging the irrigated fringes of the higher ground. Beyond this, the desert began. He looked up and across at the vast emptiness of it. The rippling orange dunes of the Sahara stretched back to the horizon, fifty miles away.

De Sauveterre filled heavy tumblers with ice from a silver bucket and then, over it, he poured the vodka from the bottle of Kubanskaya with its distinctive label depicting a Cossack riding a white stallion. He passed the glasses around and then, raising his own, made a toast. 'To the restoration of your good health, Mr Coldblow.'

The collision of crystal produced a satisfyingly deep clink as the thick glassware came together. Through the yet thicker and heavier plate glass of the window, small lights twinkled amongst the palms below. The agent drank down the cold liquor. The vodka, distilled from wheat and flavoured with a just a touch of lemon, was indeed excellent.

'Is the view not extraordinary?' de Sauveterre asked him.

'It's all extraordinary.'

'Yes, isn't it?' de Sauveterre agreed. 'Let me tell you a little about this place. Within the ridge there are a whole series of caves, all naturally formed inside this mountain. And there is an even larger cavern than this one: the main chamber. I was told about these caves many years ago by a Bedouin nomad. He told me that they were inhabited by an evil spirit which deterred even the vultures from nesting within them – but I was undeterred. There is now a road which I had blasted through from the gorge but before that they were reachable only by climbing the near vertical southern face and, as you must have done yourself of course, I did just that – though with better success at descending the shaft. With the Bedouin as my guide, I was the first westerner to have scaled the mountain and entered the cave complex. I have never forgotten my first sight of the main chamber, nor have I forgotten filling my lungs with that dank, subterranean air. The caves have obsessed me you see and I sought ownership of them for many years. Only recently did I finally succeed in acquiring them and the necessary permissions from the Kingdom to develop them as I wished. So, you see, I have devoted some time working to achieve everything here, everything that is so extraordinary.'

From the girl, the agent sensed a vulnerability. It was clear to him she'd been reluctant to be left out but, in the company of both men, she didn't seem comfortable. After her initial, confrontational attitude towards the agent, she now remained tight-lipped. As for himself, he was perfectly happy to watch the girl and to let de Sauveterre talk. He went on, proudly telling the agent about the development of these subterranean spaces.

'The entire cave system was of course naturally protected from the outside and the two massive main chambers within were unashamedly and beautifully dramatic,' de Sauveterre said. He recognised that the window he'd installed in this cave was excessive but admitted that he loved the fact. 'My vision for this place was realised for me by my architect with the same great clarity afforded by only the very best of Russian vodkas,' he said, lifting his glass up to eye level as if to inspect it, 'such as the one we are drinking.'

'But surely, you didn't go to all this trouble purely to hold lavish receptions?' the agent asked, wanting to see if de Sauveterre would lay his cards on the table.

'Indeed not, but let us come to that in a moment or two.' (The agent would have to remain patient for a while longer). 'I was about to tell you about the construction – or rather excavation – of the facility here.'

Once he'd started talking, there seemed no stopping de Sauveterre and he continued describing the challenges to the construction for several minutes. He spoke levelly now about the security of the facility. 'Of course, local people were not unaware of the substantial construction project underway on the mountain over the past few years. However, it was built by a French company who flew in a skilled work force and absolutely no local labour was used. This policy was adopted purely in the interests of security.'

'Why would you want to make such a secret of the place?' the agent asked, pushing things more than was perhaps prudent.

De Sauveterre smiled thinly at the agent. 'Security is essential for the work we are doing here, Mr Coldblow. You have inadvertently stumbled upon a rather sensitive facility. During its construction there was an unavoidable suspicion of the site from the locals and a good degree of bad feeling, even hostility from those people who desperately needed work and hoped to find it here – and we had to deal with that. Nethertheless, few people had a clue as to what was being built here and as a result, security is watertight – or rather it was, until you dropped in to pay a visit.'

'Look, I apologise for landing on you unannounced – unfortunately I underestimated the depth of that shaft I was descending.'

'And you have also underestimated me, Mr Coldblow, if that is what you choose to call yourself.' De Sauveterre abruptly quit his pally talk and now he looked pained. 'Climbers do not generally equip themselves with hand grenades and revolvers.' Clearly, he'd grown tired of the charade.

'And as a rule, gentlemen do not imprison their visitors,' the agent snapped back at him, the alcohol sharpening his retort, 'whether invited or otherwise.'

In the vacuum which followed the outburst, the agent eyed the girl for her reaction. There wasn't one.

'You must forgive me for detaining you in such a manner,' de Sauveterre said, dealing calmly with the accusation, 'but while on the subject of security, I am curious to know how it is you came to obtain the security code with which to operate the elevator?'

'If I am not mistaken, Nikita Khrushchev was born in 1894,' the agent replied flatly.

'And so he was. How very clever of you to make that association.'

The agent didn't want to beat about the bush anymore, he wanted to know more about the missiles. 'You appear to have quite an affinity with the Soviet Union don't you, de Sauveterre. But tell me, why is there a small arsenal of Soviet rockets – a pair of them armed, fuelled and ready to launch – inside one of your caves. What kind of show exactly do you have in store for your guests tonight?'

The face of the Frenchman registered no surprise (after all, the agent had made his way here undetected, roaming freely about the place and he'd been found in the first instance, albeit unconscious, almost directly underneath one of the missiles). 'I admire your pluck,' he said, without showing bias. 'And how well informed you are in matters of military ordinance. I wonder what sort of person might know about such things?'

'Let's just say I'm an interested party.'

'And which party might you represent? Certainly not the Communist Party,' he said with a little chuckle. 'Another foreign government then. Now, let me see, which one might it be? Or are you perhaps no more than a filthy mercenary?' he said, taunting the agent.

'I'm on the side of international law.'

'Good for you. Then you'll be relieved to know that our missiles were acquired through legitimate and legal means.'

The agent watched the girl. Her face was unmoving, it gave nothing away. 'And how does she fit into it?' he said, keeping his eyes on hers.

'Miss Primakova is an envoy for her country, Mr Coldblow. You see, the project here has been undertaken in collaboration with the Soviet Union – they are my partners in the enterprise.'

'Why would you build a Soviet missile base here?'

'Because doing so is advantageous for my business activities – though for what it's worth, I personally feel no particular allegiance to the East, nor do I support the foreign policies of the Soviet Republic – and what is more, I have had no fear in making this known to my Russian allies either,' he said, directing an affectionate smile towards the girl. 'I do not favour communism as a system of governance over any other system, including democracy for that matter. I tell you this because I know that people like you are keenly interested in such matters–'

'There's a very good reason why "people like me" are interested in the activities of the Soviets,' the agent interrupted, 'particularly where ordinance is involved, let alone ballistic missiles.'

'You are an Englishman. I take it that you work for the British Government?'

'I'll keep that to myself, if you don't mind.'

'No matter, I think I know exactly what you do and who you work for,' he said, pausing for a moment to address the girl. 'Excuse us my love. I wish to speak privately now to this gentleman.'

At once the false air of indifference she'd displayed throughout all the exchanges between the two men thus far was gone. The attitude she'd adopted was blown away by de Sauveterre's sudden dismissal like an umbrella caught in a squall.

'Of course,' she said but, at the prospect of finally being cut out, Valentina was left looking panicked as she turned and walked back over to rejoin the party – her departure not going unnoticed by the glancing eyes of some of the higher-ranking members of Russia's military.

'Such a lovely girl,' de Sauveterre commented as she departed. 'And now to you, Mr Coldblow – if that is the alias you like to use.' De Sauveterre refilled the agent's glass. 'Though are you not in fact, a nameless agent working for a government department so secret that it could never publicly be admitted to?'

This man was astute and equally well informed – the agent could not have described his own position much better than this. But he had a line too on de Sauveterre – now at least he understood better the Soviets' place in whatever this scheme of his was.

'What are the targets?' the agent asked him. He seriously doubted there to be any truth to the thing the girl had mentioned to him about a test – firing the missiles into the desert with no discernible target other than a random set of co-ordinates or, come to that, out into the ocean. No, from what he'd seen in the silos, he didn't believe the purpose of launching these missiles was about anything as straight forward as that.

'Listen to me, de Sauveterre, I've been down to your missile silo or cave, whatever you want to call it and I've seen how much fuel's being pumped into those things–'

'What do you imagine – that I am to threaten firing the missiles at London and New York unless some outrageous demand of mine is met before the stroke of midnight – a comic book scenario? Do you really think I would invite all these people here tonight to witness an apocalypse?'

De Sauveterre appeared happy enough at least to provide an oblique answer to the agent's question. However, the agent detected a subtle moderation in the level of his voice now – it seemed that, despite his confident manner, he didn't want there to be any possibility of being overheard.

'You tell me, but I don't believe for one minute that this is purely a show of arms – a test flight or whatever.'

De Sauveterre faltered for a moment. During their

conversation, especially since the girl had left them, the agent had become aware of the interest of the Russian Military brass in observing their exchange. Now it seemed, so had de Sauveterre.

'Actually, I couldn't care less if you believe me or not,' he said and laughed heartily.

'Did I miss the joke?'

'Mr Coldblow,' de Sauveterre said, the smile from his own private amusement still lingering, 'I feel that I have afforded you far too much of my attention already at the expense of neglecting my other *invited* guests. I suspect that you are, how do you say, a loose cannon?' The smile faded. 'I think that it is time for you to leave the party. I'll let one of my staff take care of you from here.'

De Sauveterre beckoned his man over. The Russian had been standing discreetly at a distance, coolly observing the agent throughout the discourse with de Sauveterre. He came over now and directed himself to the agent, spitting something out at him in the hard, stressed syllables of his own language.

'This is Volodya,' de Sauveterre said. 'He is in charge of my security. I would introduce you properly but I'm afraid his command of the English language is poor. His skills… lie elsewhere – where his abilities are frankly unsurpassed.'

The agent had already recognised Volodya from the airfield, where he'd seen him supervising the transfer of cargo from the plane. A mean-looking Russian, he was well built and ugly as hell. This thug was only distantly related to the specialist crew he'd seen working down below in the silo. The agent knew the type well: he was your typical ex-navy, tough nut and in Volodya's case the agent would bet on him having been a submariner – those sun dodgers were as tough as nails. Seeing him here though, up close, the agent realised that in fact the man's face looked as though he'd been out in the midday sun for much too long, and he knew at once Volodya had made a very lucky escape. The airfield at Anfa wasn't the only terminus at which this thug had been in attendance, receiving volatile shipments from the homeland. He must have been on the pier when the Star went up because his forehead was red raw and the backs of his bare arms were heavily blistered, injuries which are to be expected when a canister of rocket fuel goes up in fairly close proximity. Paraffin, my eye. He'd be surprised if anyone in the Sûreté had actually fallen for the story.

'Do not be concerned, Mr Coldblow,' de Sauveterre said. 'I do not intend for you to be harmed – I am no barbarian. Volodya will simply escort you from the installation. You will go with him now and he will leave you at the head of a gorge on the south side of the mountain. You are clearly a resourceful man and I have no concern over your ability to make your way out from there – you simply follow the stream down to where you will come to a track leading out of the gorge. But I wouldn't think of leaving you to expire there all alone in the desert. I shall instead arrange for you to be picked up from there and taken back to your Consulate in Casablanca from where you may make your report to your superiors in London. I'm sure you will relate to them a detailed account of my installation here but I am untroubled by this. Your government will in any case shortly learn of the outcome of my operation and it can make up its own mind what it thinks about it – though I do trust that, in due course, they will come to find that the failure of your mission has proven in fact to have been a blessing. In the meantime, if you will excuse me, I will bid you goodnight and farewell… Mr Coldblow.'

The Russian was armed with a pistol but the agent recognised that de Sauveterre wouldn't want a scene and, rather than pointing the pistol toward him, Volodya instead simply made him aware of its presence. He held the gun casually in his hand, his fingers caressing the cold, smooth metal as if it were benign, like one might enjoy handling a good cigarette case. The Makarov PM was a soviet-made 9mm automatic, largely based upon the qualities of the German Walther PP. It was a robust weapon and good in the field of combat. Something about this fellow told the agent that he wouldn't hesitate to shoot him if he failed to do as he was instructed. Up against the Makarov, the agent longed for his Beretta. Without it, he felt he had little choice but to go along with de Sauveterre's wishes and so, courteously, he thanked the man for his audience and said goodnight. Volodya took up position closely at his side and led the agent over to the waiting lift. The door slid softly closed behind them and the lift descended, down again into the heart of the mountain.

Chapter 18
Cold Heart

Deep underneath the summit, the lift door slid back into its housing at the terminus of the passageway carved into the mountain. The agent looked at the Russian. His features remained impassive, the eyes cold and dead. He didn't doubt that here was a thug with a particularly nasty streak – and as if to prove it, out of sight of de Sauveterre's guests, he became more insistent in his method of escort. Though he continued to brandish the weapon in the same casual manner, he now took to directing the agent with sharp, sadistic kicks to his ankles – in this way, steering him towards a door further along the passageway from the lift.

Inside the room were small changing cubicles for the staff. Volodya shoved the agent towards a row of the white, full-body hazard protection suits hanging along one wall. He stopped the agent there while he put one of them on over his own clothes. Abandoning his cavalier attitude, he held the gun pointed at the agent throughout the process, dextrously switching it between his left and right hand as he dressed. He didn't seem at all the type to worry about personal safety – perhaps the incident with the Star and the burns that he'd almost certainly received as a result of it had proven too much for even this hard man. With himself now safely suited up, Volodya offered the agent no instruction to do likewise. Instead, showing no regard for his evident injury, the Russian cruelly took hold of the agent's bad arm to propel him back out into the passageway and on through the door to the silo. This manhandling pushed the pain in his broken wrist close to his bearable limit.

They crossed the assembly floor of the silo to the far side where the vast steel entry gates were, securing the access tunnel to the gorge. Volodya, keeping a well-trained eye on the agent, punched in the code to the keypad. The motors began whining and the heavy doors cracked and groaned as they inched open. In front of them lay the paved access road, leading out to the waterfall and the gorge beyond. Volodya, with a brutal kick to the agent's Achilles tendon, signalled him to move and he limped forward. The sound of the waterfall, now echoing up the tunnel, once again rushed in the agent's ears.

***

Inside the silo, a white-suited figure returned from the access tunnel alone and once again dialled in the code to close off the tunnel. As the great doors swung back closed, he looked out onto the assembly floor through the yellow-tinted visor. He made his way purposefully over towards the blast gates surrounding one of the missiles. He walked through the open section of gate and climbed the latticed metal steps of the stairway to the first level gantry, above the giant rocket engine bells. From here, he went on up to the first of the upper-level gantries surrounding the second stage fuelling point. He inspected the pressure gauges on the fuelling pumps and noted that they were up, meaning the fuelling was still in progress. This level also provided access to the missile's control platform. Work here looked to have been completed and the technicians were now off the gantry. The access plate covering the guidance control systems for the missile had been bolted securely into place but the tools remained on the gantry – undoubtedly, one of them would be returning soon to pack them away. He wouldn't have much time. Grabbing a socket spanner, he quickly set about the task of getting the plate off before someone came back and challenged him.

A few minutes later and the agent had the plate off. He couldn't afford any chances: whatever de Sauveterre's plan was, he had no choice but to close it down. Now, with his head buried inside the hatch, he was busily engaged in inspecting the gyros inside the guidance system. It would only take a fairly small adjustment to throw the stabilising system of the rocket off kilter and so, not only alter its course from the prescribed flight plan, but render the missile unflyable. He reached down into the tool kit he had pulled up beside him, fishing about for the necessary implement. Through the suit, he became aware of a gentle pressure on the small of his back. He recognised the sensation immediately and stopped in his tracks. He had company.

The voice was soft but insistent. 'Put the wrench back down slowly and place your hands where I can see them. Don't make any sudden movements or I'll shoot you in the base of your spine.' (Though the agent had his back to the voice, he didn't need to see the owner of it to recognise that perfectly enunciated English.) 'Spinal injuries can be tragic you know, if the victim is lucky enough to even survive them. With a bullet through your spinal cord, you'd certainly never walk again but, beyond this most obvious loss, such an injury will often result in permanent and irreversible impotence – such a shame for a man like you – forevermore denying the chance of fatherhood. And let us not forget the loss of bladder control and use of one's rectal muscles. Yes, these injuries can leave a person in an awfully messy state.'

'What do you want, Valentina? If it's an apology, then forget it because you won't get one from me.'

'Don't flatter yourself to think I care about that. Get your head out of there and stand up where I can see you. Arms above your head.'

The agent did as he was told. The sleeping draught he'd given her had been a lot less brutal than a gag and she'd have simply woken several hours later – however long ago that was now – with nothing more than a bad headache. To his mind, he'd taken the most civilised course open to him and had treated her more than fairly. He could have easily chosen a more permanent option with which to silence her – perhaps he should have done.

'Now, turn around and move away from the hatch.' She motioned with her gun for him to move.

He did as she ordered, stepping sideways around the gantry towards the second stage fuelling pumps. Clearly, she had been in a hurry to catch him because she'd not bothered with donning a hazard suit and still had on her evening gown.

'Stop, that's far enough,' she shouted and then, lowering her voice, said, 'I want some information from you. I have *you* at *my* mercy now and it's your turn to talk – isn't it funny how things change?'

The agent realised there was something familiar about the line she'd used. 'What did you have in mind?' he said.

'You can start by telling me who you are.'

'De Sauveterre had it about right.'

'Tell me. You work for the British Government?'

'Yes, I don't care if you know that.'

'And that is all you have to say for yourself?'

'I could tell you which football team I support and how I like my coffee.'

'Don't try to be funny with me. I want to know what you talked about up there with him. Tell me exactly what you told him. Don't think of lying to me, because I will know.'

A typical result of the communist regime, the girl was frightened and paranoid. 'You don't need to worry – I didn't spill the beans on you if that's what's on your mind.'

'Just tell me what you said.'

The girl's anger towards him was obvious, even if she didn't know it fully herself. Her gun was straining at the leash for retribution. Though, on inspection, it was in fact not her gun at all – it was his own Beretta. She must have taken it from him while he was out for the count. Valentina had probably kept the compact little Beretta hidden away in her handbag earlier, he mused. Perhaps she thought she might need it to help force the outcome of an argument. But her need to appropriate his gun told him something more: that she hadn't one of her own and that it was likely therefore that she would not be familiar with using it.

'There wasn't time for me to say much. He wanted shot of me fairly rapidly as soon as he noticed our little tête-à-tête had attracted the interest of your generals. What's he hiding from them, I wonder?'

'He's not hiding anything,' she declared, loyal now to her lover.

The agent had flustered the girl into defending herself. 'What has he in mind for your rockets?'

'The rockets are being test fired – one will fly into the desert and the other into the sea. The exercise will simply enable data gathering from the flights which will assist him in the further development of the missile guidance systems.'

'Yes, that all sounds fine. But that's not what's really happening is it?'

'I don't know what you're talking about,' she said – but in her voice, the agent detected she was faltering.

'Come on, Valentina. You don't need to play the innocent little girl with me anymore. Obviously, your people don't trust him either – that's why they put you with him to find out. He's up to something, something else. Polyakov knew it and so do you… but you're not sure what it is yourself. That's it, isn't it? Why else would you so urgently feel the need to follow me down here and threaten me in an attempt to get information?'

'You're not the one asking the questions here. Shut up or I'll kill you right here.'

Something she'd said a few moments ago came back to him. Standing now with his back to the second stage of the rocket, the agent felt the chill from the ice-frosted skin of the integrated tanks containing the sub-zero fuel. The rocket groaned and shuddered as the super-chilled contents of the tanks churned and broiled deep inside it. Similarly, the previously frozen memory now thawed in his mind. He looked up again at the girl's elegant face.

'You're being played, Valentina – but I think you half know that already. He's playing you all.'

'What makes you say that?'

'I think he's using you, using your country – and using your missiles for his own ends, exactly as Polyakov suspected. There's more to it than the defence of your country. Surely you can't think he's built all this merely to support his business interests, supplying the Soviet's with missile systems? No, there must be more to it than that. There has to be something else. You see my dear, I strongly suspect that he's planning on doing much more here tonight than simply conducting a series of test flights for the pleasure and advantage of your mother Russia. Mark my words, he has his own plan for these rockets.'

Her face tightened. 'What plan?' she asked, doubt creeping in.

'I don't know but it could well be linked to that business of extraction. Look, I don't understand it completely but whatever it is, it's not good, I do know that. Not for you or me – nor perhaps for either of our countries.'

'This is nonsense. That was all settled before. Polkovnik Polyakov was convinced that whatever the other business was, it had nothing to do with the missile tests and I believe it – you're lying and you're trying to trick me. Your government quite obviously doesn't want our missiles pointed at the United States and, before I interrupted you, you were trying to sabotage the tests.'

'I don't need to lie to you – or to trick you. If you think you know what's going on, why did you follow me down here?'

'I saw Volodya taking you and had a queer feeling that he

might not get rid of you so easily. That's why I followed you and why I waited in the silo for him to return. I needed to be certain.'

'A woman's intuition?'

Her eyes narrowed. 'I realised that it was you who came back from the tunnel and not Volodya. He is shorter.'

'How very astute of you, my dear.'

'Don't call me that,' she hissed, and visibly increased her grip on the gun. 'You're not answering my questions nearly well enough. I want to know what Aristide said to you.'

'Oh, *him* now? Why?' he asked, but he knew why. Paranoia was why – it ran for her in both directions: she wanted to know if de Sauveterre had given anything away to him.

'That's really none of your business.'

'Okay then. He told me he thought that you were lovely. Oh, and he mentioned something about an apocalypse… at midnight, I believe he said.'

'The launches are scheduled for midnight…' she said, hesitantly.

'Well, there we are.'

'I don't believe you.'

Even with him using a bit of artistic licence to fill in the gaps, for some reason the girl still refused to see it. She'd backed herself into a corner but wasn't sure what to do. He'd give her a way out. She had clearly been won over by the man on whom she had been charged to keep watch but, however her sympathies might have grown for de Sauveterre, she was surely loyal to her country above all else. Underneath the perfect English and all of her international sophistication the girl was, after all, still Russian.

'Now listen to me Valentina, I'm telling you the truth. Put the gun down and go back upstairs to him, there's a good girl.

I'll finish what I'm doing here but you must tell your brass up there that he's up to no good, something unlawful at the very least, and that they absolutely have to shut the launch down.'

'Don't dare tell me what to do, you bastard. You've talked enough. You won't trick me into getting the launches aborted. Now, get down on your knees.'

The agent wouldn't kneel before anyone, let alone this girl. He let her rant but he stayed where he was.

'You should have stayed safely locked up in your room like a good boy,' she said, and lowered the gun towards his groin. 'Volodya messed up, but you won't get away from me. Now it's your turn to be violated,' she spat, the perfect English accent slipping under the stress of her emotion and the hard, native vocal inflection revealing itself like an x-ray showing up a hidden tumour.

She was becoming hysterical, volatile. He needed to bring this to a close: get Valentina out of the way so he could finish his work to divert both the missiles. The agent had consciously positioned himself directly next to one of the fuelling hoses where it was connected to the missile. With his arms still held above him, he felt for the ringed attachment collar.

'What are you doing?' She demanded, pulling her aim back up higher again. 'Stop it at once or I will shoot you – in the head instead of your balls.'

He'd have preferred it this way himself but he only needed to achieve a moment's hesitation in the girl.

'Look Valentina, you must realise that I'm standing in front of a giant bomb. A rocket fuelled with thousands of gallons of highly explosive propellant. Surely, you haven't forgotten what happened to the Star? If you were to fire that gun, there wouldn't be very much left of the whole bloody mountain let alone my aching head, or my testicles for that matter.'

He gave her a moment – enough time for her to absorb what he'd said and for it to worry her but not enough time for her to think what to do about it – and then he jabbed forward suddenly with his foot to connect his heel with her shin. As she went over, he knocked the gun violently from her with his forearm. It clattered away along the steel gantry. Then he had the hose collar in his hands, twisting it, then yanking the thing out bodily from the side of the second stage booster.

The girl had fallen onto her back and lay on the platform with her legs akimbo. As she'd tumbled, her dress had ridden up and shown him those elegant legs one last time. He noticed the red gash on her shin where his heel had caught her and couldn't help himself trace the line of her shin up to her knee and beyond to the soft flesh of her thigh, before it disappeared under the darkening folds of silk and lace. Her beautiful face was taken over by a noxious cocktail of shock, disbelief and fear. He caught the girl's eyes as they took in his own moment of hesitation, then quickly travelled to where the gun had come to rest. The hesitation in him passed.

Holding the hose with one hand, he trained it on the girl. With his free hand, he deftly pulled the suit's headgear back on. He looked at her through the tinted face shield. Horror poured over her suddenly yellowed face – desperation quickly followed.

'I thought there was something… something between us?' she said, pleading.

'Oh, come on Valentina. You know that's not important and it's probably not even true.'

'I think it is. You wouldn't hurt me darling, would you?' (She was doing her best).

'But dearest, you had a gun on me only moments ago – what am I to think?

The fear in Valentina's eyes was becoming unbearable for him to watch. He couldn't stand any more of this. Like a deer, shot but merely wounded, he had to finish her quickly before empathy overturned his decision. He opened the valve on the flow control regulator of the outlet housing.

'I'm afraid it's kill or be killed,' he said.

The hose released a thick column of cooled liquid oxygen. Delivered under pressure and at a temperature of minus three hundred degrees Fahrenheit, the super-chilled propellant was capable of shattering even metals upon contact. It shot out onto the girl, causing frostbite to her upper torso within seconds. The onset of hypothermia to her internal organs would be fast. The muscles controlling the regulation of her breathing were incapacitated and she began to asphyxiate. The agent played the hose onto her upper body for less than ten seconds but in that time the valves of her ventricular chambers would also have lost function and her body have begun to go into cardiac arrest. The cold heart of Russia froze and stopped beating.

The agent shut off the fuel valve. A second death at his hands in little over a week. The one in Prague had been a lot easier – he hadn't liked the soldier's manners. Valentina's death represented a loss to him though. 'You murdering bastard,' he said to himself aloud.

Retrieving the gun from where it had been sent spinning several feet along the gantry, he re-united it with his vacant holster – donned earlier in the mild hope of it being filled – then returned to the hatch and hurriedly finished making the necessary adjustments to the guidance system. Shortly after being launched, the rocket would now veer away from whatever course it had been set upon and fly uncontrollably toward the south-west where it would, most likely, crash somewhere deep in the vast wastes of the Sahara – as unpopulated a target as the agent could hope for. As he fiddled with getting the access plate back on, he heard footsteps rushing onto the lower gantry. Sirens went off. Urgently, the agent finished securing the plate.

He needed to get off the gantry now but he could see there were already figures moving up to the first level, directly below. He had no other choice but to go in the opposite direction: up. The top-level gantry was set at the level of the nose cone. This was the business end of the missile, housing the warhead. There was no other way down from here than the way he'd come up – unless he felt like free falling again. He could see more men gathering below him on the second gantry level, security staff would no doubt be among them. Like a pack of dogs waiting, poised for the attack, it wouldn't be long before they would make their assault. He was trapped. A single figure broke from the pack and came up the steps alone. Despite the spillage, this one hadn't the white hazard suit and headgear on which the others all wore – the agent had this man's suit on himself.

His hair and clothing were still wet from the soaking he'd received at the agent's hands. He thought he'd drowned him but he hadn't hung around long enough to make sure – instead he'd been happy just to hold his fat head under the tumbling water until he'd felt the man's struggle cease. After he'd stripped him of the suit, he'd summoned the last of his own strength to despatch the dead weight of the Russian over the precipice. He'd watched as it had disappeared into the dark, frothing waters below. And yet somehow, still the oaf had managed to come back from this. The agent was forced to review his opinion of Volodya. He was clearly made of even tougher stuff than he'd previously thought.

Volodya wasn't holding a gun. Though he may well have rearmed himself after his pistol was lost during the struggle, unlike the girl, he appeared conscious of the risk of discharging a firearm in the immediate presence of a fuelled rocket. The agent was keenly aware of the extreme danger presented by these volatile liquid fuels and wouldn't think about using the Beretta here. And after his close call at the pier, Volodya will have learnt his lesson. Instead of a gun, he brandished a combat knife – a Soviet NR-40 Scout's Knife, clearly recognisable to the agent from the uniquely inverted S-shaped guard. Volodya's type would of course always carry such a blade for use in close combat.

The agent suffered a couple of minor stab wounds to his leg in attempting to kick the weapon from his hand. Volodya then slashed him viciously with it, cutting the agent down and quickly getting hold of him from behind in a headlock. The man's thick, muscular arm gripped the agent's neck as tightly as a noose. He struggled but, this time and without the element of surprise in the agent's favour, the big Russian had the upper hand – probably also fuelled by the agent's earlier treatment of him. The agent saw the bright, forged steel flash in the floodlights as the knife approached him and then he felt the razor-sharp edge as it slid across his neck. Cold, Ural steel cut into him. The sensation was quickly replaced by the warmth of blood as it began to flow down his neck and onto his chest. The sirens stopped whining and, yet again, the agent lost consciousness. Only this time surely, he was about to die.

Chapter 19
Pyramid

The stinging of his new wounds brought him round. He was in a lot of pain – but he was still alive. Instinctively wanting to feel his neck, he realised that his hands were tied. What had happened? He opened his eyes and saw the master of his fate standing over him. Smoking a foul-smelling cigarette, Volodya was silently and dispassionately contemplating the agent. He wasn't the type accidently to miss the jugular – the agent had been kept alive purposely and the knife had been used superficially only to worry him. His wrists had been bound around the vertical beam he lay slumped against. But they were no longer on the gantry, they weren't inside the silo even – this was a new space.

His aching head slowly came back to life, his brain taking stock of the new surroundings. He wasn't inside the mountain any longer but on top of it, lying on the smooth, bare rock of the weather-worn ridge – though he wasn't really outside. He was within the area of the ridge enclosed by the glass of the inverted pyramid structure. Though the footprint on the ridge was small, from it the four great glass walls of the pyramid sloped outward and upward at an angle to the much broader, flat steel roof of what was a sizeable structure – the stresses involved seemed impossible and it must have been a triumph of engineering to construct. The floor reflected the beautiful yellow and orange-tinged light of the Moroccan late afternoon sun which filled the space through the east facing wall. It was a heavenly sight. The purpose of this curious space was made evident at its centre. On top of the mountain, protected by the magnificent glass pyramid, was installed a monstrously large, reflecting telescope supported on a giant, motorised mount. An observatory then, but rockets and telescopes – what the hell was going on here?

He took a moment to do a body count: there were half a dozen in view and, unlike the technicians he'd seen below in the silo, the men up here were all European. The man in charge was, of course, de Sauveterre who stood high up on a raised steelwork platform forming a ring around the telescope. A soft glow of coloured light came from the various instruments on a whole swath of control desks set around the oversized telescope. Numerous dots of colour from the indicator lamps in green, red and amber illuminated a mosaic of individual, beaten copper-coloured instrument panels set into dull grey metal desk cabinets – each panel with a pair of handles at the side, presumably to expedite assembly of the desks. There were dozens of Bakelite knobs, rocker switches and meters labelled in engraved black lettering that was mostly too small for the agent to read at this distance, let alone with a haemorrhage in one eye. He could just about make out a few of them though: *VOLTS, MICROAMPERES DC, METER SENSITIVITY (INCREASE), EXPT GYROS, SEQUENCE.* All these desks couldn't be required to operate the telescope – they must serve as the missile launch control.

De Sauveterre seemed intently focused on a particular bank of instrument panels with television screens mounted above the desking. The largest of these showed a schematic of the Earth, overlaid with what appeared to be missile trajectories. From his viewpoint, the agent wasn't able to make out any more detail than that, though it was clear enough to him that the flightpaths were, at the least, sub-orbital. Worryingly, as he'd suspected, it appeared likely these missiles were intended to be launched intercontinentally.

De Sauveterre left his position and came down the steps from the platform. Perhaps noticing that the agent had come round, he walked over to him. 'I gather you were not quite ready to leave us, Mr Coldblow,' he said solemnly. 'And so, as you are clearly so keen to stay, I have decided to allow you to watch this evening's spectacle from up here. Since you took it upon yourself to rid us of our pretty little spy, you may now take her place instead – in fact, I must insist that you do.'

'I'm hardly in a position to argue,' the agent said, motioning to the rope wound tightly around his wrists.

'Yes, a sensible precaution I think you will agree,' de Sauveterre said thoughtfully. 'Volodya will watch you from here on in, less you take it into your mind to attempt murder upon anyone else. Shame on you, Mr Coldblow, to take such a beauty away from us, and in such grisly fashion – you really are quite grotesque, aren't you? It is a great pity but poor Valentina just wasn't at all in your league – she was more of an amateur player...'

De Sauveterre trailed off, pausing for a moment while apparently in thought. 'Oh, but I nearly forgot to tell you – your sterling effort to sabotage one of our missiles has, most sadly for you, *not* been successful.' (At this, the agent's heart sank – though he showed nothing of it). 'In any event, it seems prudent now to keep you up here where we can keep an eye on you, just in case you still harbour any further thoughts of mindless wrecking. Rest assured, the gyroscopes which you tampered with have been reset and everything is back in order again – in fact, there is even a little time at my disposal before the launch. So now, let me explain exactly what you will be witness to. You see, up here I may speak more freely with you than it was possible for me to earlier at my little gala. Those fellows working down below us inside the mountain – in the engine room, if you like – are Russians. In the pyramid I have only my most trusted men – my inner circle – and you and I may speak here as if we were alone – you can forget Volodya, I believe I already mentioned that, sadly for him, foreign tongues are not at all his forte.'

'And so, you're captaining the "ship" from up here then, I suppose. The brains on the bridge and the brawn below decks – is that it de Sauveterre?'

'Precisely. It's actually quite an appropriate analogy,' de Sauveterre said, seeming to enjoy the thought of it. 'And with my guests enjoying themselves so, on the quarterdeck. All those Russian dignitaries are oblivious to the true nature of the operation which their comrades below decks are, in fact this very moment, facilitating. You see, you were of course quite correct in your assertion that the missiles were not intended to be test fired. Instead, I have appropriated them for another, altogether better, purpose.'

'Whose side are you on then, de Sauveterre?'

'I'm not on anyone's side. I'm on my own side.'

'I take it,' the agent said, attempting to impose some clarity on this increasingly tangled plot, 'that it is under the presumed authority of the Soviets that you are conducting this illegal operation in a foreign country?'

'I am breaking no laws in this country – in fact my activities here have the support of the highest office. You see, the outcome of the mission we are engaged in tonight will benefit Morocco immensely.'

'You're telling me that the government here knows what you're up to?'

'Those within it who matter.'

'And the interior minister didn't?' the agent asked boldly.

'The minister was not a party to everything, no – and for good reason. He had strong ties with the Soviets, something which suited the task he had been presented with – he was pretty much a communist, you see. But he then became aware of certain information which we believe led him to suspect another reason for the placement of the missiles here – one which the Russians were unaware of.'

'And so, you had him killed.'

'Whatever you might think of me, I am not a murderer. His death had nothing to do with me in fact, but someone in… let us say a higher office, felt that the minister might come under pressure from the Soviets to talk – and he wasn't trusted not to by that office. There were a lot of unfortunate casualties when the Star of Odessa blew up. The minister for the interior was just one more.'

'Are you saying that this goes right to the top – that the King ordered his thugs to do it?' The agent was referring to the Special Administrative Police. This was sounding messy. It might be even worse than he'd at first thought.

De Sauveterre looked pained. 'Let us move on.'

'Yes, let's – this is all starting to sound fantastical. Where exactly do you fit into it?'

'I developed the guidance systems for the new generation of Soviet-built rockets that we have here, and had these systems specially manufactured in one of my factories – my navigational systems are second to none, you understand. The ex-Minister for the Interior, with me acting as an interested party, brokered a deal with the Russian military which secured the placement of a number of these new missiles, armed with Soviet nuclear warheads, within Morocco's territory. Our Russian friends were seemingly presented with a golden opportunity to redress the missile gap with the United States. The transportation of these large rockets had to be done covertly though, so as not to attract international attention. The separate components were mostly shipped here from the Ukraine by state-owned, merchant freighters – hidden in plain view – and the missiles were quietly assembled inside the mountain over the course of the past few months. But just as you say, this is all a front and it is in fact the Kingdom alone which stands to benefit from the reality of the arrangement. The ex-minister unknowingly misled the Soviet military into unwittingly supplying the Moroccan government with the necessary armaments and hardware that I required for my operation.'

'If you're pulling the wool over the Soviets eyes as you say, then what is it that you're really up to here? It sounds to me like you're about to start a war – whether intentionally or otherwise. My understanding is that you're a scientist of sorts and that this place is supposed be some kind of research installation. Firing off a couple of rockets armed with nuclear warheads hasn't got very much to do with scientific research though, so what could you, or the Kingdom for that matter, possibly hope to gain by it? And by the way, I know that you've secured permits for extraction from the desert, but you can't blast oil or diamonds or whatever the hell it is that you're after out of the desert with a nuclear detonation. Besides, even if you did, you'd contaminate the region with radioactivity for decades.'

'You think that I am interested in mining the desert,' de Sauveterre laughed at him. 'My sights are bigger than you give me credit for.'

'What else is it then?'

'I realise that you would like to know the true purpose of my enterprise and, as I have a few minutes at my disposal, I shall indulge you by revealing my intention to you fully in due course.' De Sauveterre snapped his fingers in the air as if he were calling the attention of a waiter – which, in a sense he was.

One of the more junior technicians immediately rushed over to him. As the young man approached, de Sauveterre simply stuck a single finger in the air. It was enough for the boy to get the message and he turned on his heels, disappearing for a few moments only before reappearing again with a drink for his master.

'I would offer you another vodka, Mr Coldblow,' de Sauveterre said, 'but I fear it would prove rather difficult for you to drink it in your current circumstance.'

The man was a megalomaniac. The agent had seen this type of thing before. De Sauveterre wanted the agent to witness the abhorrence he planned to cause with his missiles and then he would have Volodya kill him. He must find a way to stop it and to escape. If the pyramid was the control centre for the launch, then the agent was in the right place to try aborting it again. First, he had to learn exactly what was going on and what the targets were. With de Sauveterre now so eager to share his secrets, all the agent had to do was listen. Without missing a beat, the man proceeded with another lecture – this time on the subject of the arms race – quickly settling into his subject and clearly feeling pleased with himself.

'As you will know, both the Americans and the Soviets have developed Intercontinental Ballistic missiles solely for military use. Armed with nuclear warheads, they provide these nations with the ultimate threat against each other and the rest of world – a threat which each is constantly aiming to counter. The escalation of arms is inevitable until ultimately, were these two countries ever to come to a state of war – real war I mean, not the cold version which permits this rather juvenile amassing of deadly weapons – then they might, between them, have the capacity to bring an abrupt end to the human race, along with most other forms of life on the planet. A stark vision, I'm sure you would agree?'

'Get to the point,' the agent replied, impatient already.

'Oh, I am sorry. I hope that I am not detaining you from, perhaps, falling off another mountain – but please do bear with me. You see, the rockets developed by the Soviets to strategically deliver a nuclear warhead to the United States have also proved effective in the pursuit of space exploration. And now also a space race has developed between the Americans and the Soviets which, if viewed simplistically, might be seen – like the arms race – as merely a competition to assert the power of nationhood, a matter of national pride. But the senior Soviet scientists – those who have led the field in designing rockets which are capable of sub-orbital flight – are not interested in such things. They are concerned only with science, with understanding.

'The carrier rocket used to put Major Gagarin into an orbit around the Earth – I'm sure the news of this cannot have escaped you – was a Vostok-K. What we have here are R-16s. They are the next generation. These rockets have been designed to be capable of being launched from underground silos – or in this case, an adapted natural cavern. They are far more advanced than anything which has preceded them. They are in fact, so new that they have only just completed a test flight programme in Russia and they have not yet been deployed anywhere... except here.'

'You're telling me then, that all this is about the exploration of space?'

'Not exactly – not yet at least.' De Sauveterre, apparently enjoying this guessing game, took a sip of Kubanskaya. 'The rockets being prepared inside the mountain here are extremely powerful and are capable of attaining Earth orbit and, as you have already correctly deduced, the missiles are indeed both fuelled sufficiently for such an orbital flight. However, they will not be used to carry a craft into space because... they are in fact both armed with nuclear warheads. Five megaton warheads to be precise – large enough to cause significant destruction to a major city.'

'Sounds fairly aggressive to me. Which city are you planning to attack?'

'As I have already told you, the rockets will not be used in any act of aggression.'

'A riddle wrapped in a mystery inside an enigma. You would make a very good Russian yourself, de Sauveterre.'

'You are quoting Winston Churchill. Now I am certain whom you work for – do remind me who your head man at Section 6 is these days.' A sickly smile appeared on the face of the Frenchman.

The agent was amused at the thought of himself working for MI6. The very idea that a secret military intelligence department which purported to be hidden from public view should even have a title was anathema to him. His chief, the lieutenant-general wouldn't be amused by the notion in the slightest. He considered for a moment the thought of him in his smart uniform stuck behind that desk, with the portrait of Nelson hanging on the wall of the fusty old office in the Section 6 building next to the park. Of him railing at the bunch of pipe smoking wags there, all dressed in their civvies and tied to their desks for the better part of the year; of the special engineering branch in the basement, spending all its days dreaming up hare-brained gismos and God knows what else. The lieutenant-general wouldn't tolerate any of it for more than five minutes. They'd be no playing around on boats – Nelson would be neatly despatched through an open window and Montgomery swiftly put up in his place. But the agent was tiring of de Sauveterre's rambling and seemingly deliberate contradictory discourse – it was time to get him back on track again.

'You're testing my patience, de Sauveterre. Are you going to tell me what this is all about or not?'

With the agent hoping that now he might finally tie it up, de Sauveterre returned to his thread.

'I am not so much intending to send anything into space,' he said, 'but rather to take something *from* it.'

'And what, pray, might that be?'

De Sauveterre stuck his fingers into his drink and fished out a cube. He held it up in front of him with purpose. 'This,' he said, before theatrically dropping it back into his glass. 'Ice.'

Chapter 20

Cold Star

Coming after the baroque speech, the simplicity of the man's answer took the agent by surprise – but he understood at once what it must mean. 'A comet?' he said. 'You plan to use the missiles to bring down a comet.'

'Bravo,' de Sauveterre said, clapping his hands together.

The agent felt a hollow in his stomach. He looked steadily into the man's wild eyes. 'You must realise,' he said 'that if you succeed in bringing about the collision of another celestial body with the Earth, it may be with devastating consequences to our planet.'

De Sauveterre gave him a comforting smile as if it were directed at a child afraid of the dark. 'Let me address your concerns–'

'My concerns,' the agent said, interrupting him, 'are that the impact of a comet would cause God knows what sort of worldwide catastrophe. You're on the brink of causing Armageddon man.'

De Sauveterre's smile waned. 'I beg to differ from your opinion but I'm afraid that your grasp on the matter is somewhat lay. Allow me to explain the details of the operation. I have been tracking the path of a particular comet for some time and, most recently from this observatory, have been able to make highly accurate observations which have been used to calculate the precise trajectory of its orbit by means of a computer. The comet in question is due to make a near-earth pass in the early hours of tomorrow morning. When it does, I will launch a missile to intercept it. The missile will escape Earth's orbit and the warhead will detonate in close proximity to the comet as it passes by the planet. The nuclear detonation will adjust the natural course of the comet and bring it into a shallow orbit with the Earth.

'A second missile will be launched shortly after the first, following a sub-orbital trajectory that will directly target the comet once it is in low Earth orbit. The detonation of the second warhead will cause the comet to fragment into several smaller objects – meteors that, upon losing their orbital velocity, will enter the Earth's atmosphere. Using formulae which I have written, the likely trajectories of these meteors have been modelled – also by the computer – and a fairly accurate prediction of the impact coordinates has been plotted. The information from these computer simulations has, in turn, enabled us to adjust the missile telemetries to bring about a collision site of our choosing. In short, we are able to control where these meteors will impact the Earth.'

The horror of it was building in the agent's mind but he needed to know more. 'How big do you imagine these meteors to be?'

'Several hundred feet in diameter each – large enough to fulfil the purpose of deliberately colliding them with the Earth.'

Multiple, directed strikes. This madman intended to use the meteors to take out a whole raft of targets. The agent spoke gravely. 'And what would that purpose be?'

'Why, to benefit both the natural environment and mankind,

of course,' de Sauveterre replied brightly. 'Contrary to your rightful humanitarian concern, the meteors will disperse over their target locations to fall on an area of uninhabited land. The impacts will form craters hundreds of feet wide, but with minimal meteorological side effects observed only locally.'

That this lunatic wasn't in fact set on destroying the world's great cities gave the agent a degree of solace. Calmer now, he spoke again. 'It sounds like pure madness to me. Perhaps I'm missing something here though – how exactly could this benefit anyone?'

'Comets contain galactic rock debris which in itself is of great scientific interest, but they also contain certain precious metals.' De Sauveterre tapped his little finger onto the side of his tumbler. The metallic clink of his signet ring resonated through the crystal.

The agent cocked an eyebrow. 'So, it's gold you're after?'

'Any gold or other metals we might find would of course be useful, but they are purely secondary commodities to me – and so no, that is not the principal benefit.'

'What then?'

'Comets are largely made up of frozen water and it is the water that I am interested in – water which might bring about the rejuvenation of a formerly sterile environment.'

'The Sahara,' the agent said.

'Bravo again, you are quite correct.'

'Desert reclamation through cometary deposition – that has to be on the edge of insanity. And what about evaporation? How long do you expect this water to remain in that oven of a desert before it simply disappears into thin air – a few weeks perhaps? What good could it possibly do?'

'In their search for oil in the Sahara,' de Sauveterre countered, 'the petrochemical companies have conducted expansive geologic prospecting programmes. Their surveys have revealed there to be vast quantities of water contained in sedimentary basins located within sandstone formations deep below the desert floor. The Sahara contains a great number of these ancient aquifers – some of which continue to supply the desert oases and others which have long since dried up. As the ice from the comet melts, the water from it will permeate the sand and refill these empty aquifers. Using specialist equipment, the water can then be drilled for and pumped back up as required. In addition, and more immediately, the impact craters themselves will be deep enough to hold onto the water from the comet for much longer than you think and will form a multitude of lakes in the desert – safe havens around which vegetation can quickly take hold.'

'Okay, de Sauveterre, let us assume for the moment that what you say is not pure fantasy. How can you be certain that this will all play out as you say?'

'The honest answer to your question is that I cannot be absolutely certain of it – how could I possibly be? I freely admit that the operation is not without risk. There is of course always risk involved when one is engaged in something which has never been attempted before. But the odds are very favourable. I would not attempt to play them, were they not.'

'Play them.' the agent exploded. 'This isn't a game of cards. You claim that this fantastical idea of yours will benefit mankind when in fact you're gambling with humanity.'

De Sauveterre remained unruffled. 'By far the most probable outcome of this operation is that the desert will be irrigated as I say and that there will not be any significant collateral damage. It is a matter of probability and my calculations in this area have been exhaustive. I have taken into account all possible permutations and deviations from the expected course of events and I have even considered technical malfunction and human error – to sum it up, everything that is possible to go wrong. And after doing so, the odds remain in favour of a complete success.'

'What are they then, your odds on not committing global genocide? I'd like to know.'

'One to five. As I say, they are very good odds. I do not intend for anyone to die tonight – not even you.'

The agent needed to keep de Sauveterre talking – something which wasn't difficult at least. 'And how exactly are you set to benefit?'

'An excellent question. Sometime ago, I acquired permissions from the government to set up agricultural projects in the Moroccan Sahara. The permissions afford me the right to cultivate the desert wherever I am able to find or extract the water to do so – provided that it is not supplied by aquifers which were known to be active at the time the permits were issued. The government department concerned presumed me mad of course but, nonetheless, they sold me the permits I required. I may, therefore, use the water brought down by the comet to irrigate the desert and grow crops around the oases that will be created. I will farm the Sahara and for the next decade the havens will provide plentiful food and water from what was previously barren.'

As de Sauveterre spoke, the agent concentrated his mind on dredging up his meagre knowledge of the Russian language. He needed to spill the beans to the other side – then he could simply stand back and let the oaf, Volodya do the dirty work for him. But de Sauveterre wouldn't allow him much of an opportunity – he may only have a moment to deliver his message before being silenced and so he must be clear and concise. He had to use the correct words – but what were they? He couldn't think.

'And provide you with a healthy income, no doubt.' he said, buying more time as the brute stood by, coughing regularly.

'I might be an idealist but I am no philanthropist. Look around you.' De Sauveterre's arm went out in a gestural sweep. 'I have made a significant investment here – and I expect a return on it. A man has to live, does he not?'

De Sauveterre looked restless now, and the interminable coughing from the Russian seemed to be bothering him. It would have to do – but all the agent had was a single word. He blurted it out. *Volshebnik* is the Russian word for magician (hopeless really, but it was the closest he knew to liar or trickster). The agent cursed himself for this paucity of vocabulary. He checked the Russian for his reaction. It wasn't what he'd hoped for. The thug looked nonplussed.

'Good try,' de Sauveterre said, a wry smile leaking out over his face, 'though a little wide of the mark, I'd say. I think it fair to boast that my own knowledge of the Russian language isn't quite so rusty, but it's better to keep these things – what is the English expression? – ah yes, under one's hat. Though for this evening's performance, I'm afraid that I forgot to bring a rabbit along to go with it.'

The French have little regard for any language other than their own and, despite de Sauveterre's evident good English, the agent was surprised that the man's linguistic abilities stretched to such a difficult tongue as Russian. But he didn't appreciate the mockery and, putting it coarsely, the agent said as much.

'So elegantly put, Mr Coldblow,' de Sauveterre said, dismissing the agent's insult. 'Now, where were we? Ah, yes, I was in the process of concluding your interview.' And he carried on as if the agent's desperate action had not occurred.

'Perhaps you were wondering what will happen after my permissions run out?'

Silence. The agent had had enough and de Sauveterre was left to answer his own question – which in fact he did.

'The process will be repeated elsewhere – I have calculated there to be a near-earth pass from another comet within the next five years. Again, it will be tracked from here and then pulled in to another area of the desert. But beyond my own interests, the wider benefits of this experiment will be to mankind by creating pockets of life in these oases. To bring about such a change to the otherwise naturally hostile environment of the Sahara will demonstrate that the process can be replicated in deserts elsewhere in the world – or even on other, seemingly inhospitable, worlds–'

The agent would prefer to have believed him, for this not to be the diabolical plot of a maniac, but that was precisely what it was and he'd heard enough. De Sauveterre was still speaking but the agent had stopped listening. Now he cut him off. 'This is pure science fiction – you're a madman.'

'On the contrary, I am quite sane but if that is your view I will not quarrel with you. The launch sequences will commence within the hour. Now that you are here, I intend for you to witness our achievement tonight so you may report its success to your Section 6 – or whichever covert government department sent you here to sabotage my operation. But you cannot stop it, not even if you somehow succeeded in killing me. You see, the guidance systems in the missiles will follow the flight paths which have been programmed into them from my computer – they cannot be reversed. Now, I think that our discussion has reached a natural conclusion and so, if you will excuse me, I'm sure you will appreciate that I have many final details to attend to.'

De Sauveterre indicated towards the thug, Volodya, who'd remained by his side, quietly awaiting his orders. 'As I said, Volodya will take care of you for the remainder of the evening,' he said and then, speaking quickly and effortlessly in the man's native tongue, he gave him his instructions. The Russian nodded and produced a pistol – another Makarov.

'You will have a spectacular view from here,' de Sauveterre said, pointing towards the vast glass side of the pyramid. You will also be well away from the launch control in case you are still thinking of trying somehow to throw a spanner in the works – as you English might say.'

The agent had nothing more to say to this lunatic – he looked resignedly at him. Silently, he watched de Sauveterre go back over to the control area and mount the steps to the platform.

Volodya took out a packet of cigarettes and coughed again, deeply this time as if to clear his lungs in preparation for smoking. The agent noticed the cigarettes weren't Russian as he would have expected but were in fact the same Moroccan brand he had bought himself in Tagadert. Volodya wore a black leather bomber jacket and he looked hot in it. His hair was oily and unkempt, his fingers nicotine-stained and the fingernails were bitten. He looked unhealthy. This character clearly smoked too much and probably drank too much vodka into the bargain. Volodya extracted a cigarette from the packet and without taking his eye – or his gun – off the agent, lit it with a squat petrol lighter – a silver affair, embossed on the front with the image of a rocket bearing the hammer and sickle. He sucked on the cigarette and watched over the agent with dead eyes.

The Earth continued to spin away from the Sun and the light, progressively refracted by the Earth's atmosphere, appeared yellow then orange and finally red. The colours oozed across the ridge and pooled on the naked rock like a gargantuan bloodstain. The sky, as vast as Russia, fell to a deeper blue and the brighter stars became visible. As the light finally faded and the sky blackened, inside the pyramid the glass began to take on the quality of a mirror. A motor whined and the giant telescope swung around like the turret of a gun emplacement. The lights inside the pyramid were dimmed and then cut as a large section in the centre of the steel roof began to retract, revealing the glittering cosmos. Out of the utter blackness, a thin beam of light snapped on from a miniature pocket torch. Volodya kept it trained steadily on the agent. He'd taken de Sauveterre at his word and wasn't taking his eyes off him for a moment.

The agent looked up through the open roof of the observatory. He remembered Valentina's description of the galaxy as being magical and thought that he could do with some magic at this moment. What he had was far from it. The comfort afforded by the presence of the Beretta nestling against his calf had been fleeting – the slight weight of the gun was absent once again. But he *could* feel, against his thigh, the small piton in his pocket still. His head ached and he struggled to formulate a feasible plan of attack.

The earlier fortification from the drink was gone and his tank was nearly empty. He needed a pick-me-up to help him think and, in the spotlight of the Russian's pocket torch, he indicated to Volodya that he could do with a cigarette himself. Despite having attempted to drown the man earlier that evening, to his great surprise and without any hesitation, Volodya took a cigarette from the packet, lit it for him and stuck it in his mouth. Custom overriding personal feeling, perhaps. Whatever the case, he wasn't fool enough to let the agent anywhere near the lighter – even with the Makarov pointed directly at him.

The agent took a long, deep pull on the cigarette. He wouldn't have considered smoking this rubbish in normal circumstances and he knew he was in a spot if it had come to this. He sucked the thick smoke into his mouth, allowing it to sting his tongue before drawing the hot, harsh vapour down his throat, letting it work its way deeply into his lungs. He held it there for a moment, enjoying the sensation and then released it slowly back out through his nostrils. He disliked anything other than English cigarettes but nonetheless the smoke did the job. The nicotine began to cast its spell and he felt his head start to clear. He thought of a way. It wasn't going to be easy and it certainly wouldn't be pretty. In fact, he didn't like it one bit – but he couldn't think of a better alternative.

The agent's wrists had been bound with rope – a length of his own climbing rope, in fact – to one of the huge, steel beams from which the angled-glass-walls of the pyramid were suspended. In the darkened conditions, Volodya had perversely and quite stupidly chosen to keep his torch trained on the agent's face (which gave nothing away) rather than on his hands. Though they were securely bound, this lapse had permitted the agent to fish out the pin and, in the cover of the shadows, he began working on the rope. By the time the lights in the observatory came back on, the rope, though it still appeared to be wrapped tightly around his wrists, would no longer offer resistance. With De Sauveterre's final observations apparently complete, the lights were faded back up and the retracting roof closed. With pure drama, de Sauveterre made an announcement to the room.

'We will launch missile number one at exactly one minute to midnight.' Looking over in the direction of the agent he added, 'Everything will be as it should – and the result will astound the world.'

The scene had been set. De Sauveterre stood at his desk, turning dials and flicking switches. The agent watched the screen above it with a blank expression as data – unintelligible to the uninitiated – flickered across it. Coughing deeply again, Volodya lit another cigarette.

There were a number of technicians seated at a secondary bank of control desks flanking one of the glass walls of the structure, but it was clearly de Sauveterre who would launch the missiles. The agent watched the launch being counted down on the television screen – large, white numerals displaying the remaining minutes and seconds were set in a sea of luminous green. Time was running out until the launch of the first missile and the agent needed to act.

Chapter 21
The Falling Man

Volodya wasn't taking any chances with the agent now. He'd rearmed himself handsomely – he was now practically a walking munitions shed. In addition to the second Makarov trained upon the agent, he had a Stechkin automatic pistol holstered outside his trousers on his thigh and there were two F1 grenades clipped to his belt. No doubt, he would have the Scout's Knife concealed somewhere on his person too. He needed to disarm Volodya quickly. The Stechkin didn't have the shoulder stock attached and so the recoil would make it difficult for the Russian to control in automatic fire. If he could acquire the Makarov, then he should be able to relieve him of the rest without too much trouble.

But he was armed with only the piton. A climbing pin is a poor adversary to an automatic pistol – he would need to create a distraction if he were to stand any kind of a chance. Lobbing one of the small pebbles he had still in his pocket over the Russian's shoulder would have made for a perfect diversion, but his captor's eyes were fixed on him as a cat's were on a bird. The agent returned his gaze, watching him, studying his movements. He noticed that the Russian's eyes would unglue themselves from him for just a moment when he coughed, which he did every so often as a heavy smoker tends to. The agent waited until the next cough for him to cast his eyes behind Volodya and toward the lift doors that were directly behind him, but he deliberately – though only marginally – mistimed this furtive glance so it might be noticed as Volodya returned his full attention to the agent. The gesture was so slight as to be either missed or ignored. The agent repeated the move with the next hacking spasm, careful not to ham it up but rather aiming for it to be almost imperceptible. He needed to make Volodya believe the look was intended to be covert. Again, it wasn't noticed, nor was it was the time after that.

Meanwhile, the clock was ticking. The agent noted that Volodya's clogged respiratory tract required him to take measures to clear it roughly every ten minutes – that gave him only two more chances at the most before the first missile was due to be launched just before midnight. On the fourth attempt, the agent got the result that he wanted. Something in the Russian's subconscious noticed what was happening and commanded him to act. It was five minutes to midnight. Almost involuntarily, Volodya wheeled his head around towards the lift doors. The agent had only a moment to release himself from his loosened bindings. Violently, he pulled his hands from the rope apparently still wound around his wrists. He was free in an instant and his good arm flew to his pocket to withdraw the piton, his index finger instinctively finding the eye hole and looping itself through. He sprang from the ground, himself now like the cat and was on the Russian as the Makarov started up. The climber in him expertly plunged the pin into that which presented the least resistance – in Volodya's case this was the most vulnerable organ in the human body.

Though the agent was under fire from the start, he instinctively had his other hand to the gun, forcing the muzzle away from him – the bullets singing as they ricocheted inside the pyramid – and was able to wrestle the pistol from the injured Russian without much resistance. One of the Russian's hands had gone to his eye, holding onto the piton embedded in it, clearly not knowing whether to wrench the thing out or not. It was a grizzly sight as Volodya danced about in agony and confusion, the blood pumping out from his eye socket. Using his good hand, the agent squeezed the Makarov's trigger and, despite it being his left, placed a single bullet into each of Volodya's kneecaps with the accuracy of a surgeon. The rug was pulled from under him and instantly he collapsed in front of the steel beam which he'd previously had the agent up against. The heavy trunk fell to the ground like a mighty Russian larch at the hand of the forester's saw.

De Sauveterre was barking orders at his men to advance but, pulling the Stechkin from the felled man's holster, the agent sent a spray of bullets in the general direction of the launch control platform, causing the technicians stationed there to scatter and take cover instead, with De Sauveterre left cowering beside his desk. The agent continued with burst fire – battling with the recoil of the automatic to target the instrument panels, the rain of ammunition sparking the electrics – until the pistol, out of ammo, stopped firing. He switched back to the Makarov until that too was exhausted, then reached down to where Volodya lay slumped, unconscious now. Quickly, he unclipped one of the grenades from the sleeping man's belt, pulled the pin and hurled it towards the control area. Having now discharged the Makarov too, he ran for cover from the impending blast.

But it had all been too slow. From his hiding place, de Sauveterre's hand had already broken cover and was now reaching up towards the large red button located prominently on the desk above him. Unmistakably, this was a firing button, responsible for activating the launch sequence for the missiles. As de Sauveterre had told him, the sequence was preset and fully automated and so the button would likely govern the firing of both missiles, launching within only a few minutes of each other. Once activated, the agent knew that the launch sequence would be irreversible.

The grenade had rolled directly underneath the telescope and when it exploded it not only shattered the internal optics but it also took out one of the giant glass wall sections of the pyramid. The noise of the detonation competed with the shrill of the heavy plate glass falling to the ground. Both noises though, were instantly eclipsed by the thunderous roar emanating from within the mountain. De Sauveterre had pressed the launch sequence button and it was too late. The first ignition sequence was underway and the rocket engines of missile number one quickly built to full thrust. The agent had earlier noticed the sound baffles installed in the silo chamber to help contain the noise of the firing but it was still deafening inside the pyramid. The ground shook as the launch cradle must have detached below and the first missile cleared the shaft and shot out the top of the mountain.

The agent watched through the broken glass as the plume rose in the night sky. Inside the pyramid the control system for the telescope was now alight. The motorised mount had gone haywire, the electrics on it sparking as the whole thing whizzed around out of control, rotating wildly at great speed on the circular rails like a waltzer at the fairground. Finally, something gave and the enormous refracting tube broke away from the mount and was hurled from it like a giant caber. Even if he were conscious, Volodya wouldn't have known very much about it. The instrument must have weighed a good ton and was travelling at a fair lick when it hit him – square on, taking him and the steel beam with it. He would have been killed instantly.

The telescope took out another large section of the south wall of the pyramid and giant shards of glass rained down – deadly spears falling everywhere. As the agent dived for cover once more, an unlucky technician was skewered through the back by one of the things. It was a few feet long. Blood sprayed like a fountain from the exit wound in his chest, spurting out at high pressure from the man's ruptured heart.

Electrical fires caused another explosion which brought down yet more glass, the splinters skating out across the smooth stone floor of the pyramid like shards of ice arcing across a frozen lake, slowly revolving as they slid away. With the critical support of the beam lost, the carefully designed structural balance of the pyramid was compromised and the whole construction had become unstable. The agent had to get out before it came down on top of him. He saw de Sauveterre make for the gaping section in the south wall and he went after him.

For centuries the ridge had been blasted by the sand-filled desert winds to achieve a smoothly buffed and rounded summit. From here, the polished stone sloped away, the incline steadily increasing, inexorably towards the south face like a giant slide,

until it finally shelved to a five-hundred-foot vertical drop. The agent watched de Sauveterre making his way along the ridge ahead of him. He followed, putting a safe distance between himself and the pyramid. Away from it now, out here on the mountaintop, all was calm.

The moment was short-lived though for, once again, the mountain began to tremble as the preset ignition sequence for missile number two fired up the rocket engines right on cue. The automated launch shot the missile up the shaft, ejecting it from the mountain only a few hundred yards from the agent. Instinctively, he flung himself down onto his stomach – burying his face onto the rock to protect himself from the heat blast as the missile screamed above him, heading skywards on its mission to intercept the comet.

Up again, and after de Sauveterre once more, the agent caught up with him just beyond the shafts, at the far end of the ridge. As he approached, he watched his eyes darting about like a trapped animal looking for an escape. But he had nowhere to go.

'Look,' de Sauveterre shouted triumphantly, pointing up towards the flaming tail of the missile, 'they're both away now, and there's nothing you can do to stop them.'

'You bastard. You know the Soviets will kill you for this, don't you – if I don't first.'

'It wasn't what they had in mind, of course, but they will see I have made a peaceable use of their technology for the betterment of the whole world. Russia will be awarded great respect from many nations for their part in it – they will forgive me, thank me.'

'You're beyond deluded. The Soviets couldn't give a damn

what the world thinks of them and they don't forgive – they most certainly won't forgive you this. But first I'm taking you back to my people in London for interrogation – there must be a good deal you know about the Soviet missile programme which should interest them – after that, you'll be left to the hounds.'

The man stared at him in disbelief. 'You can't do that,' he protested. 'I'm a French citizen and you have no authority here.'

'I don't need authority,' the agent said and took hold of his arm smartly, forcing it high up behind the man's back. It was the agent's turn to inflict his will upon another.

De Sauveterre was in agony. Struggling against having his arm forced any higher, he began cursing in French. But the arm was forced higher still in order to dislocate it and, as it went, he squealed like a pig in the slaughterhouse.

The dark sky suddenly lit up and the agent looked up. It was the comet, ripping its way through the upper atmosphere, a fireball caused by the outer layers of ice and rock being vaporised under the tremendous heat generated through the friction of entry. The comet, above him to the southeast, appeared to be in one piece still and on a collision course with the Earth. The agent could no longer discern the burn from the second missile – had, perhaps, the onboard self-guidance system failed? All he could do was pray it hadn't, otherwise this would surely be Armageddon. There was nothing to do now but await the deadly impact of this monstrous icy rock.

Distracted, the agent had allowed de Sauveterre to struggle free and now he'd taken off, running back along the ridge towards the pyramid. As he went after him again, he felt the mountain tremble below his feet and saw two gigantic fireballs shoot out from the shafts ahead, the mountain summit suddenly spewing flame like a dragon spitting fire. The fires from the pyramid must have spread to the missile facility inside the mountain and ignited the remaining rocket propellant. As it went up, de Sauveterre's 'engine room', with the remaining missiles and the entire Russian ballistics team stationed there, would have been instantly vaporised – everything going the way of the port side of the Star.

In that moment, the balance of power between East and West returned to the status quo – the attempt by the other side to level the playing field had, inadvertently, been thwarted and the allies' advantage, restored. Beyond the shafts, a giant ball of flame was visible for a moment inside the pyramid observatory before it exploded outwards, taking what remained of the glass with it. Twisted sections of the steel frame buckled and came crashing down. Ahead, de Sauveterre was thrown to the ground by the blast.

The honeycombed rock of the summit cracked open and the agent watched as the twisted remains of the pyramid sank into the void opening up below it. The mountain consumed the ruined observatory as the sea might a broken, sinking ship. Against the dark of the night sky, the spot where the pyramid had, only minutes ago, been standing now glowed orange from the furnace burning inside the mountain below it – any of de Sauveterre's men still left in there would not have stood a chance of escaping the firestorm. Flames darted out from the newly formed crater to lick at its rim. The agent was reminded of the Chimera fires he had once seen at Olympus, on a visit there years before. The flames, which are impossible to douse, have been burning on the mountain there for tens of thousands of years. In ancient Greek literature, sighting the Chimera was considered an omen of storms, shipwrecks, and natural disasters.

Above, the sky was ablaze too. The missile had found the target and the warhead split the comet open, exploding it in a spectacle of light – illuminating the night sky like a false dawn. A panoply of small, bright objects radiated out from the disintegrating comet and the whole sky seemed to be full of light now as the fragmented comet fell earthward, the vapour trails showering down over the vast arid waste of the North African interior. They shot across the sky above the agent and disappeared over the southern horizon towards their terrestrial rendezvous. He thanked God that the second missile had struck home but what was to come? Could there be any possibility that this madcap plan of de Sauveterre's might actually work? He couldn't seriously believe that there was.

To the agent's eye, one of the trails appeared much bigger and brighter than all the rest. Then he realised that it wasn't bigger at all. It was simply closer, much closer. He watched it falling before it must have crashed onto the Erg Chebbi dunes just to the south of his position. Then the noise of it came. It sounded like the end of the world – a deep, almost subsonic rumble. The mountain bucked again under him as he felt the shockwaves transmitted through it and up through his own body. The wind picked up – he knew what was coming. De Sauveterre was back on his feet but dazed now, a rabbit caught in the headlights. The agent caught hold of him just as it struck.

The air blast knocked them both off their feet and they were sent skating off along the smooth, weather-worn ridge. The agent grabbed at the rock for something, anything to get hold of but there was nothing. Just as panic began to set in, he found himself blown into a shallow depression in the geometry of the summit. It slowed his progress for an instant – enough for him to feel a small gulley. He managed to work his fingers into it and finally bring his body to a jarring halt in the relative safety of the hollow. De Sauveterre, partially disabled after having had his arm dislocated, had voluntarily anchored himself to the agent – ironically, the man responsible for this treatment. But the gale of sand travelling out from the impact site of the meteor had reached nearly ninety miles an hour and it was wrenching the agent's fingers from their hold. To hell with his people in London, now this was about survival. He made up his mind. If he were to stand any chance of not being swept off the edge of the ridge, then he had to rid himself of his prisoner. De Sauveterre had brought down hellfire and brimstone from the Gods. It certainly felt like this could be the end of the world. The man deserved to die, and to die horribly.

With one hand fighting to retain his grip in the small rock crevice, the agent fought to shake off de Sauveterre with the other, his injured right, but the pain was excruciating and he kicked out instead at his legs, jabbing his toecaps into the man's knees, shins and ankles.

De Sauveterre was clinging onto him for dear life and wouldn't let go – he opened his mouth to voice a plea but it was immediately filled with sand and his words were buried before they were formed.

The agent needed to try something else to lose the deadweight or they would both be leaving the mountaintop rapidly. He moved so that he lay on his back and, rolling backwards, drew both his legs up above him. Then, fighting to control them against the wind, he brought them crashing down simultaneously to stamp heavily on de Sauveterre's lower body – pounding his stomach and groin area, hard and repeatedly. Soon he had done enough.

Before he went, the man's face came close to his own for a moment and, this time, the words were pushed out individually, violently, against the storm. But whatever they were, this final communication, the last thing which de Sauveterre would ever say was lost completely in the blizzard of sand. And then the agent saw a look of sheer terror come into the man's eyes and he was off, clawing desperately at the polished rock, his nails screeching against it before they snapped. His efforts were hopeless and then, evicted from the gulley, suddenly he was gone. De Sauveterre was blown clean off the side of the mountain. That was the end of him.

The agent found another grip on the rock with his other, free hand and with the burden gone was able to hold on until it was over. When it was, he wiped the sand from his eyes with his bloody fingers and looked out across the desert plain. In the half light of the pre-dawn, a dark column of what must be plumes of sand and ice particles thrown up by the impact was steadily rising up into the atmosphere.

He'd have to wait until the sun came up to find a way off the ridge. For now, he could do with some rest. Inside the gulley, he curled into the foetal position to preserve his body warmth on the cold rock and tried to sleep, but it did not come easily. Instead, he thought about everything that had happened. God knows what damage the collision of the meteors must have had elsewhere – he should have stopped it. He'd failed his mission. It was a feeling previously unknown to him. But whatever course he should have taken, it made no difference now. It was done and he had to put it aside.

***

It must have been around five when the light from the imminent sunrise began to give some definition to the desert below. It awoke something in the agent's semi-conscious brain and, blurrily, he looked out. At first what he saw confused him – he must be concussed. Then slowly it dawned on him what he was looking at, the sight of it pulling him sharply back into lucid consciousness. The remains of the meteorite which had crashed onto the Erg Chebbi dunes became visible. The crater field began only about five miles away with a series of small and medium-sized craters but the largest looked to be of lunar proportions – several thousand feet across. Half buried at the centre and glistening in the early morning sun was an impossibly large, dirty snowball. Even at this distance, he was overwhelmed by what he saw. This monumental meteorite was just one part of the smashed comet – how many more titanic lumps of ice like this had landed in the desert?

As the sun came up, he could see it all more clearly and he considered again what de Sauveterre had told him. With the benefit of the scene laid out before him, he realised that he had probably been wrong about the man whose death lay squarely on the agent's shoulders. However dangerous a plan it may have been, nonetheless, it appeared the man had achieved precisely what he claimed he would. Regardless of everything that had happened, the agent began to wonder if de Sauveterre had in fact accomplished something astonishing – something as remarkable as putting a manned spacecraft into orbit around the Earth or even the dream of landing a man on the moon. De Sauveterre had willingly gone to bed with the Soviets alright but it appeared that he'd had the audacity, not only to try, but to succeed in fooling them.

And what about the agent's own place in it all? In attempting to stop de Sauveterre, he'd inadvertently allied himself with the enemy. So, had he made the wrong call? Had he failed in a different way to the way he'd thought he had only a few hours before? And then there was the girl. He brooded on the thought that if perhaps he hadn't put her in the position in which he had, then without the resulting paranoia to motivate her, she might not have gotten herself into a situation where he felt he had no choice but to kill her. She belonged to the enemy but nevertheless, he knew – even in the moment of his action – that he regretted killing her. Had she meant what she'd said to him with her last ever words or had she used them merely in fighting for her life? He would, of course never know but, in any event, he would mourn her death.

Below him lay a piece of the comet, smashed on the desert sands. He pictured de Sauveterre at the foot of the mountain, his limbs – already beaten at the hands of the agent – now twisted and torn from his body as he fell. In the splendid beauty of the desert sunrise, the agent, bitter and dejected, had set the course for his own descent.

Epilogue
The White Cliffs of Dover

Great Pluckley was a country club housed in a grand old Elizabethan pile, set in several acres of parkland and managed woods in the Weald of Kent. The club had a closed membership and boasted a nine-hole golf course. The agent was here at the invitation of one of its members, to play a round before being given luncheon.

A piano occupied a far corner of the dining room with a pianist playing one of the old wartime favourites. The room itself was a relic of a bygone era, preserved in aspic. High ceilings, oak panelling and oversized fireplaces with extravagantly carved stone mantles and great cast iron firedogs. But this historic mansion, with its leaded windows and ivy growing up to the top of the castellated walls outside, wasn't quite what it seemed. The place had burnt to the ground and had been rebuilt in the thirties incorporating the few features which were salvageable, but without the benefit of a discerning eye one would never have known.

Meanwhile, the fire burning in the grate could only manage a whimper of a flame. One of the waiters – kitted out in a get up which looked like a pastiche of a naval officer's uniform and wearing far too much brilliantine in his jet-black hair – was busy trying to get the thing going with only a stack of yesterday's menu cards to use as kindling.

'The food can't possibly be that bad,' the agent quipped as he passed on his way to the table.

The man, clearly unused to the members making such brash comments and unsure of how to respond, hesitated for a moment before allowing his mouth to form the smallest of smiles and his lungs to produce what was surely intended as a discreet chuckle but which actually sounded rather more like the clearing of catarrh from his throat.

The table was positioned in one of the large bay windows overlooking the gardens, the formal hedging leading down, away from the house, to the golf course beyond. The agent made his way over and sat down. While he'd been busy depositing his clubs in the car, his host had already settled himself at the table and the sommelier had arrived with the wine. His lunch companion had his nose stuck in his glass. He took it out smartly and grimaced.

'That's corked, I'm afraid,' he told the sommelier. 'Bring us another, will you please?'

'But of course, General.'

'Oh, for heaven's sake leave that aside, will you? How many times do I have to tell you people here not to stand on bloody ceremony? Why you must all insist in behaving as if you're on the blasted parade ground is beyond me. "Sir" will adequately suffice.'

The sommelier, suitably reprimanded, retreated towards the safety of the cellar – running off there like a spider scuttling away and disappearing under the floorboards.

The lieutenant-general turned his attention to his guest now and, without any care of being overheard by the departing sommelier, said, 'These stewards talk a lot of rot about wine and then the bloody bottle's corked – ha. Anyway, I've ordered us Dover sole. I'm not ever inclined to eat a starter. I can't see the point in messing about with some paltry serving which couldn't possibly satisfy, at the expense of delaying a main course that may very well.'

The agent had lunched with his chief at his London club on more than one occasion, so he knew the form well enough not to be surprised at this – and he tolerated the Dover sole, despite a certain distrust of flatfish. This prejudice was largely based on the fact that, as these fish lived on the seabed, both eyes were positioned on one side of the animal – a characteristic which to the agent seemed at best a violation of natural symmetry and, at worst, freakish.

'Well, your wrist has certainly mended well enough judging by your driving this morning,' the lieutenant-general said. 'I'd say that three over was more than fair on a course you've not played before, and especially on wet greens. All this rain's a damned poor show for May if you ask me.' As an Englishman of the old order, he seemed unable not to take the opportunity to remark on the weather.

'Thank you, sir. My wrist feels just fine now,' he said and, knowing what was about to come, glanced nervously out through the irregular thicknesses of the small, intricately leaded glass panes – which, incredibly, had somehow been saved from the inferno – at the wet lawn beyond. He began to say that he thought the sun might come out later but was cut short. As he'd rightly suspected, the lieutenant-general's mention of his injury was of course simply a preamble for what the agent had been dreading.

'Bloody awful mess we managed to get ourselves caught up in over there – and I have to say that, whilst I understand that your actions were taken in accordance with your brief, I do regret that, once you understood what was actually happening, you didn't have the sense to stand back and let the thing play out. The Soviet threat was neutralised by this Frenchman's scheme anyway and he could simply have been left to answer to them. Instead, we stuck our nose in and got embroiled in the whole damned thing, at the cost of our Foreign Office's relations with the new king – and not only ours but, perhaps more importantly in this instance, the American State Department's too. It wasn't a good week for the Americans – firstly they lost out to the Soviets who managed to get their man into space before the first Mercury astronaut could even get off the ground, then they had the fallout from your escapade – and they finished it off with the CIA's Cuban debacle. If you ask me, Kennedy will have to do something now to restore the country's prestige, not to mention the faith of the American public in his administration. As to the political repercussions here, well, what with the newspapermen's efforts to whip up such a bally storm over it all, it caused a proper stink and, as you well know, the Prime Minister was not in the least bit happy with the way in which the department was implicated.'

'I am truly sorry about it all, sir. The whole thing was a fiasco. I deeply regret the decisions I made.'

'Yes, well I'm afraid the backlash was simply unavoidable.'

The lieutenant-general had chosen to wait until after their game to get this off his chest and having made his view known, rather than being relieved to have done so, he now looked thoroughly browned off. Thankfully, the sommelier's return at this moment with a new bottle, served as a distraction and helped to break his sudden bad mood (they usually passed as quickly as they came). Having performed the same operation with his nose, the lieutenant-general gave the sommelier a nod and their glasses were filled. A boy who was standing by with a bucket, should the wine pass muster this time, quickly moved forward and set it up on a stand next to the table – just in time for the sommelier to deposit the bottle into the ice, while muttering something quite unnecessary about it 'maintaining the correct serving temperature' and complimenting the lieutenant-general on his fine choice of vintage.

The lieutenant-general, completely ignoring the sycophancy of the wine waiter, took a good mouthful of Sémillon and savoured it for a moment before swallowing. 'You shouldn't be too hard on yourself,' he said, '…and neither should I. It wasn't a straightforward situation, I admit, and I suppose you did your best in the end.'

'Thank you, sir,' the agent said, relieved that the inevitable dressing down had been considerably milder than anticipated.

'Well, that'll do,' the lieutenant-general said, presumably wishing to draw a line under it. 'As of now, you can consider yourself officially debriefed. Look, our luncheon is here already.'

The waiters arrived with it on a trolley which looked like it might have been one of the artefacts rescued from the fire. The agent could just imagine some poor clot of a footman running out with the great, clumsy-looking thing – with his coattails alight. The dish was presented to the table with a large, polished silver cloche placed over it – no doubt to keep the fish piping hot – which was then removed with far greater ceremony than the food was subsequently found to have deserved. The waiter proceeded to bone and plate the fish on the trolley. A waitress brought the vegetables and the lieutenant-general called for the bread boy to come back. It wasn't exactly a bad meal – the Dover sole was so-so – but it owed nothing to the new style of French gastronomy that the agent was used to seeing now in the better London restaurants. This food was old hat – firmly rooted in the past, no different from that which his father might have enjoyed, back when he too was a younger man.

Over the sole, the men talked about the nine holes they'd played and the game in general – a subject which they both enjoyed. While they ate their pudding – spotted dick with custard – the lieutenant-general returned the talk to business as he spoke now about how he saw the future of the department. To say that the agent enjoyed this conversation less, would be an understatement. After their bowls had been cleared and the coffee was on its way, the lieutenant-general picked up his cigarette case from the table and, opening it, offered it to the agent.

Surprised, the agent said, 'I don't mind if I do,' and plucked one from the case. The Turkish-blended tobacco had always smelt agreeable and had provided his chief's office with a pleasant room note. These cigarettes were certainly specially made for the lieutenant-general for, though he had studied them on numerous occasions, the agent had never detected there to be a maker's mark. He also had never been so forward as to ask who made them for him. Taking one of the cigarettes in his hand now, for the first time, he was keener than ever to know. But perhaps more than this, he was curious to understand why it was – that up until this moment – his chief had never once offered him one. Must this change be down to what had happened? With his new Ronson, he lit the lieutenant-general and then himself. At the risk of seeming impertinent, he pointed the fact out to him and asked, in the most delicate way he could think to, for him to explain why it was so.

The lieutenant-general wasn't put out in the least. 'The answer to your question is simple. Smoking, if we are to believe what the doctors have to say about it these days, is detrimental to one's health. Now, the good health of the department's field operatives has always been vital to me and so, though it might well be hypocritical of me to have taken this view given that I smoke the damn things myself, I have never wished to encourage smoking among you – nor anyone else working for the department for that matter.' The lieutenant-general took a pull on his cigarette and blew the smoke slowly out across the table. 'You're out of it now and so I don't care a damn what damage you choose to do to yourself.' (To the point as ever, the agent thought). 'It's no longer my affair, and so I can afford to be cordial.'

After they had finished coffee, his old chief walked him back out to the lobby, past the pianist who, closing in on the bottom of the barrel, was now playing *The White Cliffs of Dover*. 'Well, thank you for coming down,' he said. 'I enjoyed our morning's golf and I… just wanted the opportunity to wish you farewell.

What will you do, now that you're no longer bound by the rigors of the department?'

'Oh, I don't quite know yet, sir – first I'm going to take a holiday.'

'Spending your severance already, eh? You've not lost your appetite for foreign travel then?'

'Actually, I'm planning on motoring down to the Italian Riviera.'

'Well, the best of luck to you.'

'Thank you, sir. And… may I ask what you will do, sir?'

'Oh, don't fuss about me. I have plenty to occupy myself with. Starting with the roses – our poor excuse for a gardener has let the bloody things grow wild.'

'Well, I'm sure you will return them to good health in no time at all, sir.'

'Yes, well we'll see…' The lieutenant-general allowed the sentence to trail. Unusually, he appeared at a loss as to quite how he should finish it. He chose instead to hold his hand out.

The agent took it firmly and shook hands with his old chief. 'Thank you for lunch – it really was very good of you,' he said. 'Sir, please will you accept my sincerest apologies for the damage I have caused the department and… well, for what has happened.'

'Oh, stuff and nonsense, the man at the top always has to carry the can. You get off now, and enjoy your wanderings.'

'It's awfully decent of you to put it like that. Goodbye sir.'

The agent walked out through the heavy double doors of the lobby entrance, down the steps and onto the driveway. The pea shingle crunched under the leather soles of his brogues as he walked across the gravel towards his car. The lunch hadn't been up to much, but the company had of course been first class – he was going to miss the old bugger.

The morning's bad weather had lifted and the sky had all but cleared, though there still remained a stubborn, dark band of grey which persisted on the northern horizon. Despite the platitudes made by his old chief, the way he saw it hadn't changed. In his own mind, he'd failed his assignment, and in spectacular fashion – quiet resignation or not, there was no getting away from the fact that he'd left the department more or less in disgrace. Two months on, he still felt ashamed of himself over it and for having let the lieutenant-general down. But he was also relieved to be gone, relieved not to be that man any longer. He'd been handed the opportunity to start afresh, to begin his life again.

The sun shone now out of a nearly clear sky. The bright blue expanse would go on all the way to the coast and the chalk cliffs which Vera Lynn had sung about, and then on beyond them, across the Channel and to France, then south towards the Mediterranean. This was where the agent was heading. And what a pleasant little trip it should be – in his new sports.

The car was the first he'd bought brand new, out of the showroom. It was a Triumph TR4 – in British racing green with claret upholstery – and it had cost him well over a thousand pounds what with all the optional extras he'd chosen: Laycock overdrive and forty-eight-lace wire-spoked wheels which he'd had painted in the same colour as the coachwork. His severance money had just about paid for it all – he had justified this extravagance with the fact that, because he'd saved wisely over the years in which he'd worked for the service, he reasoned that he'd be comfortable enough on that alone for a good while at least – and anyway, if it ever came to it, he could always sell it.

His bags were already neatly stowed in the roomy boot and he'd slung his clubs onto the back seat of the 2+2, immediately after the game. He looked at his watch. He had about an hour to get to Ferryfield Airport for the Silver City Airways' air ferry service to Le Touquet. There was no time for him to pull down the Surrey top – he'd have to wait until he reached Lydd for that. He'd attend to it out on the apron before it was driven up the ramp and into the aeroplane, passing through the parted nosecone of the Bristol Superfreighter.

The agent had already run the car in but, before he could pick up the trunk road at Brenzett and properly open her up, he'd first have to negotiate the traffic heading out towards the coast at Littlestone along the New Romney road – and he knew the road to be slow at this time of year. With the world and his wife no doubt heading off to the beach for the afternoon after the morning's showers, he'd better get a move on. He lowered himself into the front seat and turned the ignition key. The little roadster's 2.2 litre, inline-four sprang to life and the agent pointed the car down the grand, ornamental box-lined driveway, steering it out through the great arched edifice at the end and onto the B2077.

THE END

A word from the author

I hope you enjoyed *Cold Star* and, if you did, I'd very much like to keep in touch with you so I can let you know when the next book in the Agent series is coming out. And also, for you to comment on my books – I'd love to start a conversation with you about them. The simplest way to keep in touch is by joining The Club (free to join). And, when you do, I'll send you a free e-book with a Club exclusive story set in the Agent's universe. Visit dickwoodgate.com to join.

Free Book Offer

Get your copy of *Treasure Hunter* FREE

Aboard a WW2 destroyer on Arctic patrol to hunt down a Nazi enigma coding machine.

For a limited period, you can download *Treasure Hunter* for free.

The story is exclusive to The Club (free to join) and features Dowling, the head of station in *Cold Star*, in an intriguing story set during his time as a young naval intelligence officer in WW2. Patrolling North Atlantic waters aboard the destroyer HMS Tartar, Dowling leads parties ashore to Arctic lands. Dowling is hunting down an elusive codex machine in a bid to unravel the secrets of the Nazi's enigma code.

Find out more at dickwoodgate.com

Review Cold Star

If you've enjoyed this book then please help other readers to find it too by leaving your review on Amazon. Amazon reviews are tremendously important to new authors like me and I'd love it if you were to take a moment to share your thoughts on *Cold Star* with the Amazon community.

Acknowledgements

Jon, for structural editing. Lovely long conversations with you about my manuscript in its various stages – developing my characters, finessing the plot. Thursday nights, wine in hand, you enthusiastically steered me in the right direction and provided the encouragement I needed to go back and rewrite the damn thing yet again. And you kept reading my drafts until the job was done. I simply could not have written this book without your help. Thank you, mate.

Susie, for line & copy editing. We've had some great discussions over minute points of grammar. Your vast knowledge of the English language has lifted my prose to a higher level. You went through my manuscripts word by word, line by line. I know how much work that is, the focus that's required. Thank you so much for doing it and for supporting my writing.

Gem, for putting up with it all. Thank you for proofreading a manuscript written in a genre that isn't really your thing. Most of all, thank you for allowing me the time to write and for indulging me in my new obsession. I love you very much. And Jon, Susie, I love you both very much too.

About the author

As well as being a writer, I'm also a furniture maker. I moved from London to rural Kent seven years ago to start a family. The skies are dark down here. I bought a telescope soon after we moved and it was this – and a love of espionage fiction, Fleming in particular – which led me to start writing my first novel, *Cold Star*.

Cold Star is the first book featuring the Agent in a planned series charting the race to the moon in the sixties. A sense of that pioneering decade of space exploration is expressed in parallel with the plot and theme of each book – I'm nearing completion of the second book, set later on in the decade in Europe, Russia and California. I hope you'll enjoy reading it as much as I have writing it for you.

dickwoodgate.com

Printed in Great Britain
by Amazon